A Deadly Snow Fall

A Liz Ogilvie-Smythe Provincetown Cozy Mystery

Cynthia Gallant-Simpson

CAPE COD COZIES & MYSTERIES, INK

P.O. Box 1115   South Orleans, MA 02662
Email:hesperus@capecod.net

1.Cozy mystery 2. Cape Cod 3. Female sleuth 4. Culinary Mystery
5. Provincetown 6. Romance

For Ken

Who can give law to lovers? Love is a greater law to itself.

Boethius, *De Consolations Philosophiae*

Thanks to my proofreader Judi Lech.

One

"No one in Provincetown liked Edwin Snow III. Well, no one but his faithful and devoted pit bull, Patton."

That was the voice of my new best friend, also a British expatriate, Daphne Crowninshield, on that snowy April morning when the village mystery began to unfold. On that chilly spring morning, as I stood with Daphne and the other villagers prevented from getting any closer to the dead body lying in the snow than the yellow police tape allowed, my world shifted on its axis. But, this is not principally a story about me. No, it is about a village and its people, old grudges, misunderstandings, love, hate and the perpetual determiner of the mood of New Englanders; the quixotic weather. I am but a participant. Edwin Snow III is the star. Albeit, a fallen star.

Spring is not coming this year…April Fool! Every year, as residents reached their limit for tolerating icy North Atlantic wind, long, gray days, snow, sleet and freezing rain, invariably there would be two or three days of pure delight. All it took for a collective sense of hope to rise was that welcome, sudden change in the weather. The promise of spring. Warming breezes, lots of sunshine and little green shoots daring to peek out of the earth all contributed to something akin a healing tonic that swept through the village. However, "April on Cape Cod is," as Daphne said in her sardonically descriptive way, "as quixotic as a wily fox on steroids."

The year of the mysterious death of Edwin Snow III was no exception. As southern New England held its collective breath waiting for menopausal Mother Nature to decide whether to bring forth spring or cling to winter for a while yet, there were a few tantalizing spring-like days. Like hermit crabs, the villagers crawled out of their winter-imposed isolation and began outdoor projects such as raking yards, washing windows, painting storefronts. The gardeners among them perused the flats of pansies in front of Daisy Buchanan's (a pseudonym for Annie Buckley

1

who was a devoted fan of F. Scott Fitzgerald's books) Narrow Lands Nursery.

Then, to the dismay of everyone it snowed.

It snowed and snowed and snowed, burying the fledgling daffodils and crocuses as well as the prematurely heightened spirits of the villagers. That year, the town meeting had voted to eliminate from the budget the snow removal at the Pilgrim Monument due to financial concerns. So, Bill Windship, the self-appointed keeper of the Pilgrim Monument and Museum, had bought a new snow shovel at the Land's End Hardware Store. The town had let down his precious Monument but he would not.

Bill Windship was the owner of the Army-Navy Supply Store on Commercial Street and a dedicated and learned historian of everything concerning the Pilgrims. He acted as if they had stayed and settled in and been the life's blood of the village when actually, they had split for greener pastures at the end of their first winter there. But for Bill, the only really worthwhile tourist site in the entire village was his beloved Monument.

Bill had opened the Army-Navy Surplus Store when he was just a young man and he had grown wealthy over the years on the WWII Navy pea jackets, canteens, disabled howitzers and other surplus he had bought by the truckload at the inception and still had not depleted. Exotic seashells from the tropics--by way of the Jersey shore—cheap Indian cotton clothing, old fishing nets hand-made by the early Portuguese fishermen and a thousand other things that tourists loved to pick through in search of treasures, kept the store full all summer long.

He closed the store the day after Labor Day each year and re-opened for Memorial Day because his wares held little appeal for the year-round population. Except that he did re-open briefly at Halloween for locals looking for something to wear to costume parties. Every fall, Bill, who was a wealthy man in his own right, considered selling his "gold mine" business and retiring to warmer climes. But every spring, his interest was revitalized. Now, in his mid-eighties, the self-appointed advocate of the Pilgrim Monument had accepted that he'd die in Provincetown.

As Bill told the story later to the Chief and I heard it after I made the fortuitous acquaintance of Officer Finneran, the Chief's right hand man, the day had started out well but quickly descended into the realm of horror for poor Bill. On that snowy, late spring day when Edwin Snow III's crumpled body was found at the foot of the Monument, Bill had disobeyed his doctor's orders.

Bill had walked the six blocks from his house to the Monument huffing and puffing. Two heart attacks had weakened the once strong man. "Light exercise" as the cardiac specialist had advised, hardly meant a long walk followed by shoveling snow. As it happened, only two weeks earlier, Bill's younger brother had forced the man to get a cell phone. "Time to move into the twenty-first century. What if you fall and can't call for help? No one will hear you from the deserted area of the Monument." Bill had countered, "So what. That's where I prefer to die, anyway." But he had acquiesced and on that snowy morning, gazing down at bloody snow, Bill had called in the death of his long-time enemy, Edwin Snow III. The two had been schoolmates.

Fortunately, the snow was light and fluffy. Bill had been working slowly. He had all day. Not that anyone visited his precious, historical site in winter. But, Bill's pride and love of his Monument drove him to clear the walk. He was making pretty good progress, he told Chief Henderson, when the shovel hit something solid. Leaning down to inspect the shock of red snow just under the light, top covering caused him to totter and stumble. The shovel stopped him from falling and he braced himself against it until he could catch his breath. Remembering the phone in his jacket pocket he called the Police Station.

Chief Chet Henderson and Officer James Finneran were there within minutes. Yellow police tape went up and Doc Hooper, the medical examiner for the lower-Cape had been summoned and was on his way from Orleans within eleven minutes of Bill's call. Before I arrived, Officer Finneran was called to an early morning domestic dispute and so, our paths did not cross on that particular day. That would come later.

The crowd quickly gathered only because Emily Sunshine, out for her regular early morning walk, happened to take a route that passed by the monument. Seeing the police car, as she told me later, she quickly ducked behind a huge oak tree from where she could see the bloodied, old and tattered tweed coat that she knew belonged to none other than Edwin Snow III.

Like Paul Revere but minus the trusty steed, Emily immediately headed back into town to spread the alarm. Had anyone heard Emily's little singsong, however, as she peered around the tree at the death scene, they'd have been either confused or…greatly disturbed.

"Humpty Dumpty had a great fall."

Had I not decided to morph into an amateur sleuth, inspired by my love of cozy mysteries, probably foolishly believing I could help, things might have turned out very differently. As Officer Finneran pointed out, once we became friends, my actions just might have ended in my being dead as the proverbial door nail, as well. *C'est la vie!*

However, not one to turn my back on a chance to dig into old mysteries, in keeping with my former career, I became privy to assorted, fascinating village secrets. One of those being, as Emily Sunshine eventually shared with me, why she'd intoned the old nursery rhyme at the scene of Edwin Snow III's death.

Within minutes of Emily's arrival back in the heart of the village, nearly every resident of Provincetown was at the death scene. If it hadn't been for the snow covering, it might have been summer and the line of arriving people a queue waiting to climb the Monument. By that time, Chief Henderson's hope that he could keep the terrible incident under wraps until the autopsy report was completed had exploded. Much later, back at the police station, he had berated Emily Sunshine to Officer James Finneran. "Damn that nosy woman. Ran all over town like the town crier calling it murder. She had no right. The man was miserable and he took his own life. End of story."

Thus, two camps quickly formed. The suicide camp and the murder camp. Neighbors pitted against neighbors over the question. Friends argued their positions on the street, in the stores, at the bars and in the privacy of their homes. The town buzzed like a frenzied bee hive. Chief Henderson was furious about how the whole incident had gotten completely out of hand. Then, on top of that, someone called the Boston papers with the anonymous tip that it might have been murder.

4

Reporters descended on the town like lemmings on holiday. Weather notwithstanding, gawkers arrived from everywhere to view what the *Boston Globe* called, tongue in cheek, "A Monumental Death." Either someone had overheard the Chief call it that or, it was so obvious a tag that it came naturally to others, as well. Windship was naturally, totally appalled.

The only good to come of it all was that the tourist season got an early start. It seemed sad to me that poor old Edwin Snow's death had only brought smiles to the villagers and no one but probably his faithful pet Patton missed him. Only much later, after I took on the persona of amateur sleuth, having fashioned myself on an amalgam of my favorite feisty, female, cozy, undercover investigators, did I discover one person saddened by his passing.

Two

I knew the old man, Edwin Snow III, lying bloodied at the foot of the Pilgrim Monument, only by sight. Actually, he had bestowed on me a look of complete disdain and disapproval with never a word uttered between us. But that will come later. As you can imagine, it came as a seven on the Richter scale when the village's least liked, most miserly and nastiest curmudgeon reached out from the grave to influence my life. To change its course, I might say.

On the morning of the death of Edwin Snow III, the Provincetown Chief of Police kindly Chet Henderson, stood looking down at the newly fallen snow (no pun intended) as if it might contain a vital clue. As if it might reveal how octogenarian Edwin Snow III had managed to climb the locked up tight, two hundred and twenty-five foot tall granite tower, the iconic Pilgrim Monument, and jumped. Chief Henderson removed his cap and scratched his head. What he saw challenged his imagination as well as his logical policeman's mind. His gout was troubling him standing there in the cold air.

Back at the station, the Chief repeated his sentiments regarding the day for Officer Finneran who later shared them with me. Standing in the un-spring-like snow, the Chief had recalled his beloved, deceased wife Trudy's quoting of T. S. Eliot each and every year at that time. "April is the cruelest month." That particular April certainly was for the dead man.

As an especially grueling winter had turned to spring on Cape Cod everyone held their breath. It was not unusual for winter to hang on tenaciously even into May. My Scottish grandmother had a saying that seemed appropriate. Granny MacLaughlin referred to anything slow in arriving as being "as reluctant as sheep to the shears." That sluggish spring, two questions hung over the seaside village like precarious icicles waiting to fall. Until that morning, foremost had been the perennial New England quixotic weather question. The second question being more of a mystery wrapped in an enigma and presenting all with a challenging puzzle had to do with a mysterious death in the village. Not at all mysterious for some, but for others, a call to arms. Suicide or murder?

Even there, at the scene of Edwin Snow's demise, the villagers began to pin irreverent labels onto the scene before them. "The abominable snow-man." "Fallen Snow." "Curmudgeon on ice." Please don't misunderstand. These were not unkind people. Far from it. They were good citizens and good neighbors. A mixed bag of long-time year-rounders composed of fishermen, shopkeepers, restaurant owners, innkeepers and the usual variety of tradespeople necessary to keeping a small village humming along. As a newcomer I had felt welcomed almost from the first. No, they were not unkind people however Edwin Snow III had tested their patience for decades. Everyone had a story about Edwin's mean and miserable ways.

In Provincetown, where tourism is king and summer fills the coffers of businesses catering to their every need and whim, there is an annual downside. Winter. However, even the downside had its upside. Winter was the time for seeing friends one had no time for during the busy season. Time for catching up on projects and getting ready for the next tourist season. A welcome respite. In winter, Provincetown reverted back to its small New England, seaside village persona. Warts and all.

Standing with Daphne in the snow as the ambulance pulled up and the EMT's prepared to take the body away I heard one old timer remark on the death of the dead man. "Well, one bad apple can sour the entire batch of cider. Frankly, I say, good riddance to our bad apple."

An elderly lady standing in her bathrobe and rubber boots spoke in a whisper to her neighbor but I heard. "Don't blame the old curmudgeon. Might do it myself if no one liked me." Her younger neighbor put an arm around her elderly friend reassuring her that she'd never have that problem.

"Daph, won't anyone mourn the poor man?" I asked.

"Doubt it. I told you, nobody liked the old coot. In fact, there were two attempts on his life not so long ago. Just before you came to town. One came from the air and one was a land assault.

7

Edwin was walking by the Canterbury Leather Shop one evening at just about dusk when a cement block just missed his head. It took out the post box and cracked the sidewalk. Imagine what it would have done to the old coot's head. The second attempt came in broad daylight on Commercial Street when a fist-sized rock was lobbed across the street missing his nose by a hair. But here's the fun part. It crashed through the front window of Spiritus Pizza and landed smack in the middle of a pepperoni pizza that Maggie and Eric Lund were just about to dive into. Rock pizza."

"My goodness, that sounds pretty scary. Was the culprit ever apprehended?' I asked, wondering if, in fact, my peaceful and safe-seeming adopted home village was safe, after all.

"Nope."

Looking across the snow at the man who'd found the body, talking to a man I would come to know as the kindly, grandfatherly Chief Henderson, I realized that I'd had an uncomfortable encounter with the former just the week previous. "Daph, who's the man leaning on the shovel?"

"Oh, that's Bill Windship. Owns the Army-Navy store."

"He stopped me in the library just last week to correct me when I asked if they had any books on the local Indian tribes. Gad, you'd think I'd touched the Queen!"

"Not surprised. He's always correcting those who are politically incorrect."

"Don't give me that raised eyebrow look. I'm British. We still call them "Indians"."

Ignoring me as if she'd been born in Dubuque, Daphne continued. "But he's just a harmless history fanatic. He takes care of the Monument. Found the body this morning while clearing the snow."

I happened to be on the scene only because Daphne had phoned and dragged me out of a lovely sleep-in so that I wouldn't miss the village's excitement. "Get down here pronto, Liz. It's like a movie scene. When they do make it I want to be portrayed by."Keira Knightly.

I turned my gaze upward, way, way up to the top of the Pilgrim Monument. Just the thought of jumping from such a height and flying through the air without the confidence of a reliable parachute made me shiver. Looking back down at the hump of bloodied and snowy tweed covering the old man's twisted body I thought about my favorite childhood rag doll. Even if no one liked the old man, that was a horrible way to go.

I took a couple of gulps of the fresh, if frosty, air and attempted to release my mind from the scene before us. "Don't quote me but I can only say, Daphne, looks like it's a monumental death."

"Too late, Shakespeare. Chief Henderson beat you to that proclamation. Good though, I'll give you both that. Great minds think alike. Do you know the Chief, by the way?"

"No. Is he single, handsome and sexy?" I asked.

"Single, scruffy, but good looking for a guy close onto seventy. He's also a whiz bang at Scrabble and appreciates good scotch. Nice guy if you need a father figure." Daph smiled her wily smile. "That's him in the dark green parka, over there." She pointed at the chief who looked like Santa Claus with less hair.

"Right up your alley I'd say Daph. Didn't you tell me your father is the template against which you measure your men and none so far have measured up? And, think of the hours spent playing Scrabble all winter to pass the time while sipping on a twelve year old blend."

This type of repartee had become an intrinsic and most enjoyable aspect of my friendship with the charming, if now and then caustic, Daphne Crowninshield. Although I hoped her habit of trying to sound American did not rub off on me. Her version of the "lingo of the rebellious colonists" as she put it, resulted in a hash of bad, nineteen forties movies and Hollywood mafia impersonations. But, I loved her and depended on her to keep me from being all too serious. We were a good mix.

My eyes were suddenly riveted to the dead body lying in the snow. Something was not right. I am no forensic expert but I was sure that what I saw did not fit. As the EMT's carefully picked it up it was obvious that it was frozen like a Popsicle. There was a lot of blood on the snow under the body but what particularly caught my eye and my imagination was the man's head. The skull had obviously been crushed. From the looks of the damage, I surmised that the man had landed head-first. Why that somehow didn't seem right I could not have said at that time. However it niggled around in my brain for days afterwards, demanding recognition.

The sight of Edwin Snow's twisted limbs made me shiver. I couldn't help but wonder what it must it be like in the seconds after you take flight to make such a fall? Do you immediately regret your choice? I could imagine arms and legs flailing in a kind of desperate attempt to fly in the hope of cancelling the plunge you'd been so sure of just moments before.

My feet were cold and the villagers were beginning to disperse as the ambulance took away the body. Time to go. "So, want to come along to the Stop & Shop Daphne? Can't abide another shriveled turnip or limp decaying bunch of lettuce and whoever invented the plastic tomatoes that are the specialty of winter produce bins in America ought to be flogged."

"Sure. Fun's all over here. Let's stop at the Hot Chocolate Sparrow first for cappuccino. Love their gooey pastries."

"Daph, is there ever a time or a situation that puts you off your feed?"

"Not yet. Let's go, I'm famished."

The ambulance pulled onto the road and Daphne and I jumped into my new, lemon yellow Jeep headed for Orleans. Since coming to the village, I had bought locally as much as possible. However, sometimes I had no choice but to drive the twenty odd miles up-Cape to the Stop and Shop Supermarket.

We left the gruesome scene behind us and headed for foodies' Nirvana. Or, at least the best source of fresh produce, that side of Boston. That morning, as the villagers dispersed to their homes for their much needed first cup of coffee and a hearty breakfast on what was more like a winter than a spring day, three vital questions hung in the frosty air.

Naturally, and probably the primary question, was in regard to the weather. When would spring arrive in earnest? An ages old New Englanders' query. Second: Why had the miserable old man who was so disliked and shunned waited until his ninth decade to "cash in his chips", to quote my irreverent friend, Daph.

Before more urgent concerns distracted the villagers, there was the final question regarding the two close calls for Edwin

10

Snow. Again, there were two camps on the open question. Had the "incidents" been nothing more than simple harassment or had they been attempted murder? Poor aim or just a warning? Leading to the ultimate question: Suicide or murder?

As a devoted fan of cozy mysteries, I could not resist giving the death scene a title. Having been beaten to the obvious, *A Monumental Death,* by Chief Henderson I went with the weather related tag. Being rather fond of double entendres I titled it, *A Deadly Snow Fall.* The appellation would come back to haunt me in the weeks to come.

Three

Before we move on to the real meat of the mystery of Edwin Snow III's enigmatic demise, allow me to introduce myself. I, like unwary Alice, had been thrust through the Looking Glass by Dame Fate to find my life transformed. One day uncovering ancient sites and the next, *voila!* making beds and cleaning bathrooms. A little literary license there but, in retrospect, it sometimes seems that way.

My name, Lady Elizabeth Ogilvie-Smythe, I clipped to just plain Liz Ogilvie-Smythe when I moved to the quaint seaside village of Provincetown on Cape Cod to become an innkeeper. A turn of events that could not have taken me more by surprise if I too had found myself shrinking small enough to slip through a rabbit hole.

Born and raised in London, I grew up among the crème de la crème of British society. My mother sat on the board of the Tate Gallery and my father, who worked for the Queen, had a job so top secret even Mother did not know what he did. However, his job brought us into the fold of the royal realm. Our life was a whirl of fancy dress affairs like the ballet, the opera, the theatre, cocktail parties in magnificent homes in the city and hunt weekends in the country. Not to mention the annual dinner with the Queen. By the age of ten, I was the possessor of as many ball gowns as Princess Di and enough jewelry to sink a battleship.

After graduation from Oxford with a degree in literature, I spent a few years living on my own in Hasting running a small, private library. A sweet village but hardly where I wanted to remain into old age. Finally, spurred by reading about digs like Chichen Itza and the supposed ruins of Troy, I entered grad school. Two years later, armed with a degree in archaeology and a determination to put many miles (continents) between me and my snooty family, I was headed to South America to work on a dig of ancient ruins with my esteemed professor. Unfortunately, my dream career came tumbling down only twelve weeks later. Rather than rooting around in the earth I was in a bed at Massachusetts General Hospital in Boston being a pin cushion for the world's foremost expert on malaria.

Finally, I was released with a satchel of drugs to be taken for the coming six weeks and then, if I did not feel like my old self, I was told to report back for more tests. I checked into a suite of rooms at the elegant Ritz Hotel in Boston's lovely Back Bay section. There I read cozy mysteries, walked in the Boston Commons and Public Gardens, watched cooking shows on the telly and waited for an epiphany regarding what to do with the rest of my life.

My doctor had expressed in no uncertain terms that to return to field work out in jungles and all the other favorite habitats of malaria-carrying mosquitoes would probably result in my death. The little nasty insects had become my arch enemies. As it turned out, I went on to dubious fame in the *New England Journal* of *Medic*ine. It turned out that my immune system's reaction to the disease was most unique. And, not in a good way.

My dreams smashed and scattered, I could not imagine what to do with the rest of my life. I was a trained and dedicated archaeologist who was not allowed to dig unless it was in a safe environment like Hampstead Heath! It was a truly difficult time for me. I had anticipated a long and rewarding career as a field archaeologist but it was not to be because of a member of the insect family, *Culcidae* of South America.

But, the answer to my dilemma was on its way. That answer could not have been more of a surprise than if the Queen herself requested that I come dig up the Garden at Buckingham Palace in search of Viking ruins.

Checking at the front desk of the Ritz before heading out to explore the historic city of Boston on a pleasant mid-summer day, I found a letter waiting for me. It was a summons from a Boston attorney to meet with him at his office in Pemberton Square. The letter was well-travelled. It had gone to London, on to South America and then to the hotel thanks to my dig leader who had my new, if temporary, address.

Two days later, I was sitting in a lawyer's office in a handsome old building totally mystified about why I was there. The letter had been most ambiguous but it had mentioned my, dropped-from-the-august-Smythe-family-tree-aunt, Elizabeth Smythe Huntley. Aha, she hadn't added a hyphen when she'd settled in America.

So, there I was sitting looking out of a floor to ceiling window onto a small green space and thinking about doing some shopping on trendy Newbury Street, as soon as I could escape. Finally, the smartly dressed attorney addressed me.

"Aha, yes, well, how nice for you Ms. Smythe, er, or is it Ogilvie-Smythe, then? My, my, yes, interesting."

I smiled rather sardonically having grown used to the American reluctance to accept the validity of hyphenated names. The lawyer, sounding like every member of the renowned American royal family, the Kennedys, proceeded to read the terms of a will. To my open-mouthed surprise, "Libby" (the Elizabeth for whom I'd been named) Smythe Huntley had left me an inn on Cape Cod.

All I knew about my estranged aunt was that she'd been disgraced and therefore, expunged from the Smythe family tree. The dear lady had fallen in love with and then (gasp!) actually married an American car salesman. I'd never met her and her name had been virtually mud in the Ogilvie-Smythe aristocratic, snobbish family. The will named me as her sole heir!

Through the haze of my utter amazement, the nasal tones of the attorney's voice pulled me back to reality. An inn. Cape Cod. Perhaps a summons from the Queen *and* a sterling silver shovel might not have been quite so shocking, after all.

"Of course, a young, well-educated woman such as you are will not want to bother with running an inn. The town is dead as a dormouse all winter and in summer is flooded with quacks and tourists...many of them interchangeable." He paused as if to say something else, appeared to dismiss the thought as irrelevant and then, blurted it out. "Full of queers. The Greenwich Village and Fire Island crowd flocks there these days. A disgrace."

I didn't feel that it was my responsibility to correct the ignorant, homophobic man on his choice of the term "queers". My

14

complete intolerance for homophobia, on a par with the social inequities subscribed to by family however bubbled over as I listened to the obnoxious man. I longed to leave the presence of the prejudiced and officious man. But, there was more to come. I bit my tongue and persevered.

He pointed to a map on the wall behind his desk. "We summer in Chatham. A lovely, quaint town with excellent architecture, fine beaches, the best restaurants and shops, but Provincetown is well…let me put it this way, an offensive dumping ground for…"

My taser-like eye contact with the annoying, tiny-minded man put an end to that speech.

Regaining his balance however he shot me a few more bullets.

"That degenerate Eugene O'Neill and his cohorts turned Provincetown into a sordid gathering place for socialists. That radical writer John Reed and his tramp mistress Louise Bryant hung out there." Blah, blah, blah.

Conversely to his intentions, everything he was saying meant to discourage me was rather, intriguing me. I conjured up an American version of Penzance in Cornwall, England. A favorite seaside place in my childhood.

The man babbled on in his efforts to convince me that I ought to sell the inn immediately, take advantage of the favorable real estate market, wipe my hands of the whole affair and pocket a goodly portion of money, etc., etc. I began a little fantasy in my head. Wouldn't it be fun to contact my parents with the news that I'd fallen in love with a Boston chimney sweep and I would be bringing him home to London to meet the family; complete with broom, bucket and sooty face? It would serve them right. My poor, dear aunt. Ostracized for falling in love *outside the realm*. I figured if she had chosen the little seaside village way down the peninsula of Cape Cod then it was probably a far more real place than where she came from. One more reason to like the woman I'd never met but wished I had.

According to the lawyer, my aunt's American husband died soon after they settled in the village and with his life insurance she had bought the antique, distressed house and, doing much of the work herself, restored it to its eighteenth century beauty. She supported herself by taking in summer guests and then in winter by teaching piano to the locals. She had been a pillar of the community, served on the library board and more recently, until her untimely death, had been chairperson of the Provincetown Historical Society. As my admiration for my dead aunt increased, the man's words floated by me, unheard. Blah, blah, blah.

Spotting some photos poking out of the file in front of the lawyer I asked, "Are those photos of the property?" Was that a harrumph?

Pulling them toward me I saw a solid, four-square white house with deep front veranda. Four stalwart chimneys, gleaming windows framed by deep cranberry painted shutters and a front yard overflowing with wildflowers filled me with enchantment. The white wicker furniture set out on the front porch for the guests to enjoy the evening salt breezes called to me. I found myself slipping into a love affair with a house. When my eye fell on a huge, ancient tree overhanging the yard and a sturdy limb just perfect for an old fashioned rope swing I knew I had to live there.

All through my childhood I'd wanted a rope swing like the ones I saw in storybooks. Of course my request for one was anathema to my parents' ideas of propriety. "But darling, you don't want to look like the bumpkin child of the help." I never fully understood who it was who was going to see me and pass judgment on one small girl enjoying a swing.

Looking at the photo, I wanted to walk right in, brew a pot of tea and sit on a wicker chair to read Beatrix Potter. Well, the old girl showed them, didn't she? She made a good life for herself despite her family's odious treatment. My affinity for this courageous woman blossomed as I leafed through the photos. Then, sending a shiver down my spine, I was face to face with myself. Yes, the hairdo was dated and the flowered summer dress would be a big hit in a vintage clothing shop but otherwise there stood I. My father's sister and I were so alike I wondered how my parents felt when they looked at me. Did they have second thoughts about ostracizing her? Probably not.

"Please read me the details of the property, how many rooms, etc."

16

Was that a groan of annoyance I'd heard? Okay, two can play at this game I said to myself. If this man was going to be annoyed by my interest in a property legally belonging to me, one that he was ready to simply hand off to the highest bidder, I would make him earn his fee. The man was getting on my nerves, big time.

"I'd like to hear every tiny detail. I assume my aunt lived there, therefore, there must be an owner's flat. How many rentable rooms are there and what is the going rate in season? I'd even like to know the population of the village. I am sure your secretary can quickly Google that."

With a deep sigh the man looked to the file folder and pulled out a sheaf of papers. I was feeling quite satisfied to have brought him to his knees, so to speak, by forcing him to let me run the show.

"Well, the building was built in 1748 by a sea captain named Joshua Eldredge and lived in by the same family until your aunt purchased the property and converted the private home into an inn. It has ten rentable rooms all with private baths, a sitting room, gathering room, formal dining room and a kitchen…considerably outdated according to the surveyor. Your aunt called the place the Cranberry Inn Bed & Breakfast and yes, it has a spacious owner's apartment and the furnishings are in excellent condition if terribly out-dated. It says here that it is a "turnkey operation." Therefore, I am sure you can unload it fairly quickly.

My look, icy though I tried to make it, appeared to have no effect. The man only rolled on to issue more dire warnings.

"If you were to take on this business you would need to hire a breakfast cook, cleaning people and a bookkeeper and you must be made acutely aware of the upkeep expenses demanded of such an old structure. In addition, this is a seasonal business with no income for probably nine months of the year thus, blah, blah, blah."

Thank goodness, I thought, I took that great course at the Cordon Bleu in Paris the summer of my junior year. What fun to try out all those great recipes I've been collecting for years. If my cooking skills haven't grown rusty in the intervening years.

As the bombastic man prattled on with the litany of reasons why I should want to wash my hands of this whole affair as expediently as possible, I asked myself one simple question. Why not go for it?

The man nearly tumbled off his chair when I announced, "As far as the cooking goes, I can whip up the flakiest *croissants* and *pain au chocolate* your mouth will ever wrap around. My soufflés are like clouds and I am sure I can hire help to do what I cannot manage. By the way, as far as expenses and seasonal income are concerned, I am sure that you are well aware that my finances will allow me to hang on, do the improvements and, if necessary, lose money—if I so choose."

I didn't bother to feed into his chauvinistic attitude toward me by mentioning that I had not one iota of how to run an inn beyond the possible fun of exercising my cooking skills.

If looks could kill I'd have been slumped in that handsome Windsor chair with my tongue lolling out. But I was a match for the condescending man. Although I did expect a harsh parental issuance of a punishment to fit my crime. *Young lady you are grounded for two weeks due to your complete failure to comprehend the magnitude of my sage advice.*

"Sounds just perfect. When can I take possession?"

Four

Truth *can* be stranger than fiction, now and again. The mystery that took hold of the little seaside village of Provincetown fell like a shroud and hung around stirring up trouble, for some time. That it would come to involve me was another earth-shaking happenstance. I was new to the village. Not unlike the weary, ship-worn passengers on the notable, tiny and inadequate ship the *Mayflower* had been. I too had arrived in an unknown land unsure of my welcome by the natives. A compressed course in American history I'd found in a tourist pamphlet for the Pilgrim Monument had been very helpful for this transplanted Brit. It told me that Provincetown was the first landing place, in 1620, of the ship-weary Pilgrims. After a rugged winter and the question of whether the sandy soil would be good for planting, they moved across the bay to Plymouth. It was there that the rag-tag band stepped back on land or at least, onto the iconic Plymouth Rock now enshrined in that colony.

One can imagine the native people waving farewell from a high sand dune, grateful not to have to deal with a pack of miserable dissenters from a faraway land. But that is, of course, only a fanciful hypothesis for which I alone take credit.

Driving back from Orleans on the morning of the death of Edwin Snow, with Daph busy reading *People Magazine* to stay on top of the latest secrets and scandals out of Tinsel Town I had time to contemplate the "case." As the dead man's body had been lifted onto a stretcher, my second thought after wondering if the snow was ruining my expensive Italian leather boots was about the day I "met" the village curmudgeon.

Passing the Provincetown Town Hall, a stately Greek Revival building in the center of the village, I'd stopped to pat a handsome white and black pit bull. I checked his collar and found out that his name was Patton. We were having a fine time making friends when suddenly an old man stepped up and yanked the dog's leash that had been trailing on the sidewalk. I'd looked up and smiled. After all, I was brought up to be polite. However, the wizened old man only stared back at me as if I'd been beating his dog. Then, he pulled the dog away and off they went. So much for everyone in the village being friendly.

That was when I spotted Frank Kavanagh the reporter for the *Provincetown Banner* the local, highly acclaimed daily newspaper. "Hi Liz," Frank greeted me. "So, you've met our local Scrooge."

"Hi, Frank. Not a nice person, I'd say. Who is he?"

"That, my dear lady, just happens to be the least liked man in Provincetown, Edwin Snow III. My guess is that after sucking on far too many lemons combined with rarely practicing his smile, his smile muscles simply atrophied."

"Why is he so hated? Does his dog hate him, too?"

"Ah, Patton, poor fellow, absolutely devoted to his master. Good old dogs, if you want a best friend who'll love you unconditionally, get a dog. Even a mean son of a bitch can be loved by a dog."

"First person I've encountered in the village with not even a smile to offer a newcomer. Maybe he mistook me for a tourist and he doesn't like tourists." I laughed and Frank smiled broadly.

"Nope. Our Edwin doesn't like anyone. Beginning and ending with himself. But he is one of our local celebrities At least, in his own mind. Claims he's writing a memoir of his glory days when he hung around with that artist fellow Edward Granger who spent a few summers in our neighbor town of Truro. Granger and his wife Ellyn, a New York theatre critic, rented a place in the hills of Truro to which their hard-drinking city friends came to visit. If you've ever seen Granger's paintings then you know that he painted the outer Cape in a rather Gothic style. Often wondered if he only painted when drunk. Might explain his odd take on the place. "

"Yes, I agree. I was in Boston when his recent show came through. I saw it at the Museum of Fine Arts. He certainly saw Cape Cod through a rather stilted lens, didn't he?"

"That, he did. It seems, at least according to our local crank, that Granger and his hard-partying New York friends wandered into our fair community looking for the entertainment and watering holes not to be found in sleepy Truro. To hear Edwin tell it, he slipped under Granger's wing and had a rip roaring old time. Also, according to the old guy, he's in possession of certain secrets and scandals that are about to come to light. He's writing a book that will set the literary and art world on fire." Frank laughed and tossed his Green Genie Coffee Shop paper cup into the nearby trash receptacle.

"Gotta go; deadline to meet. Nice talking to you, Liz."

"But wait, Frank. The man isn't hated just for that, is he? I mean plenty of people write that kind of book. In fact, wouldn't you think that, in light of how desensitized we have become to scandal that what he has to reveal will be *ho hum* to readers? After all, Edward Granger and all of his friends are long dead or too old to care."

"Right on, Liz. Unlikely anyone will care. But the old guy is unpopular for lots of other reasons. It didn't take his announcement of an up-coming sizzler to get him on the list of nastiest people ever. His old man, Ned Snow, started the ball rolling. Mean and greedy and obviously without a scintilla of conscience was old man Snow. Made millions grabbing property for unpaid back taxes, overdue mortgage payments, whatever. Turned folks out into the cold without a by-your-leave. A real Simon Legree. Real clever though. Knew just how close he could come to the line between legal and illegal in his machinations. Like a hyena smellin' carrion, old Ned swooped down and grabbed houses, land, everything he could. Built himself a grand Victorian manor house up on Pilgrim Lake Hill Road where he lived in splendor looking down on all us peons. Everyone says that Edwin not only inherited the old man's fortune but his nasty disposition, as well. Hey, by the way, Liz, how's that book club doing?"

"Terrific. Want to join?"

"Nope, I read the blood and guts stuff exclusively. And I heard you gotta' cook. I live on beef jerky and popcorn unless my

mother stops by and fills the freezer with casseroles. Well, gotta go."

We parted and I continued on my way to Souza's Portuguese Market. Tish Souza, the owner with her husband Manny, was behind the counter and in a questionable mood. Not that Tish Souza was a grouch or anything like that but there were certain customers who just grated her. Entering the shop on the departing heels of one of her testy customers could land you in the middle of a gray mood. Although they never lasted long. As it turned out on that day, Edwin Snow had just left and she was still smarting from his visit.

"Hi Tish, how are things?"

"They'd be a lot better if that miserable old coot Edwin Snow would move away. Like to Timbuktu. Sorry, Liz, don't mean to take it out on you but the man just drives me to distraction."

Having spotted old man Snow and his dog turning the corner at Seashell Lane as I reached the market, I guessed who'd set her off. I gave Tish a moment to recover by checking out a shelf of new teas. When Tish's smile returned, it seemed to me that it might be a good opportunity to get another opinion on the old man with the nice dog. Basically, I am an insatiably curious person. Interested in what makes people tick. Having come face to face with the old man on every villager's most hated list, I felt it behooved me to know more about him. Ironically, that curiosity would become a useful skill when I most needed it in the coming weeks.

Tish wiped her hands on a towel and straightened a tray of sausages that didn't need straightening. "Everyone else in town tries to be pleasant. It's a small town and a long winter so it makes sense for us all to make an effort. You know what I mean? But not that old bat. I just don't understand why he bothers to come in, except to bug me." Tish handed me a sample of a new cheese. It was delicious.

"Frank Kavanagh gave me a little rundown on the man but tell me what you know about why he is so miserable? Usually, someone who acts that way is just plain unhappy and takes it out on everyone around him. Is that his excuse, do you know?"

"Let's sit down, Liz. Just made a pot of caramel chai and my daughter Shelley made a coffee cake for breakfast. Never got a chance to try it because I had an early delivery to unload. Join me?"

"Love to, thanks. As long as I am not taking you from your work."

"Hey, after a session with that nutcase I need a break. He comes in here about once a week when he comes into town for his meager rations. Not that he ever buys anything here. Just looks around, makes a few critical comments, and leaves. However, never without saying, under his breath, *'They ought to go back to Portugal where they came from.'* Hey, Manny is from New Bedford and I'm from Quincy. The man is unstable and just plain mean."

"Do you think he really is writing a book about Granger the artist?"

"Well, someone does and someone is mighty upset by it, I'd say."

"Why do you say that, Tish?"

I never heard her answer since the shop was suddenly very busy. It was the day Manny put out the newest batch of homemade Portuguese sausages and the rush was on. After all, not only were the sausages terrific, but there was a finite supply every Tuesday morning. They were always gone by noon. Later, I joined the anxious throng, rising early on Tuesdays to be there first.

What Tish would have gone on to present as evidence that someone was upset about Edwin's real or imagined book, Daphne filled me in on, a few days later at the scene of Edwin Snow III's fall into the snow. The man *had* been, if not physically attacked then at least had two close calls. First came from the roof of the Canterbury Tales Leather Shop when a cement block fell within inches of his head. But that didn't mean that it wasn't meant to hit him. The cement block was not part of the structure that had come loose and fallen. No, it had been dropped. The second attempt had come in the form of large rock tossed across Commercial Street, again missing him by just inches. *Curiouser and curiouser.*

Five

When I'd told my mother about my inheritance, she was far from pleased. "But Mother, you know I love the sea and I can have a little sailboat and swim every day and I've always wanted to live in a small village. In addition, I can finally put to use those lovely cooking lessons from the Cordon Bleu. Owning and running an inn really appeals to me."

My mother, Lady Gwendolyn, let out a loud harrumph that travelled all the way from her townhouse in Holland Park, London, across the wide ocean and into my ear like a trans-Atlantic taser. I held the cell phone away from my head for fear of hearing damage.

I had put this off for days but finally, I had no choice. The call to my parents to let them know that I was beginning a new career had to be faced. I didn't kid myself that they would be pleased. Particularly my patrician mother.

"Sometimes I do believe that you are not my child. Why must you do such a foolish thing as go into *that* business? Serving people, no less. Her tone might have been in response to my announcement that I was driving a rubbish truck. "Darling you were not born to take on a subservient business. Running an inn is like being a skivvy. Darling, you will be a servant. Does your trust fund not provide enough for your needs, my darling? Tell me how much you need and MaMa will send it, I have more than I need. Or better yet by far, do come home and marry that lovely man who has adored you since childhood, Cecil Bottomley. Have a few little ones and learn to garden. But pleeeeze, darling, not commerce."

But, by then it was too late. I was settled in and enjoying my new life as innkeeper. My aunt's very capable manager, grad student in hotel management, Katy Balsam, had quickly immersed me in learning the business when I arrived on a lovely August day. The inn was full and the town was, as Katy described it, "a zoo with all the animals un-caged and on the rampage." I rather liked the crush of tourists. They added a carnival air to the little seaside village. Katy was an excellent instructor. In fact, in the interim since my aunt had died she had carried on so well, that, as she said, "I don't mean to be disrespectful, Liz, but it seemed important to me to continue on doing my job in such a way that the guests would never suspect that Mrs. Huntley had *checked out.*"

When Katy returned to school that first autumn of my new career, leaving me in charge, I actually enjoyed myself. Perhaps, if I'd known what was waiting for me in the not too distant future, I might have run like a rabbit. But, maybe not.

That first winter, I put my own mark on the inn. Never having painted a wall in my life I took on four bedrooms turning them from my aunt's evidently favorite colors of lilac and aqua and blushing pink to Williamsburg Blue, Tanbark Red and Scrivener's Gold. The white woodwork had been fairly recently done and was just fine so I left it in place. The shiny wide pine floors were lovely, needing nothing more than the handsome striped Dash and Albert cotton rugs that I ordered on-line.

I turned a long sunroom off the kitchen into an office that did double duty as a sitting room. There I could work at my laptop and read on sunny afternoons. The room had six long windows that offered wonderful light on all but the darkest, stormiest days or serve tea to friends. I bought a wonderful, antique pine hutch where I stored, out of sight, everything related to running the inn. I replaced the old brown tweed, cat hair-infested couch with a glove soft, navy blue leather sofa and added two deep, comfy wing chairs. Thus, over time, the Cranberry Inn Bed and Breakfast was transformed from a charming, if out-dated, summer hotel into a nautical-style oasis. The addition of framed nautical charts on the two windowless walls completed the picture along with a wicker coffee table and two matching lamp tables. As a house-warming gift, Daphne had painted six white cotton duck cloth throw pillows with assorted nautical themes. A wonderful antique brass sextant from a local antique shop sat proudly on a side table and an old ship model graced the mantle. The Great Age of Sail meets Ralph Lauren in a nautical mood.

It was during my re-decorating period that I'd met Daphne Crowninshield who was to become my dearest, new friend in the "new world." I was becoming more American every day.

25

Not that my giveaway British accent matched the transformation but I was one more lump in the "melting pot."

I'd popped into Daphne's art gallery called *Galimaufry*, on my way to Souza's Market one morning that first autumn. I was greeted by a statuesque runway model obviously impersonating a struggling artist. "Good morning. Welcome to *Galimaufry*. I know, a weird name but a good one nevertheless, I assure you," Daphne said by way of introduction.

Immediately, I liked her. "Hello. I am Liz Ogilvie-Smythe. I just love your work. So…local."

We laughed and became immediate friends. "After all," as Daphne said that day, "we bounders must stick together while in the colonies." Although I wondered at her butchering of the King's English, I found her to be great fun and always a breath of fresh air. Even when things got mighty weird and there were days when I wondered if I just might have to return to England and marry simpering Cecil Bottomley.

Daphne told me that *Galimaufry* was an archaic term meaning "a mixed collection of things, a kind of hodgepodge of unrelated objects." She explained that her goal was to bring in different styles of painting, eventually. We spent an hour and a half bonding and then went off to the Lobster Bowl for lobster rolls. "The best on the east coast," proclaimed Daphne. She'd been quite correct. Yum.

I told her how I'd come to end up in Provincetown. She told me that she'd known and very much liked my aunt. We talked about art and I told her about attending the Edward Granger show at the Boston Museum of Fine Arts while temporarily staying in the city. She told me that she liked most of Granger's work except for his local paintings. I laughed until my sides hurt when she commented on her impression of the paintings Granger had done while summering on the Cape.

"Sort of American Gothic without the pitchfork. Or, Norman Rockwell meets Grandma Moses on the day the Valium ran out. I don't really think the area was ever so forlorn and seeming to be waiting for true life to begin."

We'd been good chums ever since. The day after Edwin Snow III's body was found in the snow, Daphne and I met for breakfast at Beasley's fifties-retro restaurant. Known for the best breakfasts for miles around as well as superior comfort food, Beasley's was run by a family from New York grown sick of the hustle bustle of the city. Daphne told me that it was where Edwin Snow III had eaten his breakfast every day for years. She'd added that none of the waitresses but DeeDee Bradford would wait on the difficult old man. It seemed to be a place to start.

As it was not very busy, I asked DeeDee if she could tell me a little about the dead man. She looked around to see if any of her customers needed her and finding that everyone was still busy eating, she sat with us in the booth.

DeeDee's story was captivating. Even Edwin Snow's eating habits were weird. "Every morning at seven minutes to eight he arrived. Folks could set their watches to his schedule. He checked around until he discovered a booth or table where a previous customer had left the daily *Provincetown Banner* or the *Boston Globe* and there he sat. I was the only waitperson who'd still wait on him by the time he…died. The others refused to go near the fussy man."

"What was he so fussy about DeeDee?" asked Daphne.

"Everything, but mostly his food. If you could call what he ate food. I mean, he ignored all the great stuff on the menu and ordered the very same thing, every day. You know, sometimes I'd start feeling sorry for the lonely old man and he'd just go and do something so outrageous I'd go back to disliking him. But, I was sweet as honey and always smiled at the old goat. Might have saved up those smiles for a rainy day. He never smiled back, of course."

"What did he order?" I asked Dee Dee.

"Three pieces of burnt toast with no butter but with a 'thin skin' of orange marmalade. He'd say, 'As thin as tissue paper.' Trouble was, he said the exact same thing, day after day, as if I was a dumbbell with a lobotomy and couldn't remember something so damned simple. Then he'd add, 'And don't knock off any of the crispy edges, I want my full money's worth'. Can you

27

imagine that? How'd you like to face that first thing in the morning, ladies?"

"Did he drink coffee or tea?" My inner amateur sleuth was most certainly awakening. Burgeoning inside my head. Every question was meant to add a new detail to the profile of the recently dead man. I was becoming a hybrid of my favorite small village sleuths. Then it struck me like a welcome thunder bolt. If I could not dig into ancient tombs and catacombs and buried religious sites, I could, however, dig into a possible murder. A surge of delight raced through my mind as I was pulled back to the fascinating subject at hand.

"Get ready for a really good laugh." DeeDee laughed herself as we awaited some gem.

"He always ordered a cup of hot water and the ketchup bottle. Yup, made his own mix-in-place tomato soup. Is that a hoot, or what? Guess you're not supposed to laugh about the dead but, hey, the man was a trip. Get this, he paid in small change. Yup, had an old leather change purse full of it. Never carried a single bill. He went to the bank every other Monday regularly and withdrew forty dollars in small change. My sister works at the bank. The man was a rich as Croesus and he lived on next to nothing. Hey, maybe I should have married him and inherited all that sweet dough."

DeeDee drifted off for a second then returned to the present. "I was just remembering something odd I once saw when he went to pay the bill. Never tipped, of course. Mrs. Beasley always slipped me what the tip ought to be. Well, anyway, he pulled out some dimes and nickels and in the process he dropped something on the floor. I leaned down to pick it up for the old coot. It was a torn in half Tarot card. That creepy one with the Grim Reaper on it. The Death card."

DeeDee went off to wait on another customer and Daphne and I sat talking. Daphne had her own Edwin Snow stories to impart.

"Everyone knows the man inherited a bundle of money from his equally mean father. But, get this, the man was so stingy he refused to pay for either rubbish pickup or a dump sticker and instead, he snuck around after dark to put it in Tish and Manny's dumpster."

"Did the Souzas mind him doing that?"

"I would, I'll tell you that. It's the principle of the thing. However Manny just said, 'Not worth dealing with the nutcase. Got better things to do.' So, the old bat never even got a slap on the wrist. Chief Henderson knows by heart the complaints Edwin has made over the years. He and Chief Garrett from Truro meet for lunch once a month at Beasley's just to compare notes and more often than not it is something that old madman did or said that gets them riled.

"You see, the Snow mansion is not actually in Provincetown but in North Truro. However, it's closer to us than the tiny center of Truro. Not much of a center as it consists of a small library and a poky, little general store. So, whenever Edwin had a complaint, he took it to Chief Henderson."

"How annoying for our chief to have to deal with the man whose property taxes were paid to different town."

"Get this. Our charming Edwin had a long-standing dispute going with the neighbor to his east who's a lobsterman. Edwin was forever complaining that he could smell the lobster traps and demanding the man get rid of them. Right, just go out of the business that had supported his grandfather and father before him! Imagine the nerve of the man. The nut even took his neighbor's dog hostage. Claimed he wouldn't return the poor pup until the traps were moved. Chief could find no laws regarding dog-napping so they settled the issue by covering the traps with tarpaulins and poor old Skippy the hound was returned."

"Sounds like a truly crazy man, no doubt about it. I sort of feel sorry for him though, don't you, Daph?"

"Not really. Get this. Other neighbors were harassed, as well. Oh, you are going to just love this one, Liz. Edwin complained that another neighbor's cat trespassed on his property with *malicious intent*! Chief Henderson hooted over that one, I can tell you."

We laughed heartily about Edwin Snow's irritable character and seeming driving need to cause conflict. Simultaneously however, I was experiencing a growing need of

29

my own to bring the old curmudgeon a measure of justice. Posthumously.

My amateur sleuth meter was racing. I was intrigued by all that I'd heard about Edwin Snow III. But did I dare jump, possibly right up to my neck, into something I had no business getting involved in? In the village where I was a virtual newcomer? Food for thought.

Six

Paying no heed to my own misgivings, I found myself surreptitiously asking a few questions about the old man around the village. Simple curiosity in the wake of his death. At least, I hoped no one would suspect my real motives. *"What a tangled web we weave when first we practice to deceive."*

Gertrude Nickerson, who ran the Needling Around Yarn Shop told me that Edwin Snow had been a few years ahead of her in school. "The boy was a whiner and sniveler. Got himself a fine education at Yale however. He was a pre-med student and yet, after graduation he came home to his father's house and never left." Gertrude told me this as she sat knitting without ever moving her eyes from my face to her wildly moving knitting needles.

"He never went off to make a life for himself?" I asked.

Gertrude put down her knitting briefly. She smiled slyly and I waited, knowing she was about to share something either cute or shocking.

"Edwin did absolutely nothing to discourage the opinion by all that he was the spitting image of his nasty father; a similar apple fallen from the family tree. So, everyone just assumed that he was just like old Ned. It was assumed that such a father could only have spawned a horned, cloven-hoofed, flesh-eating, devil-vermin." She laughed and picked up her knitting.

I sat shocked to hear the tiny white-haired grandmotherly woman speaking like the television narrator of a program on werewolves and Big Foot. We laughed together and then she went to make us some tea. I came away with the gift of a lovely silk ribbon knitted scarf in shades of turquoise from pale to deepest blue-green.

Back at the inn, sitting in the sunny sitting room, coming up to a fortnight (two weeks, in American vernacular) after the mysterious death of Edwin Snow, I questioned my motives. Also, my good judgment.

31

Chief Henderson had called it a suicide and closed the case. Oughtn't I just leave it at that I asked myself? However, inside my head I heart the flinty voice that sounded to me like how M.C. Beaton's feisty sleuth Agatha Raisin would sound if she were real. She disagreed with that last thought.

So, you plan to just rot away in that little American village? Toss away your skills for digging? Become a drudge and grow old never having diverted your fine education onto a new, useful avenue? Digging needn't be limited to the earth. Here before you is the opportunity to dig into murder. No trowel required.

That brought me up short. I'd ask Daphne's opinion. She also loved cozies. Coincidentally, that evening was to be the first meeting of the newly formed Cozy Mystery Book Club. A temporary name until we voted on a proper one. A book club with a twist that would probably backfire on us. Nevertheless, we planned to give it a try. Except for Daphne, the founding "mothers" were all great cooks. As it turned out, we attracted the most delightful mixed bag of gender orientations from straight females to lesbians to transsexuals and one...no I'll hold that surprise for later. The by-laws would say that the monthly hostess would be required to serve a three course meal before the meeting and book discussion. No simply brownies and cookies at our cozy book club meetings.

Daphne got a by. Since she could not, as she'd admitted, "make a Marmite sandwich without guidance" she would be allowed to hire her favorite village caterer for this task. Bama (short for Alabama) Hutton of Hutton's Gluttons Catering Service lived and worked in the village and joined the club.

Growing up in London, my family had a cook who could roast a beef or a bird and was adept at mashed potatoes but lived in fear of any but canned vegetables. For years, based on eating at friends' houses, restaurants, country houses to which I was invited for weekends and even at university, I came to assume that I had inherited some recessive genes not found in my parents. I'd never heard them complain about Meaghan's cooking although of course, they were pretty self-absorbed so that might explain their lack of interest in the meals set before them.

32

I am the child of parents who, I often imagined in my mind's eye, woke up one morning to find a baby girl lying between them and having no idea of how she got there but being essentially good people, raised her anyway. That's my story and I am sticking to it.

I'd begun reading cookbooks in my teens when my friends were reading the popular trash. The summer I'd spent in Paris learning from the finest cooking teachers in the world had certainly come in handy when I suddenly, unexpectedly, but to my pure delight, became an innkeeper. Being a *chocoholic*, I chose a very special recipe for the evening's dessert. Custard-filled, chocolate *ganache*-frosted cream puffs. To hell with the caloric impact; this was to be a special night.

The main course would consist of my favorite quiches. For the vegetarians a filling of pears, green onions, spinach and gruyere cheese. For the carnivores bacon, tomato, grilled fennel, feta cheese and fresh basil from the tall plant in my sunny kitchen window. There would be a tossed salad, various spicy condiments and freshly baked baguettes brushed with garlic butter. The wines from the local vintner, Truro Vineyard, were bright, sunny and reminiscent of a visit I'd made to Tuscany.

Everything was ready by five-thirty. I popped into the old claw-footed, porcelain tub for a leisurely bath. Forty minutes later, rising from deep, lilac-scented bubbles I was ready for a fun evening. Daphne had picked up a couple of new members who were unknown to me, so new friends would be made over good food and good books.

I made a plait of my hair that needed a trim. Maybe some lighter streaks for summer. I had to ask Daphne who did her hair locally. As the evening was cool, that wily, quixotic fox still fooling around with the season, I donned a black cotton turtleneck sweater and rust-colored, butter-soft suede jeans. A half-dozen silver bangles and large silver hoop earrings and I was ready.

I lit candles and did a final check on the food. The wine was chilling. It promised to be a fine evening. Daphne outdid herself by arriving on time. At seven sharp, she and three other women arrived. Right behind them came my next door neighbor Alice Kline and two women I'd seen around the village but never met. After introductions, we enjoyed appetizers in the living room.

Everyone enjoyed the dinner and finally, it was time for the dessert. I suggested we all retire to the sitting room for the final course and tea and coffee. I delivered the shiny, chocolate ganache-frosted cream puffs on a large, blue, Provencal platter to happy applause.

"Oh Liz, they look so scrumptious. Promise me there's not a calorie in them," Mary Ellen pleaded.

"Not a one, dive in." I answered.

Sated and nursing our hot drinks and/or after dinner cordials, it was time for getting down to business. Licking the chocolate ganache from her lips to get every last morsel, Daphne opened the business meeting. "I suppose the group ought to have a name. Any suggestions?"

"Oh, I know, I know. How about Les Girls? It's got such a nice ring to it." That was the newest member, Geraldine.

"Yes, but what if we get some male members?" I asked and was immediately challenged.

"Oh pleeeeze, no. Men are beasts!" Geraldine.

Daphne smiled at the handsome, big-boned but very attractive woman dressed in a smart pant suit and the two high-fived in female solidarity. I'd liked Geraldine right from our introduction when she'd admired the wall and furniture colors and complimenting me on my good taste.

"Now, we all know men are beasts but necessary beasts. Anyway, we might uncover some intelligent, well-mannered, interesting bibliophiles, even here at the end of the world." My attempt to broaden the perspective. I might have been proposing the admittance to our lofty club of warlocks and vampires if Geraldine's look was any indication of the extent of my crime against the nature of good sense.

Daphne's sly grin I knew only too well. What was she up to, I wondered?

"Listen up, girls. Geraldine ought to know about men. After all, *she used to be one.*" Daphne waited for the reaction.

"You were, Geraldine, that's great. It's like having a double agent in the group. Oh, there is so much you can teach us." You could have knocked me over with a feather. The lovely woman who reminded me of the sixties Swedish actress Anita Ekberg from movies my mother used to watch had formerly been a man? Amazing. Naïve me asked, "Was it very painful to make the change?"

"Just a few chemicals and a snip here and a tuck there and *voila*! Most fun was buying lacy bras and underpants." We all dissolved into laughter, the conversation drifted off in many directions and we never came up with a name for the club.

Seven

The next morning, as I was taking a batch of chocolate coconut biscotti from the oven, the old-fashioned wall phone in the kitchen jangled. The Pointillists, the local needlepoint club named for the nineteenth century French art movement characterized by applying points of paint that resulted in works of art, had hired the dining room for their meeting that afternoon. I'd offered to donate the pastries and coffee and tea. Good for business but also because everyone in the village had made me feel so welcome. It was the least I could do.

"Good morning, Ms., um, is it Ogilvie or Smythe I should be calling you, ma'am?"

"First, let's establish to whom I am speaking and then we will get to my name, Sir."

"So sorry. I am Officer James Finneran at the police station, ma'am."

"Well, Officer James Finneran, nice to meet one of the village guardians. By the way, no need for the ma'am, and it is a hyphenated name; therefore, the hyphen joining the otherwise two separate names makes it one name. Ogilvie-Smythe."

"Ah, and as I can tell by the lovely accent you are from my general neighborhood. Allow me to properly introduce myself to you ma'am er, Ms. Ogilvie-Smythe...James Finneran late of Dublin, Ireland. Not too fond of your Queen but I hope that doesn't get in the way of our being friends."

James had a habit of adopting a deeper brogue when talking to women. Although it seemed to turn men off, women seemed to "gobble it up like treacle," he once commented to Chief Henderson who laughed so hard he spilled his coffee all down the front of his uniform.

I could not help but smile; he sounded like the quintessential leprechaun. "Don't quote me, please, but, quite frankly, some days I'm not so fond of her either. And the behavior of her offspring. Oh my, a pack of spoiled *Brits!*"

"Isn't that just grand. I see that you've got yourself a fine sense of humor. Well, now, is it Ms. or Mrs.?" Right to the point.

"I suppose that depends on the reason for this call. If I have a parking ticket I do not know about or you saw me pinching the fruit at Souza's market, then it is Ms. Ogilvie-Smythe. If you want a donation for the policeman's ball or want to book a room for your mother visiting from the old country, then it is definitely Elizabeth. Should we ever become good friends, I have no problem with simply Liz."

"It will be my extreme pleasure to look forward to Liz. For now I must let you know that there is a lawyer here from Boston who would like to talk to you. When it's convenient, of course. However, he would like it to be today."

"A lawyer. So, you *do* prosecute for fruit pinching."

"Oh, Ms. Ogilvie-Smythe, you are a card."

"Mr. Finneran, or should I address you as Officer? I can be available at one this afternoon if that works with the lawyer. However, might I know what this is all about? I've never been fond of surprises."

"As you may know, we recently had a tragedy in town. Old man Edwin Snow...jumped from the Pilgrim Monument. According to the lawyer, it seems he named you in his will."

I was glad he could not see my face at that moment since he sounded good looking and I was anxious to take his measure. But if a look of surprise could be measured on a scale of one to ten, then mine was easily a fifteen.

I hung up the wall phone and simply stood there utterly dumbfounded. Then, I grabbed it back and punched in Daphne's number.

"Hi. Something really, really odd is going on."

"Yes, and your point exactly? This is P-town where odd is *de rigueur*."

"No, seriously Daphne. I just got a call from the police station about a lawyer who wants to meet with me to tell me about...It just has to be a mistake, that's it."

"Blimey, Liz, will you please get to the point."

"It seems that odd little man who jumped from the Pilgrim Monument left me something in his will."

Silence.

"Aha, so you and the old guy had something going, did you? After his money were you?"

"Get serious Daphne, I've got enough money to buy this entire town so what would I be doing with a weird little man whom everyone disliked?"

"Damned if I know. Perversity? A long, celibate winter?"

I hung up and smiled. Yes, a long, celibate winter, indeed.

I walked to the police station hoping the Irish policeman would be there. He sounded so delightful on the phone. It *had* been a long time between men. Daphne had been right on. A long, celibate winter and longer still since I'd met anyone worth even washing my hair for!

I walked into the Town Hall, looked to my left and saw the reception area for the police department. To my right a door was open and a well-dressed, gray-haired man sat at a reproduction Governor Winthrop desk leaning over a pile of official looking papers. Definitely the attorney. No sign of the leprechaun.

Introducing myself, I had my most skeptical face on. The whole idea that a virtual stranger, the town curmudgeon, had left me something was way beyond ludicrous. Surely, there'd been a big mistake.

"How do you do, I'm Elizabeth Ogilvie-Smythe and of course, there has been a mistake. I did not know the man who died and he did not know me. Therefore, he had no reason to leave me anything in his will."

"How do you do, Ms. Ogilvie-Smythe? Allow me to introduce myself, Anthony Wilder from Wilder, Fitzpatrick and Cohen, Boston."

The tall, well-dressed attorney exuded an air of frostiness that I could feel right through my forest green cashmere jacket. I was sure that this was a mistake that could quickly be remedied.

Ignoring my objections, the lawyer motioned me to a chair. "Kindly take a seat here," he pointed to a chair placed at an angle to the one next to it, in between which was a small, handsome *piecrust* edged table on which was sitting a dainty porcelain teapot and two delicate cups. Pretty nice stuff for a police station interview room, I thought. Looking around at the fine wood paneling on the walls and the tin ceiling I had to wonder what purpose this room had served in the old town hall.

"Tea?"

Being offered tea by a humorless city attorney who obviously had me mixed up with someone else, thus keeping me from more important things, really grated. However, the familiar fragrance of one of my favorite teas, Oolong, won me over.

"I do realize that this perhaps comes as a surprise, Ms. Ogilvie-Smythe, but I assure you this is legitimate. Mr. Edwin," he looked down at the papers on his lap. "So sorry, I had to step in just this morning on the fly as my father was stricken ill. Ah yes. Mr. Edwin Snow was my father's client for many, many years."

"So sorry, is your father going to be alright?"

"Pardon me? Oh, yes. Just a bit of gout. Nothing serious. Except, of course, to poor father." He tittered. I grimaced but he either missed it or chose to ignore my human emotion as it was probably alien to his nature.

"Now, let us move on here. Mr. Edwin Snow III has specifically named you as heir to his manuscript. His home and the bulk of his monetary estate he left to the American Pit Bull Advocate Society but this box belongs to you."

Reaching for a leather box about the size of a small valise, he pulled it toward him, hesitating for a moment as if trying to judge my worthiness. Looking directly into the man's pellucid eyes, I wondered how this crazy error might have occurred. My natural cat-like curiosity however kept me glued to the chair.

The sun slanting in through the tall, many-paned, not too clean window was warm and spring-like. In the past, I would have nipped off to the Caribbean or the Côte d'Azur to avoid the discontent that can come with the long, gray days of a London winter. I had surprised myself by my state of contentment that winter. Maturity or simply novelty? *Whatever.* As Daph would have said.

At last, the stuffed shirt spoke. "This case contains the manuscript formerly belonging to Edwin Snow III. It now belongs to you, by order of his will."

I simply offered a perplexed look and sat there hoping the cute sounding Irish cop would suddenly appear. We could maybe pop off to kiss the Blarney Stone together.

The attorney removed an envelope from the folder in front of him. I sipped my tea. Sun motes danced in the slanted light. No Officer Finneran came to my rescue. Damsel disappointed.

He handed me the letter and I took it as if it was on fire. A pause followed that, despite its insubstantial nature, felt like a chill blanket that encased us and altered the fiber of our corporeal reality. The room shifted and then shifted back but this latter only because one of us chose to speak into the yawning void.

"Oh, my, pardon me, how stupid of me not to notice this. Ah, yes, well now, that changes things quite dramatically doesn't it?" Attorney Wilder appeared either agitated or constipated and anxious to remedy that situation.

"Aha, at last, there *is* a mistake isn't there? This is not my inheritance but belongs to someone else entirely. Therefore," I rose abruptly, "I shall get on with my day. Good day, Sir."

"No, please wait. There is no mistake about this." He turned toward the box. "Yes, it is to be yours. Oh my. Not just yet. It seems that Mr. Snow added a codicil to his will just nine weeks before his death. It seems that he feared for his life, told my father that, according to this file and so...Interesting, very interesting."

I had never been famous for having a high patience threshold and this ludicrous meeting had just gone on far too long for me. The expression, *cat on a hot tin roof* came to mind. I knew that I would have to leave or I just might pop this fellow in his snooty nose.

"Look, why don't you just burn this or put it on e-Bay or let it blow on the wind because, quite frankly I have lost interest in this matter and I do have a busy day ahead of me. Gazing at my watch I declared, "Well now, look at that, it's almost tea time. Talley ho, got to go."

"Ms. Smythe, please," the man's tone made it abundantly clear that he was totally disinterested in what I might want and, in addition, he'd gotten my name wrong. I began to bristle like a hedgehog.

"I think that you will want to hear this, as it explains everything quite succinctly."

I groaned audibly and resumed my seat.

"Evidently, the man was a close friend to your aunt. A Mrs. Elizabeth Smythe Huntley, late of this community. As the man was evidently fearful for his life following certain 'attacks' to his person, he added this codicil to his will just nine weeks ago. My, my, this is strange. Yes, indeed."

I snapped. "And did you wish to share this oddity with me or simply keep it to enjoy later at your leisure? So, the tragic old man knew my aunt, did he? She is gone and I was never even properly introduced to the man so this makes not one iota of sense. Why me?"

I considered faking a faint. Anything to bring the strange meeting to an end. But there was something more. Something so farcical this scene fit more appropriately into a British drawing room comedy than my life. These kinds of things don't happen in real life. At least, not in my life. But I was wrong.

"In effect, it states here that you do not receive the manuscript until you find his *murderer*!"

"What?" I fell back into the chair like a popped balloon.

Eight

I'd walked home in a daze. The snow was gone but there were little reminder traces of the surprise snowstorm up against places that did not get the sun. Along the way my spirits, if not my confusion, lifted as I noticed lots of pale green shoots in front gardens. Signs of spring.

"Find my murderer." Why in the world had that unhappy old man chosen me for the task? Where did he get off demanding such a thing? From a virtual stranger. I could only suppose it was just one of his nasty plots to cause discontent. Because I'd patted and befriended his dog? Surely, that could not have been enough reason to foist such a ridiculous duty upon my head. Therefore, I would simply ignore the codicil. I'd classify it as the final trick of a sick and paranoid man and forget I'd ever heard it.

Back at the inn, the architect and the builder who were in charge of renovating my Aunt Libby's 1950's kitchen were just arriving as I pulled up in the Jeep. They left after we made a few changes to the plan. I made a cup of Jasmine tea and headed to the sunny sitting room. Just what I needed, right then. If this were a tennis match, I thought, the point would have gone to the old man. He had managed to set my nerves on edge. Nothing like the comfort of tea. The chamomile tea's soporific effect took me from contemplation of my strange meeting with the attorney who'd, in effect, arranged a posthumous encounter between me and the old grump, Edwin Snow III, into a lucid daydream.

Find my murderer!

Wearing a handsome, black London Fog trench coat and a muted paisley Liberty scarf I moved stealthily through the village in search of clues. Calling upon my newly formed friendships, I surreptitiously inquired about the dead man while carefully disguising the reasons for my interest. Best not to arouse their suspicions that I was on a mission to find a murderer.

One by one the clues accumulated until I had the case solved and only then did I go to the police with my findings. They applauded my efforts as the case had stymied them for so long. I was thereby appointed a special ex-officio detective. A sort of crime consultant.

The chiming of the old grandfather's clock on the landing brought me abruptly back to reality. The sun had lost its gloss and the thick, dark clouds that had rolled in looked most unfriendly. More rain? What is this, London? I asked aloud although there was no one to answer me, and, just as well. The silly, little daydream had stirred up the memory of what I'd seen that day when Edwin Snow lay broken in the fresh fall of snow. I couldn't shake the feeling that the incongruity of his crushed skull just could not be so easily set aside as the Police Chief had obviously done. But, who was I to question the highest law in the village? Chief Henderson had closed the case after calling the death suicide. I needed professional information. Fortunately, that excellent advice and possibly some helpful guidance was only an international call away.

Being an inveterate list maker, I took pen in hand and sat with a pad of yellow lined paper to get my thoughts and impressions organized.

Suicide or Murder: Edwin Snow III

1.   How did the old man gain access to the Pilgrim Monument? Daphne said that Bill Windship practically owns the tower and he has the key. Sleeps with the key, she surmised.

2. How did Edwin Snow manage to climb all of those steps at his age? It would seem that suicide would be a moot point since he should have had a heart attack and died as a result of the climb.

3. Why choose that method of suicide, anyway?

4. Who would gain from his death?

5. What part does his manuscript play in the plot?

6. Will reading the manuscript help to solve the case and if so, how can I get my hands on it without first solving the case????
Catch 22.

Next question I spoke aloud to the silent room. What on earth am I doing? This is just plain crazy. What does it matter to me how the old coot died? Then Agatha Raisin with her "little bear eyes" and "great legs" came vibrantly into my mind. As if she was sitting across from me, her steely voice echoed inside my head. *How can you even think of not getting involved? Are you not a decent, compassionate, civilized human being? Even miserable, nasty old curmudgeons who are hated by everyone ought to have an advocate if and when they are murdered. That's why you must, I reiterate MUST get involved, bloody fool!*

Then, almost as if Agatha herself had taken pen to paper, I wrote: *I must investigate this case because I seem to be the only person in the entire village, including the law, who saw something irregular at the crime scene and that irregularity could be the difference between the verdict of suicide and MURDER.*

I picked up the cell phone and punched in Daphne's number.

"Hi. How about sharing my humble dinner. Daphne?"

"Hi. Sure. Got to eat somewhere so might as well be your place. See you about six, got to drive to Barnstable with a painting for a show at the Cape Cod Art Association gallery. Toodleoo."

In the kitchen, I took four jumbo shrimp out of the refrigerator and set about making a potent garlic stuffing for them. This mindless work gave me more time to think about the challenging conundrum. Did I have what it takes to be an amateur sleuth? Could I weather the repercussions if I found the murderer and it was someone well-loved and respected who'd just lost it and, in a moment of passion, tossed the old man over the side of the Pilgrim Monument?

Wait a minute! Smashing six elephant garlic cloves, it occurred to me that this might not have anything to do with his real or imagined manuscript full of real or imagined scandals and secrets. Of course. It made no sense whatsoever that the frail, old man chose to jump to his death from the Pilgrim Monument. He might have been annoying and difficult but he wasn't stupid. If he'd wanted to end his life, there certainly were easier ways. I could come up with no reason for his choosing to climb hundreds of stairs in an icy tower on a snowy night to make the fatal jump.

Thus, I engaged a helpful theory learned in university physics class. William of Occam's, Occam's Razor, in modern vernacular, KISS, Keep It Simple Stupid, states that once you discard everything unlikely what you ought to be left with is the truth of the matter.

Applying this to the case of Edwin Snow's death, it seemed to me that the truth was that someone either forced or carried the old man up those stairs. Either way, didn't that point to someone younger and stronger? Insert that fact and what you get is that it was unlikely that the killer was concerned about the possible revelation of old secrets and scandals.

Daphne's arrival put an end to my sleuth-related contemplations. "Tea or coffee?" I asked her.

"Gin." said my glamorous friend.

Then, "What's for dinner?"

"I've prepared a shrimp scampi, risotto with a mild pesto sauce, spinach, mandarin orange and purple onion salad, Aunt Libby's wonderful squash dinner rolls and her favorite pie, cranberry pecan. Will that do, my food compacter friend?"

"Sure. Why not? Hey, everyone loved my painting and I think I might even have already sold it to the gallery director who grew up in this village. She simply drooled over it."

"Messy, I'd say."

"Very funny. Getting out this afternoon was impossible. I had to clip Kilty Goldfarb's nails, just couldn't put it off another day. She's shredded the house. Thankfully she was in a particularly good mood since I promised her a few sardines if she cooperated."

"I keep meaning to ask you, Daphne; why that weird name for your poor innocent cat?"

"Read it in a novel just before she wandered in with her lovely gray coat all full of knots and an infected sore on her paw. Just seemed like an omen. Kilty was a difficult person with psychological knots ergo…"

Just before Daphne's arrival, I'd attempted to reach Nigel Hoppington in London. The longer I put it off the more it would niggle around in my head driving me to distraction. Reaching only his voicemail, I left a brief message telling my old friend that I would call again the next day.

45

As we sat sipping our gin and tonics, Daphne was full of stories picked up at the gallery. I tried to concentrate on her words but my mind kept drifting off. Pulling myself back to the present and my loquacious friend, I asked, "Did you do the cat grooming in that getup, Daph?"

"Can't you tell by all the gray hairs on this skirt?" She stood, did a quick perfunctory shaking of the skirt, sat down again and picked up her glass exclaiming, "Okay, sock it to me. What happened at the meeting with the Boston attorney? Did the old guy leave you his Gothic mansion because he liked the cut of your jib, matey?"

Rather than answer her, I simply held out the letter. The letter from the old curmudgeon who'd had the audacity to demand that I find his murderer."

I sat quietly while Daphne read it. I watched the expressions on her face change like badly timed traffic lights.

"You have got to be kidding. Wowzer. Why?"

"My question exactly, why me? I just don't need this. I have a nice life here and I don't need some old coot interfering. Probably as a big joke. Black humor."

"But, come on, Liz. Aren't you salivating to read that enigmatic manuscript?"

"Daphne, I doubt that anything in that man's writing is worth reading. In fact, I suspect it is more like a list of complaints. Probably an inventory of every slight, every insult, ever rebuff the man ever encountered from the villagers. Not worth the paper it's written on."

"But, Edward Granger. What if the old guy had hung around with him? Maybe even partook in a few spicy scandals with the Granger gang from New York who came to stay. You cannot discount that the writing might be worth reading. Granger was a paragon in his time. The man inspired an entire movement in art that still shows up in local galleries. His subjects were so...angular."

"Angular?"

"Well I mean, rooflines and shingles and the general architectural lines of nineteenth century New England buildings were so damned serious. So unrelentingly angular. After growing up around charming stone house with crenellations and towers and curved windows and arches covered in strangling vines, one can't help but notice the difference in *New* England. What were those Pilgrims thinking? I prefer our softer, more aesthetically pleasing architecture but you have to like the man's style."

"Daphne, it occurs to me that you know just about everything about me, my icy parents, my lonely childhood, my school experiences, even my lovers and yet you have revealed very little. Time to dish the dirt. Crenellations, towers, etc. Are you a princess?"

"Hardly. Just a happy-go-lucky refugee from an extremely wealthy family. No big deal."

"Interesting. We shall return to that subject. For now though, time to eat."

After dinner, we returned to the subject of the Edwin Snow letter. "So you must see, Daph, after reading the crazy old man's letter, in his usual fashion he intended to stir up trouble even after death. I am hardly going out looking for a murderer that might not exist."

"Whatever. But, consider this, pal of mine. This is your chance to be one of your favorite cozy sleuths. Charge!!!" Daph stood wielding the antique walking stick with a carved eagle head for a handle that she pulled from among my growing collection standing in a tall crock next to the side table.

"Damn. Oh Daph, maybe you're correct. I suppose I would be *out of my squash* if I didn't go for it, to use one of your favorite expressions."

"It's *out of your gourd,* but anyway, close enough. Tell me honestly. In your gut what do you believe? Suicide or murder?"

"I have toyed with the following scenario; some old timer in the village decided to have it out with Edwin and finally tell him all the things that have annoyed him over the years. He intended it to be strictly verbal but it got out of hand. Before he knew it, their encounter turned really sour and without knowing what he was doing he just lost it and tossed him off the top of the monument. Not pre-meditated but a crime of passion. He's probably a wreck about what he did. Of course, that leaves a really big question unanswered. Why on earth would two old men climb hundreds of stairs just to have a chin wag?"

"Exactly." Daphne grinned like the Cheshire cat. "Although, old people get some pretty strange ideas. Maybe the two old men, just for something different to do, climbed the hundreds of stairs in the frosty tower to have a smoke. Hey, I've got it. Yes, this is much better. When they were young they shared their very first smoke up there at the top of the Monument. Back then it would have been a lark; the steps would have meant nothing to the boys. But this time, it would have been too much for them. They would have been tired and grumpier than usual when they arrived at the top so when Edwin said something nasty, the other guy, we'll call him Georgie, lost it and tossed him. Then he climbed down and went home to feed his dog."

Laughing like fools felt really good. I chose not to tell Daph about the international phone call I still had to complete before I could even consider taking on an Agatha Raisin or Miss Marple persona. Best to wait until I had all my chickens in a line or was it ducks? I guessed I'd never really sound American.

After Daphne headed home, taking with her the leftovers from dinner that she planned to enjoy the next night rather than a T.V. dinner, I sat to re-read nasty, presumptuous Edwin's letter, again. A combination of annoyance and thrill of the hunt overtook me.

Dear Elizabeth,

May I address you by your given name? Well, if you are reading this, then I am already dead so this is a moot question. We have not been properly introduced although Patton showed his approval of you and that carries weight with me. This bequest will surely take you by surprise because you do not know the history behind it. Thus, let me begin at the beginning.

When I was a young man with endless promise, I met and befriended the artist Edward Granger and his lovely wife Ellyn. We met at the Atlantic House bar one stormy summer night and after a few drinks we became the best of friends. In those days, the drinks were cheap and the regulations about public imbibing were few. Thus, the partying never ended and no one was censured for their behavior. Ed was a heavy drinker. We had a lot of good times, many laughs and much alcohol in that long-lost summer of my youth. Eventually, they and their heavy partying New York theatre friends returned to the city. I took the train into New York one weekend that following winter only to discover that ours had been only a summer idyll.

My death is the result of what I know and what my murderer does not want to reach the eyes and ears of the world. I knew your departed aunt, Libby. She was one of the few people in this cruel town who was kind to me. Libby was far too good for a town overrun with immoral artists and socialists. Eventually, we had a falling out, one that could not be mended and so we parted with bad feelings. What she foisted off on me was too, too unfair and unkind. For the rest of my life, those angry, displaced spirits plagued me. My death will end their hold on me. Or, perhaps not. I suppose I shall be one of their ilk. Despite the bitter ending of our friendship, I had intended to leave my manuscript to darling Libby. When she died before me, I despaired that all of my hard work would be lost. Thus, when her will named her niece, I regained my hope.

Now, you must solve the mystery that I leave behind me. Perhaps, the revenants will return to their original home and they shall be yours to placate. Keep this manuscript or toss it out but think on this; therein lie truths that will earn you (and posthumously, I) fame and glory.

As you now know, via my Boston attorney, my life has been threatened numerous times. Now, obviously, the murderer has succeeded. Curiosity drives me to wonder how the man will finally take my life. That is for you to know---if you have the courage. Libby was a courageous woman. I suspect you are, as well.

FIND MY MURDERER!
Edwin M. Snow III

Nine

First thing the next morning, I picked up my cell phone from the bedside table. I needed to catch MI6 Forensic Agent Nigel Hoppington before he departed for his usual long lunch at his favorite pub the Whistle and Owl in the shadow of Tower Bridge, just steps from the famous Black Friars. I was well aware that I was opening a Pandora's Box but it could not be helped. I needed Nigel's expert advice. Nigel and I had grown up together. Both children of preoccupied parents who'd left our rearing to hired help. We had ridden to the hunt, side by side. Competed in steeple chases. Taken jousting lessons and dancing lessons and even gone to the same summer camps for rich children. I always knew that Nigel loved me. Well, I loved him too but not that way. He still expected me to get through my independent phase and come home to marry him. It was not going to happen.

A wave of homesickness rolled over me while I waited for Nigel to pick up. I envisioned Big Ben's mighty face looming over the Thames. Boats of all sizes passing in the noonday sun or mist as the case may be in that flighty London climate. The ubiquitous tourists crowding the sidewalks and Ben's magnificent peal ringing out over the city. For a fraction of a second I was achingly homesick.

Then, reminding myself that the Cranberry Inn had become more homelike to me than any place I'd ever resided except for my wonderful years at Oxford, I quickly nipped that false emotion in the bud. Sure I missed the city. That city. But red, double decker buses and telephone booths, deep fog and dank rooms, the Haymarket Theatre and straight as a rod Buckingham Palace guards had been replaced by white sandy beaches, rusty fishing boats, crimson lobsters and sandpipers dancing along the shore. London, a great place to visit but Provincetown was now home.

"Agent Nigel Hoppington here."

"Hello, Nigel, its Elizabeth calling from America."

"Darling girl, how are you, Lady Elizabeth? Long time no word. So nice to come home to your melodious voice, *cara mia.*" Nigel spent all of his holidays in Italy and loved using his second, if generally butchered, language for emphasis.

"Drop the 'Lady' Nigel, I live in America now where such titles, like wearing fur, can get you splashed with red paint. However, I am in fine fettle, running my sainted aunt's little bed and breakfast in a quaint seaside village, writing a cookery book and having a jolly good time of it. However, I have a question that only you, my darling, friend can answer."

"Oh, beloved woman, just the fact that you've come to me makes me weak in the knees. Anything. But please make it, *Will you marry me Nigel and come to live with me in my seaside village?*"

"Maybe sometime, ducks, but just now I may be about to, perhaps foolishly, plunge into a quagmire that will probably be my undoing in my seaside village. But after all, as my new gal pal Daphne Crowninshield would say, what is the point of having a life if one does not go for all the gusto? Nigel, something has occurred here that has pulled me into a little mystery. Perhaps a murder mystery. Before I go ahead, however, I need you to clear up something for me."

"Did you say Daphne Crowninshield? *The* Daphne Crowninshield, multi, multi-millionairess of the Crowninshield South African mining fortune?"

"Damn. I knew that name sounded familiar. *NO.* No, she couldn't be. Could she?"

"Unless there is another, but I can tell you that when the old man died two years ago she took off and only her family knows where she is and the fortune just keeps on growing. Is she tall, slim as a reed with an angular but striking face and a gritty kind of voice? Sexy, I'm sure, to some, but for me only your angelic voice trills in my heart."

"Nigel, that describes her exactly. She has been very circumspect about her roots and her past but I never guessed... Well, well. She is very dear to me so I will respect her need for anonymity…for now. May have to use it to blackmail her sometime though."

Nigel laughed with delight. I knew all too well that I had to tread carefully since this sweet man was so dear to me. However, not dear in the way he would have liked. Since childhood, both children of busy parents who'd left the job to nurses, governesses and school masters, we'd been thrown together often. My parents and his had been best friends thus we were more like siblings than just friends. I, however, still considered him brother-like while his feelings were quite different toward me.

"I say, cara mia, why don't I just pop over for a holiday? Weather here is frightful. You could show me your village."

That would not do. "Nigel, at the mur…death scene of a man who the police assumed took his own life by jumping from the top of our very tall Pilgrim Monument. I saw something that has been niggling around in my fertile brain for days. Something that seemed, at least to me, to be incongruous. Only you can clear this up for me before I jump in and get involved in a possibly dangerous situation."

Silence. Then, "Oh, darling girl please do not put your magnificent self in danger. I can fly right over and be with you to protect you." Nigel's voice, so concerned and sincere, melted my heart as always and I wished that I could return his love but chemistry being what it was I simply could not.

"Thanks, ducks. Tell you what, if it gets too sticky then you will be the first one I'll call in. But for now, I need information. I need to know how a person who took a plunge off a two hundred and fifty-two foot tower would land."

I heard his snicker but waited for the humor to pass and for him to regain his professional stance. "Well, darling girl, I can tell you right off the bat that the sound would be *splat*. But I suppose you mean how would the body meet the hard ground, correct?"

"Yes, Nigel, my swain, that's what I am asking. Is there a formula or something that determines how a person hits depending on the height from which he falls or is it an individual thing or what?"

"The structure of the human body combined with the automatic physical response to such a fall pretty much predetermines the outcome. Let me explain. No matter how determined a person is to jump and end it all, the mind clicks in once the flight begins and there is a most definite physical response. Even deep despondency rarely overrides and obliterates our natural human survival response. No one makes such a fall with their arms pasted to their sides as they wait to hit solid ground. Arms and legs flail like a fledgling bird taking its first flight. I can tell you with certainty, my darling girl, that a person would have to be trussed like a Christmas turkey not to flail in flight."

"But, more specifically, would he have fallen face-first or on his back?'

"That would depend on his movements as he approached his landing site. There would be some effect upon the landing depending on the body's movement and whether the jumper was still conscious. However, it would be a toss-up. Like tossing a coin. Well, I mean I could get into the mathematics of it but that's probably not necessary."

"Thanks, Nigel. That is precisely what I'm looking for. So, unlikely he'd come down like a bomb with his head like a heat-seeking missile that would hit and crack open upon impact?"

"Mercy no. Whatever gave you such a Hollywood idea?"

Not bothering to address his question, I moved right on to the next one. "Well, before I leave your charming company, Nigel, please tell me this: What would cause someone to land squarely on the top of his head if he jumped or was pushed from a two hundred foot tall tower?"

"Angel girl, stretching my imagination I suppose I could propose a hypothetical situation. However, I'd rather not describe it to you; rather not cause you nightmares if I'm not there to comfort you."

"Nigel darling, I do really need to know. I can take it. Tell you what, let's suppose that the victim was already dead or at least unconscious and set it up for me, please."

"The murderer might have tied the victim's ankles together with a rope. Thus, when tossed over the side of the tower the trajectory would be guaranteed to end in a head-first landing."

"I see."

53

"Is that helpful, darling? Did your victim land head-first?"

"Thanks so much, Nigel. Let's get together next time I'm in London. Cheerio."

"Wait, Liz, what..."

I felt terrible about hanging up abruptly, but I was suddenly on pins and needles. Agatha Raisin was screeching inside my head and Miss Marple was sitting on my shoulder, carpet bag in hand, advising me as to my next move. This sleuthing business could be hard on the nerves.

Next stop the Provincetown Police Station. I jumped out of bed and quickly dressed in jeans and a white t-shirt. I added a rust colored linen blazer to add a bit of professionalism to the casual outfit. Maybe not for the city but perfect for the village. Having pulled my hair into a ponytail, I began to think about the Irish cop with the great, sexy voice and pulled off the elastic. I fluffed my newly trimmed and gently streaked, "sun-kissed" Daphne's hairdresser had said, shoulder length hair and checked my eye makeup and lipstick. Subtle, soft, feminine but with a definite edge that says I'm a serious-minded woman in search of answers. Hoping to, as the saying goes, kill two birds with one stone, I set out for the Town Hall. I would ask some questions pertaining to the Snow case and at the same time check out Officer James Finneran. Oh, how I hoped he was not married, covered in warts, had long, protruding canine teeth and was only five foot three feet tall. Well, I had considered that he was a leprechaun. Be careful what you wish for.

The weather was the loveliest it had been in weeks. The gentle, salt breeze off the harbor reminded me, as it always did, of why I loved living there. Then, my mind slipped to a day on the Thames when my history tutor and I boarded a river boat to take the ride all the way to Greenwich. We were studying British naval history and so we were off to view the Meridian and check out the naval museum. A great plan that soon went awry.

Boarding the boat in the shadow of Big Ben with tourists from everywhere, I bought a little book telling the story of how Greenwich Mean Time had been established. I remember how it

54

seemed odd to me that anyone could mess around with time. Time just was, or so I thought until I read the edifying little book.

But the real high point was yet to come. Once out on the water, the loquacious tour guide related funny and historical stories about places we passed. I, however, had my eyes on the water watching the things that floated by. The Thames is a catch basin for everyday and also unspeakable things. This thing of which I speak fell directly into the "unspeakable" category.

After counting five wood planks, a broken kitchen chair, a blonde wig and what appeared to be a child's stuffed Kermit the Frog toy minus its stuffing, a lumpy, plastic bag awkwardly floated by. Sticking out of a hole in the bag and gently "waving" at me as the passing boat wakes tossed it around, was a hand. A human hand.

The police boat was summoned and we all went on our not so merry way. The day was ruined for all but one little red-haired, freckle-faced American boy who kept asking his mother if they could see the "friendly bag" again.

The Provincetown Town Hall was quiet as I stepped inside. Turning to my left, through the dust motes highlighted by the tall window, I spotted the handsome Irish cop. I took a deep breath. His dark rust-colored hair was a bit longer than police regulations warranted but, after all, it was an unconventional village. I stood quietly watching him working at a computer. Intent on his work, it took him a bit of time to realize I was there. Turning toward me and rising, gentlemanly, I was immediately aware that there was neither a wart nor a protruding canine on- view. First impression, wow! Then, Officer James Finneran smiled. I thought only silly women swooned!

Now, I thought, if only he's single and available. My day was looking better and better. This sleuth stuff was beginning to pay off. If I hadn't become involved I'd probably have had to get arrested to meet the gorgeous Irishman.

"Excuse me, may I speak with you? Officer Finneran, is it?"

Turning toward me and grinning from ear to ear, the handsome Irishman responded in a deep, lilting brogue, "Ah, as I live and breathe, Ms. Ogilvie-Smythe, I presume. Unless me granny's talent for the knowin' skipped me by."

I put out my hand hoping it would not betray me by shaking. "I think we can proceed to Liz, Officer Finneran."

"Delighted. And it'll be James if you please, just James. At last we meet. Sorry I didn't know you were coming or I'd have baked a nice Irish soda bread like me Granny always did for drop-in folks."

My knees felt like jelly but I clamped them together for better support. Get a grip Liz, I told myself; this is not a cotillion and you're not thirteen.

"Sorry the place is a mess. But there's coffee and it's not half bad."

"James, I wonder if you might be free to have that coffee at the Green Genie? I'd like to speak to you in a more private setting." Looking around, I could see that there was not a single other soul but the two of us and, yet, something about the walls of a police station felt like an environment of perpetual eavesdropping.

James nodded to me, walked over to a partially open door and spoke to a woman in the adjoining office. "Mrs. Cannon, the Chief I assume, will be along in a tick. So, if you are not needing me, I'll be stepping out for a bit." Mrs. Cannon's response revealed that she'd been privy to our every word. Perpetual eavesdropping. "Please bring me a nice cup of that lovely Puerto Rican coffee Mamie is offering these days. Just black, dear. Have a nice time."

We sat at a window table overlooking MacMillan Wharf. It was a busy morning as fishing boats prepared to go out on the incoming tide. Unless the Green Genie was bugged by the FBI, we could talk freely. James and I were the only ones sitting to enjoy our drinks. Everyone else was a takeaway customer, in and out again.

Might as well get right to it. I looked James right in the eyes and presented my question.

"Despite the suicide verdict in the death of Edwin Snow, is there any suspicion at all that he might have been murdered?"

James' eyes did something that I later learned to read. At rest, they were an amazing shade of azure with a hint of the Irish green. When he was particularly intrigued, they flashed with a king's ransom worth of golden glints.

"Liz, what I am about to reveal must stay between us. At least, for the time being."

"You too have your doubts, don't you, James?"

"Off the record, way off, I do believe that the Chief chose to believe the man took his own life principally to extinguish the volatility of the situation for townspeople."

"Do you mean that the Chief of Police might be covering up what really happened to quell the town's likely reaction of turning on one another with accusations of *murderer*?" My voice was edgy.

James clicked back into professional cop mode. He chose his words ever so carefully. I could almost hear his mind whirring. In that stretch of weighty silence, rather than any words he might have uttered, his concentration served to forge a special bond between us. In those significant moments, our partnership gelled like a nice tangy, tomato aspic. I was not only terribly attracted to the charming and handsome cop but I respected him, as well. A perfect package.

"The Chief is a saint of a man. He loves this town like it was his child. Whatever reasons he had, and still has, for his position in the Edwin Snow case, they are not for me to question."

"Sorry, if I sounded accusatory and disrespectful of the Chief, James. It's just that, if Edwin Snow *was* murdered, couldn't that mean that we have a murderer running free in the village?"

"Well, Liz, let's look at this in another light. This is a close-knit village. Everyone knows everyone else and everyone's dog. I suspect the Chief feels that this death, even if it was murder, is unlikely to turn into a killing spree. For now, best to let the dust settle and see what comes along."

"Does that mean that he has considered that the old man, Edwin Snow, might have been murdered but it was an act of passion rather than pre-meditated and therefore, the killer is not a danger to anyone else?"

"You are good. Might you be in the wrong career, lovely lady?"

"Perhaps I need to explain myself a bit, James. I was trained in archaeology. I love the work but I contracted malaria on my very first dig out of university and innkeeping kind of found me. I didn't choose it. I was told not to return to the field or I might not live to see my second dig. When my aunt died and left me her business, the Cranberry Inn, I was in flux. However, as sometimes happens in life, serendipity makes our decision for us. On another note, I was reading British murder mysteries practically in the cradle. Agatha Christies was my surrogate mother. I moved on from her wonderful stories to cozies and, I do believe, I have the equal of a police academy education in crime solving." I smiled, sure he would laugh at such an outrageous claim but he did not. In fact, his face lit up with what I could only interpret as delight and approval.

"I don't think we have an open slot at the station but you might try private detective work as a side career." Now, he was pulling my leg. Oh, what a lovely feeling.

"I wonder if you might "off the cuff" share what you seriously feel about the case, James? Suicide or murder? "

The smile the gorgeous Irish cop gave me felt like a bear hug. If smiles could hug.

"How about we first discuss the deceased, Mr. Snow, to try and put together what might have led up to his death however it might have occured."

"Fine. I like that idea. In fact, I will begin with a question that has been on my mind since I learned a bit about the old man, following his death. As I am sure, you have heard the many stories about him and his propensity for making a general nuisance of himself. Therefore, I am curious about why Mr. Snow, Edwin, returned to the town after college and never left? Never had a career? I know he was wealthy but most young men find something to do with their lives. But, he just vegetated here. Despite how obvious it had to have been to him that he was terribly unpopular. To say the least."

"No idea, at all. I'd say you'd have to talk to some of the people who were here back then. There are still some old timers who have been here since Hector was a pup, as my Grannie used to say."

So, we had that in common. I loved calling upon my Grandmother's wonderful, old sayings. One day, we'd have to share Grannie stories, I thought.

"James, do you think he was murdered? Just between the two of us."

"Sorry, Liz, but I'm afraid I cannot commit myself to that proposition in light of my professional involvement. Would you like to talk to Chief Henderson and give him your take on the matter? You might convince him to re-open the case."

"The fact is, I'm not really so sure that I have a worthwhile take on the 'case'. Right now I seem to be motivated by an…intuitive feeling. I have a very active and most often, reliable intuitive sense. Please don't laugh. I know men put little faith in female intuition but…"

"Not me, lovely lady. Me Granny had the power of knowin' and the entire village came to her for answers. I have nothing but respect for your female intuition. In fact, I envy it."

Where had this man come from, I wondered? Sure, Ireland but also from an alternate universe where they produced the men women only dream of and rarely meet. Definitely a keeper.

Eventually, I knew I'd have to share MI6 Agent Nigel Hoppington's take on how Edwin Snow happened to land directly on the top of his head. In opposition to the way gravity would have landed him without a yet to be named action that affected that landing. But, my inner sleuth wanted a bit more time to solve that mystery.

Out of the blue, between one breath and another, James asked, "Liz, I wonder if I might take you to dinner at my favorite Provincetown restaurant on Saturday night? That is, if you are not otherwise engaged?"

"James, I'd love to. I fear that when the inn fills up I will probably not see daylight for quite some time so, as my Scottish Grandmother would have said, I must *make hay while the sun shines*."

"So, you too had a clever Granny? I knew we'd have lots in common besides geography," said charming James.

I returned to the inn and James went off to check on the report of a dead harbor seal on the beach behind the Lobster Bowl. "An elderly man called into the station to say that a bunch of boys were seen poking it with sticks. The man is fearful they'll be making a mess on his section of beach. Not exactly spurred by a belief in humane treatment toward one of Mother Nature's fallen creatures. Until Saturday, Liz. And don't be goin'off searching for murderers without me, lovely lady."

Ten

Back at the inn, I made myself a thickly sliced tomato sandwich with home-made mayonnaise on Portuguese bread from Souza's Market. The wonderful tomatoes were locally grown at Daisy Buchanan's Land's End Nursery greenhouse. Her first crop of the season. It was clear to me, even without his proffered words, that James also suspected murder.

However, he had to abide by the rules or find himself unemployed. So, it looked as if I was on my own. I could only hope that a contingent of tough, courageous, spunky female amateur sleuths had my back.

Next on my list was learning more about the dead man. Surely, how he'd lived his life would contain clues to how he'd died and why. A good sleuth did not leave one stone unturned or one villager unquestioned. I only hoped that I would not find myself left outside slammed doors when I went seeking answers from the villagers. After all, I was still, and would always be, what the locals called a "wash-ashore." I had learned that the longer you remained in the village the more the villagers tended to blur the distinction between newcomers and regulars but had I been there long enough to earn that blurring? I doubted that less than a year qualified. Thus, I'd begin with the one person I knew had fully accepted me. Well, besides Daphne. Tish Souza.

"Good afternoon, Liz. What can I do for you today? I've got some lovely freshly made chorizo sausage Manuel just brought in. Here, try this new cheese." Handing me a thick slice to sample, Tish Souza wiped her hands on her oversized black and white striped apron and smiled, waiting for the verdict.

"Oh, Tish, that is wonderful! Oh, give me a pound of that and I'll take a pound of the chorizo."

"How are things going with that cookbook of yours, these days? Can't wait to read it."

"Don't hold your breath; it's still in the planning stages."

Another customer came into the store as evidenced by the little jangling bell on the door. I didn't turn around since I was too occupied salivating at the sight of a pile of gooey, sticky, sugar encased, gorgeous, Portuguese, fried dough twists called *malassadas*. Could just one be wedged into my day without adding saddlebags to my hips? The woman, whom I didn't recognize, came to stand next to me to talk to Tish. She turned and smiled at me pleasantly. I, too, smiled and then returned to my bargain with the calorie devil.

The woman did her purchasing and left. Once again, Tish and I we were alone in the store. I had questions for her that I preferred to keep private between the two of us. I knew she was the soul of discretion and also, that she'd been in the village for almost forty years. Just the kind of information source I needed.

"Tish, what do you know about that poor man Edwin Snow that might have led to his...death?" I would keep the "M" word to myself for the time being.

"I know what you mean by the term "poor" but the man was very, very rich. I say, no wonder he jumped. What took him so long to depart from this world? Oh, I know that sounds heartless, Liz. Sorry. But the man was just a damned old pest. He was the most obstinate, difficult, annoying and bullying man in town. Got to admit that it's difficult for me to feel sorry for the old coot, even posthumously. So, the term "poor" is better applied as, *poor everybody who had to deal with him.*"

"You said bullying. Whom did he bully?"

"Kids. He'd send one of them to buy him a newspaper while he sat outside the town hall and promise the kid a dime for doing the errand but he never paid. He'd say the paper was folded wrong or ripped or messed up in some way and just shout at the kid telling him he'd done a lousy job. Imagine. Well, of course, that was years ago and all those boys are grown now but they remember how it was and once the word got around no one would do any errands for him."

"Did anyone consider him their friend? Somebody he grew up with, maybe?"

"No, wait. That's not quite correct. There was one. The sweet old lady who grew up next door to the Snows. Told me once she saw the goodness in the man or, as it were, the boy. Goodness my ass. Sour as a pickle and mean as a wasp in heat."

"What is her name, Tish?'

"Mary Malone. Salt of the earth. Generous to a fault and the sweetest lady you could ever meet. Knits little caps for all the babies born in town and bakes for scholarship bake sales. Mary is the quintessential grandmother. Although, when she and Edwin were young, according to Mary, she actually was in love with him. Hard to believe but coming from Mary I'm sure she was the only one who dug far enough to find his sweet spot. But then, I'm sure she'd find something to admire in Jack the Ripper."

"She really liked the old coot then? Is she a credible person, Tish?"

"Credible as dawn is dear Mary Malone the quintessential grandmother. You ought to talk to her if you really want the lowdown on the old bat. What's your interest though, might I ask, Liz?"

Quick, Liz, too soon to give away the plot. "Oh, I'm just a very curious person and I'm interested in what makes people tick, that's all. So, do you suppose he never pulled one of nasty tricks on Mary?"

"Oh, he played with her head, as well. The only person ever to treat him kindly and he blew it. How about this? Once, Mary told me, Edwin shaved her cat because he claimed it put hair all over his new roadster napping on the hood."

Tish wrapped my purchases and put them into the canvas bag I always remembered to bring with me to the market. Her clever daughter Shelley had designed the bright red logo of a sausage dancing with a wedge of cheese on top of a crusty loaf.

"Do you think that Mary Malone would speak to me about him?"

"Sure, why not? Mary's a love. But be prepared for a pretty jaundiced view of the old scourge."

I knew I could trust Tish so I quickly decided to share with her the old man's bequest to me. She might have some idea of why he'd done so such a ridiculous thing to a complete stranger. "Tish, if I tell you something very, very private would you be willing to keep mum for a bit?"

"Sure. You pregnant, honey?"

"What? Oh no, Tish, nothing at all like that. Oh my goodness, no. I am just interested in Edwin Snow because I inherited, for reasons I will never understand, his manuscript."

"Come on. Why?"

"As I said, I don't have a clue except for the fact that he knew my Aunt Libby."

"Doggone, I'll be a monkey's uncle. So, what are you going to do with it after you read it? Get it published? Hey, that would be fun, of course if it's any good. You could put your name on it. Serve the old duffer right."

"Here is where I need your secrecy for a while until I have time to check on some things. He *commanded* me to find his murderer! Also, I don't get my hands on it until I do so."

"I'm just flabbergasted, Liz. Murderer? What does the Chief have to say about that?"

"I don't believe he knows and I thought I just might do some investigating first to see if there is enough to convince him to take another look at the case. That's why I came to you to see if you might have anything that might be helpful."

"Sure. Let me think a minute. Well, there is the mystery of why that beautiful young woman Rosita Gonsalves wanted to marry him."

"He was married? Why hasn't anyone ever mentioned that? Is she still alive, Tish?"

"The Gonsalves had eight children and they struggled to keep this store going before we bought it. It was just a regular neighborhood store back then. I'm sure they weren't able to give Rosita pretty clothes and stuff so she probably just decided to get her hooks into the richest man in town. It happens. Oh sorry, no, I have no idea if she is still alive. Left town right afterwards."

"Afterwards?"

"Yup, left him at the altar. All dressed up and no wedding to go to."

"Oh. Do you know why?"

"Nope. Of course, I guess there was a lot of speculation at the time. One rumor was that she was with child, as they used to say, and it was not his. Some thought it might be Edward Granger's since she cleaned the Granger's house in Truro in the summer."

"Interesting." A possible suspect? By why wait decades to come back and face him? Hypothesis: She came back to the village one last time knowing that she only had a short time to live and called upon him hoping time had softened his anger. Together they climbed the Pilgrim Monument for old time's sake and he accused her again of fooling around with the artist, Edward Granger and she pushed him over the side. Stranger things have happened. I had one more question for Tish before I left her to her busy day.

"Speaking about his money. Did he ever do anything charitable with it? Contribute to the Fund for Lost Fishermen's Families or give to the Christmas drive for poor kids or anything?"

"No way, not our Edwin. I remember one time I was working the booth at the Blessing of the Fleet and Edwin came by and when I asked him if he'd like to donate to the Fishermen and Fire Fighters' Widows and Orphan's Fund he actually spit in the can with the money in it. I had to wash all that money."

Tish's face grew red with old anger remembering that experience and added, "Quite frankly, and do not mistake me for one of those atheists who don't revere life, but I for one am just delighted that he jumped off the Monument. Only thing makes me sad is that poor Bill Windship had to find his bloodied body. Bill's had a couple of heart attacks and the shock couldn't have been good for his health. Even if there was no love lost between the two of them going back to childhood."

Aha, another clue to run down. Just then, four customers arrived at once and I said goodbye to Tish, thanking her for the great food and the information.

So, he and the old man, Bill Windship, who found Edwin's crumbled and bloody body in the snow at the foot off the Pilgrim Monument, were long-time enemies. Interesting.

Daphne was just locking up her art gallery next to the wharf after a couple of hours of painting in her studio when I walked by. "Hi Liz, where are you off to?" Leaning in toward the bags in my arms she inhaled deeply. "Mmm, let's have a picnic."

"Come back with me to the inn and I'll make you a marvelous panini with chorizo and a magnificent new cheese from Souza's."

After a tasty lunch, Daphne and I sat in the sitting room finishing the bottle of Truro Vineyard's latest offering Purple Plum Vino. "I'm considering calling my family's attorney in London to see how I can get Edwin Snow's manuscript released from the instructions in Edwin's codicil based on the very real possibility that it may contain important, vital clues to a murder case."

"Murder! Oh, how tasty. Speaking of tasty, any more left in that bottle. Hand it here, girl."

"Did you know that Edwin was once engaged to be married, Daph?"

"Correcto mundo, woman."

"Daphne for heaven's sake, will you please speak English. At least when you are with me. You sound like a crazy rapper." A big, deep breath.

"You know I think you should move in with me for a while until this blows over. I have a little pistol and my neighbor is a weight lifter." Said Daphne, offhandedly as if she was offering to lend me a pair of shoes.

"I'll be fine Daph. Anyway, I thought you viewed this whole thing as a fun game with no potential for danger."

"What fun is a game without danger, woman?"

"So, you agree that I might be in danger if I pursue a sub-rosa investigation to try and determine if Edwin was murdered?"

"Only in danger of looking like a nosy parker like that meddlesome Emily Sunshine at the Fairies in the Garden Shop. But, hey, go ahead and be Provincetown's answer to Miss Marple. I'm sure that handsome Irish cop James Finneran will protect you if you smile at him just right." Sly grin. Reverse psychology always did work on me and Daph knew it.

"Don't underestimate me, Daph. I don't need protecting. I can do this on my own. "

"Right." Daphne held the wine bottle over her glass encouraging the very last drop of nectar to fall.

Finneran and Ogilvie-Smythe Detective Agency did however have a nice ring to it.

Eleven

The knock on the front door of the inn set butterflies to dancing a tarantella in my stomach. My first date with James Finnerran. I was as nervous as a schoolgirl. It had been a very long time since I'd felt unsure and awkward with a man but that was how the delightful James Finneran affected me. Where was the sophisticated Londoner who'd once had men trailing in her wake regardless of the cool shoulder she turned toward them? Wouldn't my mother love this, I thought. Dating a lowly bobbie. Even a palace guard would be better. But not much.

Opening the door, I was greeted by his honey lips dripping with poetry. Oh, they had thrown away the mold after they made darling James.

Good evening, lovely lady. *'Hard is the heart that loves naught May.'* Geoffrey Chaucer's immortal words ran through my head as I approached your front door. Such a perfect evening, is it not, my lady?" With that, he executed a deep bow and rising, handed me one miniature sunflower tied with an equally sunny yellow ribbon.

Naturally, I was momentarily speechless. When I caught my breath I said simply, "Oh, James, one of my favorite flowers."

Not knowing just how formal the Red Inn was I'd dressed for mid-range in a pencil thin olive green linen skirt topped by a muted paisley silk shirt in shades of olive, pumpkin, gold and cream belted in by a wide natural tan rope belt. I had tried boots with the outfit but they weren't right so I slipped into a pair of tan leather very simple pumps with two inch heels that felt like gloves. At five foot ten I'd sometimes been taller than my dates; however, handsome James topped me by two inches. The shoes brought us nose to nose, eyeball to eyeball...lips to lips.

Avoiding those tasty looking lips was not easy however I managed to head to the kitchen for a tall vase. James followed me.

"Whereever did you find a sunflower so early in the season, James?"

"Have you been to Daisy Buchanan's Land's End Nursery? Have you seen what is growing in her greenhouse? It is like the secret garden come to life."

"Oh, I mean to call Daisy to come and create a lovely garden here at the inn. My thumbs are not as green as most Brits. I am going to need some help."

"If it's help you need, lass, just call old James any time, day or night. I am at your service. And, I'm not a half bad gardener, either." The man obviously shared my fondness for the double entendre.

"I like you, James."

The Red Inn was delightful. The food wonderful. The ambiance, looking out over the harbor at the sprinkling of early to their moorings boats, sandpipers dancing along the shore in search of snacks and a couple of fishermen casting lines in the afterglow of the sunset was breathtaking. One of those times that ought to be cast in amber to last forever.

"Between the two of us," James said after his first sip of Irish whiskey with soda, "I've been doing some private research. In fact, I spent most of last night digging into dusty files that no one has touched in decades. I was looking for anything about Edwin that might help us."

That "us" felt like a kiss. James continued after a second sip. "Of course, if you could get your hands on the manuscript, we might have everything we need. The old guy probably named names right there. In fact, that is what confuses me about his codicil. If the manuscript is actually in-depth and honest it would reveal his enemies and so, it would be..."

"Hold up a tick, James. How do you know about the manuscript? I never told you I inherited it. The only person who knows besides the lawyer and me is Daphne and she is as discreet as a tree. Although she is a whacko and sounds like a bad western, I trust her and love her."

"Ah, yes, sorry. I came upon the information professionally. That stuffed shirt lawyer felt he had to tell the Chief

69

in case the bequest put you in danger. The man had a good point, I'll give him that; possessing it could make you a target. Especially if you got it into your lovely head to take on the old fool's challenge."

"But I don't possess it. It's in a safe in Boston and I will probably never even get a glimpse of what the old man wrote."

"Forget not, lovely woman, this village has eyes and ears everywhere. Also, the villagers have a tendency to embellish. Facts get altered to make them more interesting. I expect, by now, everyone believes that you have read every word and are privy to every secret the old man wrote. That is why I ask you, dear, lovely lady, don't go getting ideas about being a private investigator. Despite the old man's command. Not worth it. And, it could be dangerous."

"So, I suppose you want me to go voluntarily into the witness protection program." I laughed but the handsome cop's eyes did that color-changing thing. The glints flashed like heat lightening.

"Oh really, James. I am a big girl and I have a fairly good brain. I can also protect myself just fine." What on earth was I saying? I wasn't living in a cozy mystery. We weren't characters in a book. It was real life. I could be putting myself directly into harm's way. Like standing on a railroad track facing the speeding train.

I changed the subject and got James talking about his childhood. The rest of the evening, we managed to avoid talk of either the murder or my possible involvement.

The evening ended back at the Cranberry Inn where I made us espressos. "Are you alright with a big shot of caffeine this late?"

"What can caffeine do that hasn't already happened to me? I could dance on water at the moment." With that, my leprechaun did a little Irish jig right there in my kitchen.

That first date night extended through the next day. We were having too much fun together to part. Sitting on the soft leather couch in the sunroom after returning from dinner and despite the espresso, we had slipped off to sleep in one another's arms. Awakened by a large slice of bright sunshine coming in

70

through the windows James took a deep breath of my hair exclaiming that it smelled like a lemon tree. "Is this heaven? Ah, and *begorra* it must be since I am awakened beside an angel."

"Oh James, where did you come from?"

"Dublin." That amazing smile. Were those dimples? I couldn't be sure with my head snuggled into his chest.

"Are all the boys in Dublin as sweet as you or were you hatched from a sugar egg?"

"Oh, you do flatter a fellow now don't you, pretty lady?"

Kissing my neck, my ears, and my lemon tree hair, he repeated like a mantra, "Delightful. Delightful. Delightful."

"You'll never guess what time it is, James? It's eleven-twenty."

"Actually I do not know what century it is. And, I don't give a damn. Come up here woman and let me kiss you properly before it is eleven twenty-one." I moved up so that our noses touched. Then our lips. Like sipping from a honeycomb.

James's stomach let out a great, leonine growl that said it all. So we headed for the kitchen. "How about pancakes, James? I've got a great recipe for cornmeal and cranberry pancakes and a few days ago I made a batch of hazelnut maple syrup."

"I've not only slept on a cloud with an angel but she cooks, as well. I must have been very, very good this year." He kissed the tip of my nose and went scouting through the cupboards looking for mugs.

"I also cook. Have I told you that, fair maiden? I have secret recipes to share. However, you will need to keep me around to learn them all."

Oh yes, I said to myself. You, James Finneran, are definitely a keeper.

Digging our way through a pile of pancakes and two pots of coffee, sated and happy, we sat in my sunny kitchen. I told James about my plans for up-dating the old-fashioned space and how I was toying with the idea of perhaps giving some cooking classes come winter. He heartily approved.

Finally, I knew that I had to be honest with the lovely man. Keeping secrets from him would only endanger our chances of a future together.

"James, I have a confession to make. Perhaps you'd like a stenographer present for this." I smiled and he cringed.

"I knew it, my Mam warned me about vixens like you. So, you've got yourself a husband back in jolly old England. Perhaps a brood of little blighters, as well. Here it comes, get ready, James. I finally found the perfect woman and she's a fraud. Mam was right; I must return immediately to Ireland and find me a nice local girl with eight ways to cook potatoes."

"James, *I* can cook potatoes fifteen ways. Not to worry. And, there is no husband and not a single blighter. Just a suggestion. Since we….mesh so well. I thought we might consider working as a team on this case. We both believe Edwin Snow III was murdered but *how and why,* that's what remains to be discovered.

James' face flashed through an assortment of reactions; relieved, deeply thoughtful, briefly doubtful and then, what I'd been hoping for; agreeable. Also, something more but at that moment I chose not to explore that last fleeting emotion because if we were going to work together better not to muddle things with that particular feeling, just yet. Quickly, James returned to the business at hand.

"The old man, Ned Snow, Edwin's father, put families out in the cold but he always had the law on his side. He knew just how far he could go and still be within the bounds of the law. A slick bugger. The son did not follow in his father's "professional" footsteps, and I use the term disparagingly in this context, but instead Edwin was headed on a course toward medical school. Learned that from the dusty folders. When he showed up back in Provincetown and just never left, everyone was shocked and confused. Probably even disappointed. The boy had always been trouble. He was rich, privileged and never had any supervision. Old Ned left him to grow up like a wily weed after his mother died. Well, she died at his birth. Stands to reason the boy grew up mean and nasty. No one to love him and rear him and steer him onto the path of proper behavior."

"Do you think someone he knew when he was young killed him?"

"It has crossed my mind that maybe the offspring of someone cheated out of house and land might have exploded with the need for revenge. Stranger things have happened. Family grudges have a life of their own, sometimes."

"That's good, James. Yes maybe. Tish told me about Rosita Gonzales who left him at the altar. Should we try to find her, do you think? If she's alive.

"That's right. Tish and Manny bought the Gonsalves' store. Their daughter Rosita cleaned for Edward Granger and his wife in Truro for a couple of summers. Might be worth trying to find her, sure. I'll look into that when I get to the station tomorrow. I'll ask around."

"Absolutely splendid James. I'd say, you ought to go into police work!"

Twelve

The bedside clock said three-sixteen when I suddenly burst into wakefulness from a deep sleep. Rosita! Of course, Rosita, how could I be so dumb? She had cleaned the Granger's house? So that's how he came to paint her. The rare portrait Granger painted of a beautiful girl with creamy café au lait skin, raven hair and eyes like blueberries, if blueberries were black. He'd called the lovely painting *Rosita in the Morning Light*.

Leaping out of bed as if it had been in flames, I headed to the computer. Pushing aside piles of notes for my cookery book, I waited impatiently for the boot up. Facts collided in my semi-groggy head. Rosita could surely have introduced her boyfriend, or perhaps he was already her fiancé, to the Grangers. Logical. So, what does that prove? Thoughts tumbled like bits of shattered glass from a broken kaleidoscope. I was grasping at straws but somehow I knew that I was on the right trail.

Then, there on the screen was the painting of a lovely young woman just as I'd seen it at the show in Boston. *Rosita in the Morning Light*. So that was Rosita Gonsalves. Cleaning lady turned portrait subject. Granger, it said, had only painted two portraits during his long career and the other one had been lost in a gallery fire on Newbury Street in Boston in the seventies. Crawling back into bed a plan began to gestate and I spent the rest of the night sleeping fitfully between dreams in which I raced through the tangled back streets of London pursuing a killer in a lilac wig and swam in the Thames holding hands with a plastic bag.

Time to beard a certain lion in his den. Or hers, as it were. I had walked by the Fairies in the Garden shop many times and never been tempted to enter the front door. Daphne had mentioned that Emily Sunshine knew everything worth and probably not worth knowing in the village. As the official village fortune teller Emily, as Daphne had kidded, "Knows where all the bodies are buried." Therefore, I hoped that she might know more about what

74

might have motivated someone to kill old Edwin Snow. Not that I had ever believed in what the woman did for a living but sometimes, one must suspend one's own reality in the cause of justice. I noticed that my thoughts were beginning to sound like Dashiel Hammatt.

Daphne had said, "Emily Sunshine is a bit of a weirdo but really sweet. I have to admit that she sure surprised me more than once with things she knows. Once, she stopped me in the street to tell me that I really ought to get a doctor to look at the mole on the sole of my foot. I didn't even know I had a mole on the sole of my foot. The next time I went to Doc Emory for a checkup I pointed it out to him and he sent me right off to Hyannis to have it checked. Well, I no longer have a mole on the sole of my foot because it was removed due to it being *very suspicious*. You've got to admit the woman is not to be discounted as a total nut. I myself am very grateful to her. Gave her a painting to thank her. She's your oracle."

Stepping into the thick smog of the shop where the miasma created by the combat of dozens or more flowery and spicy scents vying for dominance created a sinus-blasting blend of Biblical proportions, I gasped in search of a clean breath. Finding none, my decision to get out quickly was reinforced tenfold.

Emily Sunshine was busy waiting on a customer so I wandered through the crowded shop where angels, fairies, worry beads, incense, scented candles, scented cards, and even dangling earrings that were guaranteed to waft their scent as one walked, filled every shelf and crevice. The air in the place could have brought an army to its knees. How *did* the woman spend her days in the thick haze, I wondered? Every breath was painful. I wanted to flee like a lemming. I reminded myself that every case has its drawbacks and a good sleuth must suck it up and proceed despite the difficulties. This is for Edwin Snow III. Justice must be served. Charge!

Moving away from a heap of little net pillows labeled "Lavender Love," "Mint Magic" and "Patchouli Passion", among other gag-producing names, I backed smack into a life-sized fabric angel doll with pink gossamer wings. The doll fell forward and her movable arms enfolded me.

"Isn't Mirabelle lovely? She's our mascot, blesses the shop and spreads ever so needed joy on this miserable skeptical world. Was there something special you were looking for, dear?"

"Oh, hello. My name is Liz Ogilvie-Smythe, how do you do?"

"I know who you are, dear. This is a very small community. So nice to meet you, at last. I'd like you to meet my *familiar,* Jasmine. Not just witches have cats as their animal spirit advisors, you know."

Looking down I saw a pretty charcoal gray face looking up at me. One double paw reached out to stroke the leg of my jeans as wide yellow eyes took my measure.

"She's lovely. I am particularly fond of cats but my life to date has been too peripatetic to have one."

"No better companion or confidante than a cat, dear. Now, what is it that you are seeking? The Tarot?"

Tread carefully, Liz, I told myself. Don't give too much away until you know what this pretty, tiny, pink and white lady knows. Although, to tell the truth, I had the very real sense that Emily Sunshine was already reading my innermost thoughts.

"Emily, I am writing a book about the artist Edward Granger. Not a memoir like Mr. Snow's, but a scholarly book about the effect of Granger's art on the art movement of his time."

"Oh dear, why waste your efforts? You must have other more important things to do with your time."

Thrust and parry. The joust had begun.

I chose to ignore Emily's belittling of my fictional excuse for being there. "It would be very helpful to my research to better understand Edwin Snow since he seems to have known the artist well." Sneeze, sneeze, sneeze. Emily handed me a tissue. I continued. "Sometimes writers like to get readers' opinions so they ask friends to read the material in progress. I was just wondering if Edwin Snow might have asked you to read it to get your take on it." Naturally, I was basing that on nothing. But, in for a penny, in for a pound.

"Oh no, my dear. The nasty man was not a sharing person."

"I see. Well, perhaps you could provide a little insight into him since you've lived in town for so long."

Jasmine yowled and marched away as if either disgusted or called away to investigate a sudden vermin invasion. The cloying air choked me.

"Do sit down, dear. Over here at the table. We'll ask."

We'll ask? Who will we ask, I wondered? Then, I saw it. Something I'd only ever seen in movies. Bad movies. Hokey movies. A crystal ball. Not exactly modern technology but who was I to question one's method of information gathering. Next to the orb sat a pack of Tarot cards with their weird pictures in harsh colors. Five sneezes in succession. Emily handed me a box of tissues.

"Have you lived here all your life, Emily?"

"No, I have only been back in town for a few years. But I almost got born here. My mother left when she was young. However, before leaving, she conceived me. Therefore, I believe I have the right to call myself from here. "

"Yes, I agree." Three more sneezes. I ached for fresh air. "I wonder if Edwin ever shared stories of his youth…things that would add interest to my book. Do you know if he deserved the bad feelings of the villagers? Or did he simply inherit his father's blackened name and reputation, by association?"

"I'll let you decide, dear. One time, he let something interesting drop. When he was just a boy attending the one room schoolhouse, the other kids made fun of him and called him Eggy. Because of the shape of his head."

"The shape of his head?"

"Yes, it was oddly shaped, just like an egg. Narrow at the top and broader at the chin so that he looked as if he had an egg sitting on his neck. In fact, as the story goes, one Halloween a bunch of his schoolmates walked up Pilgrim Lake Hill Road and tossed eggs at Edwin's house. They called out, *Humpty Dumpty, come out and meet your relatives.* Well, you know how mean kids can be. They meant that the eggs were his relatives."

Emily gave me a look she might have directed at someone not too bright, who, without clarification, might miss the obvious joke.

"Yes, I got it, Emily. Mean kids. Yes, poor Edwin. So, he must have been disliked, even back then?"

"He could have tried a bit. But, never did. His father was hated and it seems, Edwin just added to the family reputation for nastiness and stinginess."

"Do you happen to know why and approximately when Mr. Snow began his book? It was way back in the forties when the Grangers were around. Do you have any idea of what possessed him to wait so long to write it?

Six shotgun sneezes. Emily appeared to be annoyed by my sneezing. Evidently she had developed a helpful immunity to the terrible miasma of competing scents. Otherwise, she could not remain in that business.

"So sorry, allergies. I was just wondering if you might have an idea of what inspired the old man to write about the artist, Edward Granger, six decades after meeting him?"

"Well, in fact, I know just when he began to write it and why. I was the conduit for the fateful message."

"The fateful message?"

"Yes, Edward Granger spoke through me to Edwin. Well actually, through Eloise who is a conduit for those passed on to the alternate universes. I deliver what she tunes into."

"Eloise?"

Emily reached out to move the crystal ball closer to her and, cupping it gently in her tiny hands, she gazed into its smoky depths and then back up again at me. A tremor of fear rolled across my shoulders.

"Liz, meet Eloise. Eloise, meet Liz. She tells it like it is. No sugary coating. Can you take the unvarnished truth, Liz?"

I know. I ought to have run like the proverbial scalded cat. Bad imagery but so was a talking glass ball named Eloise.

"Edwin had no choice but to do what his old friend commanded."

"So, Edward Granger told Edwin Snow to write a memoir or biography or whatever? Was that their only communication...through Eloise?"

"No, there was one other time when they spoke about the ghosts. But that was the last time, the time when…no matter, not important."

"Ghosts?" I was rapidly descending into monosyllabic babbling.

"Up in that old arc of a house where he lived. You wouldn't catch me stepping beyond the front door. Full of angry spirits."

Do not, absolutely *do not* pursue this line of foolishness, I cautioned myself.

"Came here in the dark of night, by the back door. Heard knocking but as it was a stormy night I assumed it was the shutters banging. Eventually, I went to check and found him there drenched and as angry as a wet hen. I made him tea hoping to calm the man so that he could tell me what had brought him to my door on such a terrible night."

"What had brought him, Emily?"

"Ghosts. They had been particularly uppity for weeks and were keeping him from sleeping. Man was obviously sleep deprived."

I struggled to keep my expression noncommittal but it was not easy. Between a crystal ball and a story about ghosts I wondered if I might be in a sleep deprived emotional breakdown state, myself.

"What could I do but recommend a priest? An exorcism. But, alas, he'd have no truck with priests. Begged me to do it. I refused."

I bit my lip. Could I bring myself to ask questions pertaining to ghosts? I jumped when Jasmine's hopped up onto my lap and began kneading to make herself a comfortable place to sit. I didn't need to speak as Emily continued.

"Then he demanded I contact Granger again because he needed help with the book. He insisted that he had to get the artist's permission to include certain things in the book he'd been ordered to write. 'Things of a delicate nature,' is how he explained it to me."

"And you helped him contact Granger that night, Emily?"

A flash of light beamed out of the crystal ball, hit a mirror on the wall across the room and then re-bounded back into my eyes causing me to blink hard. My eyes felt burning hot and they stung like a million bees had struck. The flash caused me to jump nearly out of the chair and with an angry growl, Jasmine was gone like a shot. Obviously a stray sunbeam had collided with both objects and the stinging, although I'd have liked to blame it on something otherworldly, was most definitely a reaction to the thick, flowery, spicy atmosphere.

Emily said not a word. Had she even seen the flash? Had she been aware of my reaction? I assumed not. Finally, the stinging settled down and our conversation continued as if nothing had happened. If Emily had been aware of what happened she showed no sign. But I knew that she had tried to frighten me away. Or had it been Eloise?

Looking at Emily I saw that she appeared to be in a trance. I had to listen closely to what she said next. "Perhaps since he's dead, I can share this in the interest of justice."

What happened next I still wonder at although Daphne insisted, when I told her, that the woman was a magician thus, such things would have been natural for her. A way of throwing me off of the case.

Another far brighter flash issued forth from trusty Eloise. This time, it hit a tall blue glass bottle just about a foot from where I was sitting. The bottle exploded into smithereens. Blue glass flew like confetti. I ducked but my hair was full of it. Fortunately, neither of us was cut. But only I had screamed. Emily sat silent, motionless and seemingly transfixed. Unaware and somewhere else entirely.

"Humpty Dumpty had a great fall." Emily's voice sounded unearthly. I tried to shake the bits of glass from my hair but kept my eyes glued to the tiny woman. Emily's face twisted and paled. Her body seemed to implode. Her shoulders fell as if under a great weight and her chest sunk inward. As if the plug had been pulled on an inflated doll. My first thought was that the flying glass must have hit her and caused the cave in. Was I losing it? Had the tiny woman cast a spell on me?

"Are you ill? Did the glass hit you?" I reached out and touched the tiny, soft hand that lay palm down on the lace covered table"

"Oh my, my. I am so sorry but I cannot tell you what the artist said to Edwin that final night. Edwin forbids it. Sorry, please excuse me, I must lie down."

Emily rose and headed through a glass bead screen that evidently led into her private quarters. I heard the cat jump down from a nearby shelf. I felt a sudden rush of wind that came from nowhere. I could see no open window or door. Our session had ended. What else to do but leave. The air outside was life-saving. I gulped at it hungrily.

Thirteen

"Daphne, it was like a movie or the telly. I simply cannot get my head around what happened. But I can tell you that Emily Sunshine is hiding something vital to this investigation."

"Aha. So, now it is an official investigation. Well, well, should I send off for one of those silly Sherlock Holmes hats and a high-powered magnifying glass?"

"I know I sound as if I've gone off my rocker, Daph. You needn't point that out. But, I know for sure that sneaky Eloise is hiding important information. I just don't trust that crystal ball."

"Right. You don't trust a crystal ball. Listen to yourself, detective girl. Tell me, how do you feel about your microwave? Trustworthy or just a sneaky, back-stabbing kitchen appliance?"

"Bite me, Daph."

We laughed until the tears flowed and our stomachs hurt, but somehow the frivolity did little to erase my confusion. I was sure that Emily and her sidekick Eloise knew a lot more about the murder than they were willing to share? However, the very idea of returning to that shop and its thick, suffocating smog brought on a string of sneezes.

The next day, I checked my list and knew I had to visit Bill Windship. On the phone he was gracious but hesitant about sitting down to talk to me about the dead man, Edwin Snow. "I have nothing to say that can help you, young lady. The man lived a boring, empty life, so, what's to write about?"

I'd told him that I was doing a free-lance article for a newspaper. As that lie slipped out, it occurred to me to hope that he and Emily Sunshine were not pals. I'd told her I was writing a book. Oh, well, the trials and tribulations of an amateur sleuth.

Bill's sardonic laugh echoed out of the phone and I knew he'd be a tough sell. Although, if I could get him to open up, I was sure he did know, as Daphne would have said, *where all the bodies were buried.* We set a day and time.

Walking along Commercial Street toward Bill's house two cautionary thoughts collided. If Nigel Hoppington was correct, and of course, he was, then someone had set it up so that Edwin would fly off the top of the Monument and land on the top of his head, cracking it like a fragile egg. A Humpty-Dumpty scenario if ever there was one. Didn't that clearly hint at an old, childhood enemy? Who else knew about his nickname, "Eggy" but a childhood foe? Secondly, what if that foe was Bill Windship? They'd grown up together.

This led to, what if he kills me and bricks me up in his cellar wall and no one finds me...for centuries! It occurred to me that I'd told no one, not even Daphne, where I was headed that day. I tried to take comfort in Daphne's, "Bill's bark is worse than his bite so don't let him intimidate you. It's just that he is a quiet and private man and very focused. Maybe if you dress like a Pilgrim you'll get more out of him."

As I approached the wonderful architectural gem that was the Windship family home, I admired, while simultaneously disapproving of, someone's attempt at up-dating the eighteenth century home with fussy Victoriana trim.

Knocking with the brass ram's head door knocker I happened to gaze up and saw, in the shadows of the overhanging eaves, something that reinforced my sense of impending doom. Staring down were two gargoyles that belonged on a European castle or, at least, New York's Dakota Hotel. Why on earth had one of Bill's ancestors or, perhaps, Bill himself, added such incongruous things?

The door opened and there stood Bill Windship. Dressed in a wine velvet smoking jacket and paisley ascot, the man looked more British than Winston Churchill.

"Miss Ogilvie-Smythe. Do come in. Come back to the sunroom. Still too damned cold outside. The blood thins with age. Should have moved to Florida with all my old pals years ago when they did. Old age robs us of natural insulation. Don't know why I stay here. Not a soul left to talk to who remembers the place before it got all befuddled with those Greenwich Village fairies. This way, Miss."

Bill's voice was modulated and pleasant, hardly the voice of Count Dracula. Maybe I'd escape alive, after all. Homophobia probably did not constitute a danger to my person. Just my senses.

A sunroom sounded promising. I followed the man down the longest hallway I'd ever seen in a private home, even in the great homes of England. Finally, as I began to fear that I'd slipped into an endless wormhole, we entered curtained French doors and there it was. Light, sunshine and the security of a door out of which I could dash should I need to. Unless it was locked. Well, I could always break a glass pane and make my escape.

We sat in old, real wicker chairs, not the new plastic kind that can be left outdoors, for eternity. The cushions, covered in leaf green and white palm frond patterned cotton had been warmed by the sun. A teapot sat under a matching tea cozy. The scent of warm pumpkin scones caused me to salivate. I wondered if he had a live-in cook. "Would you like tea? I just made a fresh pot?"

I smiled and accepted a cup. A good start. Maybe he would open up and I'd leave with lots of answers, after all.

"So you are interested in Edwin, are you? Not much of a story there. Boring old curmudgeon. Except in his own mind, of course. Keeping secrets and scandals? I hardly think so. A lot of balderdash. The man was insane and delusional, mark my words. Knew him all my life. That artist fellow, Granger, wasn't any better than all those communists with their propaganda and free love and such. That socialist writer, John Reed and his tramp girlfriend, Lousie Bryant and their pal Max Eastman were all commies, too. None of them worth the powder to blow them to hell. Not to mention that guy who put on those depressing, immoral plays out on the wharf. Eugene O'Neill. Bad apple he was. Muck and slime, every one of them. So, Edwin hung around with Granger; not exactly a badge of honor. Bunch of heavy drinkers and fornicators, all of them, Edwin included."

I bit into the delicious scone and took a sip of the excellent tea. "But what if someone else believed him and felt threatened by what he was about to reveal? Or, at least believed he was?

"Look Miss, this fair town has been a dumping ground for riffraff like the aforementioned for years. Secrets and scandals go with the territory. On top of that, now we've got those fairies and I don't mean the kind Miss Emily sells but men who dress in tutus and wear silly wigs like a bunch of flamingoes in heat. Nothing shocks Provincetown any more. Much to my chagrin. Used to be a nice small town, with nice people, *normal* people but not anymore. I've lived too long."

Time to steer the conversation onto a new course or risk being there all day discussing Provincetown's sociological history. "Do you believe that he took his own life?"

The air around Bill seemed to crackle as if a storm was brewing and I waited for the man to issue a sharp retort. Instead, he spoke in a tired voice, as if I was taxing his strength by my questions.

"So, I suppose you belong to the murder camp. Don't waste your time. I assume, since you are doing some improvements on the old Cranberry Inn, that you plan to stick around awhile. So, let me advise you, young lady, drop this right now."

"Could you clarify, Mr. Windship?" I asked knowing pretty much what he'd say.

"If you go around stirring up the town with a crazy murder theory, ask a lot of questions and plant a lot of dangerous ideas, you just might as well put up a for sale sign and pack your bags Ms. Ogilvie-Smythe."

"So, you are firmly in the suicide camp, then?"

"Edwin killed himself. End of story. No mystery, no intrigue. Why he had to besmirch my Pilgrim Monument in the process we will never know. No, that's not exactly accurate. The man hated me, for reasons that are none of your business young lady. It would be just like him to do that, just for spite. Miserable coot."

"Did you do it, Mr. Windship?" Had I said that? It was as if someone had spoken for me. But, it was too late to take it back.

"Did I do what?"

"Kill Edwin Snow III? Did you kill him because of years of anger and injustice and finally it was one more thing and you lost it and threw him off of the Pilgrim Monument?"

Bill's deep baritone laugh resounded off the glass walls of the sunroom. Taking a deep breath he spoke very slowly as if I was an intellectually challenged adult. "Young lady, you look like a bright woman and I have heard nothing but pleasant things about you since you came to town to take over Libby's inn but you are barking up the wrong tree. I kill Edwin! Please, Edwin died years ago. It would be, quite simply, redundant to murder him. No one can murder a dead man! He died when that pretty girl dumped him. Isn't that what you young people say, *dumped*? Certainly creates an image of a romance turned to detritus and hauled off to the town disposal area."

"You must have known Rosita Gonsalves, the girl who left Edwin at the altar, Mr. Windship?"

He took a deep breath and I thought I saw a welling up of tears. He pulled a crisp white handkerchief from his pocket and with a quick swish, wiped them away.

"Knew her? I loved her. She left him for me. Of course, then she left me."

Interesting. I was getting a whole new perspective on Rosita Gonsalves, for sure.

"Do you happen to know where she is now? Whether she's alive or dead?"

"Not a clue. Not interested either. Haven't given a thought to her in years." But his misty eyes belied his tough words. He suddenly looked smaller and almost frail.

Any residue of fear I might have had up until then suddenly evaporated. The man seemed quite harmless. Unless, of course, I planned to damage his Pilgrim Monument. I suspected that, in direct opposition to his words, Bill Windship thought about Rosita Gonsalves every single day.

At the front door, just before I stepped out onto the stoop, I decided to ask one more question. "Do you know anything about ghosts in my inn? Or at the Snow house?"

He laughed and after a brief hesitation, "Libby always insisted there were ghosts but she could be a fanciful woman. Old houses always retain residue emotions but actual wandering spirits taking on misty forms of their former corporeal selves, no. Sorry to disappoint but I do not buy into that theory. However, should

86

you discover some, please call me. Anytime, day or night. I'll bring some holy water and a crucifix. Good day, Ms. Ogilvie-Smythe."

Stepping onto the sidewalk from the brick walkway lined with happy daffodils and narcissus, I looked up as if pulled by a string, puppet-like. Of course, it was my fertile imagination but I was sure that the gargoyles' expressions had changed from ennui to mocking. Yes, I just might be losing it, I warned myself. Not only was I hearing fictional sleuths inside my head and discussing ghosts but now I thought the stone expressions on carved stone faces had changed.

Having outworn my welcome with Bill Windship, it was time to do some research into birth certificates.

Fourteen

Sitting in Daphne's gallery on a paint spattered stool, I watched my best friend put the finishing touches on a scene duplicated right out the back window. Like looking into one of those fun house mirrors wherein the scene is duplicated endlessly. This, however, was just the original and the duplicate on canvas. "It's just lovely, Daphne. Is it a commission?"

"Yep; money in the bank. So how's the murder investigation going?" Daphne put her brush into a Mason jar half-filled with turpentine and wiped her hands on an apron that could easily have been hung in any gallery and mistaken for an original Jackson Pollack.

"Brace yourself, Daph. It seems, according to a reliable source, Bill Windship, that he, Bill, was the man Rosita left Edwin for on her wedding day. If we can believe him. Imagine how embarrassing for poor, old Edwin all decked out in his wedding gear, the pews full of guests, the organist ready to strike the first note of the wedding march and *ta da,* no bride."

"Maybe old Bill was worth more than Edwin and when she found out she jumped ship. Maybe the lovely Rosita was just a gold digging opportunist." Daph laughed and sat next to me on an upturned antique wooden lobster trap.

"How about this, Daph, what if the lovely Rosita had an affair with Granger while he was painting her and she got pregnant? If he refused to leave his wife she might have grabbed onto Edwin? What man would refuse such a gorgeous woman if she was also very clever? She could have convinced poor Edwin that she loved him and pulled off the bun in the oven thing. Then, at the eleventh hour, she regretted it and just split."

Daphne shook her head and reached over to pick up a fallen paint brush. "So, old Bill wasn't exactly the source of enlightenment, gal pal?"

"Not exactly. He's cagey, but he's not fooling me. Mark my words: Bill Windship knows more about this murder than he's willing to share," I said in my most engaging and confident amateur sleuth-speak.

"Hey, how about this idea? Rosita came back recently to hit up old Edwin for long-overdue child support, still insisting the kid was his. Maybe they'd had a romantic moment up at the top of the Monument six decades ago so, she convinced him to return with her there. When he refused to hand over the dough she pushed him over the side. Splat!"

"So, Daph, you think two octogenarians could have climbed the Pilgrim Monument in the throes of old remembered passion and Rosita convinced the old man to hang over the edge and carve their initials into the side of the monument so she could give him the final shove? If only I could find Rosita and talk to her, it might clear up a lot of things. If she's still alive. This is giving me a real headache. By the way, on the subject of heads, what *is* that color your hairdresser foisted on you this time?"

"This gorgeous shade of my lush, magnificent locks is called the Strawberry Fields Fade. It's the Hollywood rage. The "fade effect." See how the soft red at the top of the hair shaft gradually moves down to become a gentle, golden brown as it approaches my shoulders. If you, my dear, were a fashionista like *moi,* you'd know that."

"Oh, right. I really want hair that looks like some kind of hard candy. How can I find Rosita?"

"Google her. Facebook her."

"Of course. Do you have your laptop here?"

Daphne rummaged under a pile of rags, paint spattered smocks and brown paper bags to retrieve a leather case that looked as if it had come over on the Mayflower.

"Rosita Gonsalves. But what if she married and changed her name? I'll start with Facebook."

Suddenly, there on the screen was a photo of the most beautiful and glamorous octogenarian imaginable. "Look at this, Daphne. She's still gorgeous although she must be at least eighty-three. We should look so good at that age."

"Hey, I should look that good right now. Well, so there she is, the vixen who went around town breaking hearts and leaving grooms red-faced at the altar. What does she say about herself?"

"Let's see. She lives in Asheville, North Carolina, but she gives Massachusetts as her birthplace. She a writer. Oh my gosh! Do you believe it, she writes romance novels? Well, *write what you know*. She's widowed. She has a daughter who lives in New Hampshire. Edward Granger's lovely portrait model. *Rosita in the morning light*. Makes me wonder if they ever...."

"Quick, send her a message. Ask her about her memoires of Provincetown in the good old days. Tell her Edwin bit the dust or, more appropriately, the snow. Ask her who put the bun in her oven." Daphne jumped up, clapping her hands like a teenager anticipating a new technology toy.

"No, not just yet. I have to think about this before I go off half-cocked."

"A bit of advice, gal pal. Considering her advanced age, better to go off half-cocked than not cocked at all. She could pass on any minute and then you'll have nothing."

Daphne pulled on a ratty looking sweater at least two sizes too large for her and headed for the door. "I've got a hankering for a lobster salad roll. How about you? Let's saddle up and hit the trail."

I turned off the computer, slipped it back into its case and put it on a shelf alongside a pile of blank canvases and assorted tubes of oil paints. "Imagine the lovely Rosita still savvy in her ninth decade. We might just be getting somewhere, Daph."

"The only where I want to get to right now is a table by the window where I can dig into the best lobster roll on the east coast. Saddle up, Liz."

"You know, pal of mine, you are beginning to sound a lot like Hollywood westerns. *Bad* westerns. And, you're influencing my vocabulary against my will. Maybe I will just have to stop hanging around with you. My father always said that I was too easily influenced by my peers."

"Just trying to fit into the colonies." Daph put on a smug expression.

"Right." We headed out of the gallery and down Commercial Street. "What should I ask Rosita first, Daph?"

"Let's see, how about asking her if she did it? If she adamantly says "NO" then ask her for a list of likely suspects. Don't forget to ask her for an alibi."

"Duh. Brilliant, Daph."

"Just trying to be helpful. Did you stop to consider that he might have dumped her and not the other way around?" Daphne asked.

"Sure, and then he got into his wedding finery and showed up at the church just asking to be pitied. Get a grip, gal pal." *Why not?* Agatha Raisin asked.

I stopped dead on the sidewalk while Daphne marched ahead salivating for lobster. Realizing I wasn't next to her, she turned back. "Where are you, girl? What? You look weird."

"Let's suppose that Edwin did find out the night before the wedding that she had shacked up with Granger and the baby was the artist's and not Edwin's. She might have begged him to marry her anyway. She was, after all, quite a catch for "Eggy." But, he stood his ground and dumped her, in a rage. Then, Edwin showed up for a wedding he knew was not going to take place? But why? Who would do such a dumb thing?"

"Damned if I know. A fondness for wedding cake frosting?" Daphne asked as she pulled me along the sidewalk.

"Consider this, Daph. Men fell all over the gorgeous Rosita. Probably had fistfights over her. Yet, Edwin had the chance to marry her. All he had to do was look the other way about the baby and pretend to be the little blighter's father. It is done. Rosita would have been quite a brilliant feather in unpopular Edwin's cap. However, at the very last minute Edwin showed some pride and refused her."

"Damn, you just might have something. Now, let's discuss it further over heaping lobster chunks mixed with finely diced celery and drowning in home-made mayo on a toasted Portuguese roll."

"Daph, you will be thinking of food on your deathbed."

"Planning right now to be laid out on a buffet table surrounded by the stuff. Do you think that will put people off the lovely food?"

I groaned and followed Daph to the Lobster Bowl. "Daph, you are seriously in need of professional help."

Sitting at a window table, gazing out at three catboats gliding along, I mulled over my new idea. As we waited for our orders to arrive, Daphne offered, "So, he turns Rosita down flat. But, not to be outdone, the lovely lady turns to number two, or rather number three, Bill Windship. Also a man smitten by her beauty and charm. Then, she dumps him for who knows? Maybe a traveling salesman. But we still have a very strange situation unresolved. Why would Edwin Snow, Provincetown's bad boy and least favorite son, show up for a wedding he knew was not going to happen?"

"For the very reason that you just pointed out. Being so unloved and unpopular what better way to earn the town's pity? At least pity is a human emotion. Maybe the poor guy was willing to take anything he could get. Even if it involved utter humiliation."

"Right." Plates heaped with chunky lobster arrived and we dug in silenced by the delectable food.

"By the way, I need to tell you what I learned from a trusted scientist colleague and old friend from childhood. He is a renowned forensic scientist employed by MI6. He told me that if Edwin jumped he would not have landed squarely on the top of his head but on his front or possibly his back but never the way he landed, point blank on the top of his cranium." Like Humpty Dumpty.

Daphne's quizzical look was so profound and so full of confusion that I couldn't help but take satisfaction from it. I was about to make a big, fat point in our continuing jousting.

"How do you know he landed on his head? How could you know that? Did you witness his fall or were you in attendance for the forensic investigation? What are you talking about, Liz?"

"None of the above. I, just as you did, watched the E.M.T's take the body away. Obviously, however, you are not as observant as I am, although you certainly ought to be since you are an artist, Ms. Crowninshield."

"Touché friend. Sorry I wasn't captivated by the blood on the snow and checking out the head of a man who'd fallen over two hundred feet to his death. Yuck, brain mush on ice. You *really* checked that out?"

"Of course. Agatha Raisin would have been that astute. Miss Marple would most certainly not have overlooked it. The very top of Edwin's head was horribly broken from hitting the ground. Like tossing an egg. In fact, according to my friend Nigel, that indicates that someone tossed him off the top of the Monument probably with a long rope tied around his ankles. Let's hope the old man was already dead or at least, unconscious. That would have guaranteed his fall, head-first. 'Like a heat-seeking missile', as Nigel put it.

"Ouch." Daph winced.

I suddenly jumped up and headed for the door nearly toppling the half-filled glass of iced tea I'd been sipping.

Daphne grabbed what remained of her lobster roll, plunked down some money on the table and raced after me. "Hey, was it something I said? Do I have parsley between my teeth? Hold up Liz."

"Daphne, I've got to go up to the top of the Monument. Want to come?"

"No."

Arriving at Bill Windship's house, I knocked and knocked but no one answered. "Have to see if he's at his store; come on."

We headed back along Commercial Street toward the Army-Navy Surplus store. I spotted Bill outside the shop talking to a man dressed in overalls and carrying a tool box.

Going right up to the men, I stood waiting for them to finish talking. Bill gave me a frosty look and then turned back to the carpenter. "Thanks, Henry. Like to get the work done just as soon as possible. I'll look forward to seeing you on Tuesday."

"What *do* you want Ms. Ogilvie-Smythe? I'm a busy man. I have nothing more to say to you."

"Mr. Windship, I need to get up in the Monument. Today. Right now."

"Sorry Ms. Ogilvie-Smythe but the Monument is closed for the winter. As is the museum. Come and see us after Memorial Day." He turned but I grabbed at the arm of his jacket.

"Look, Mr. Windship" I quickly rummaged around in my mind for a reasonable excuse for my urgency. "My editor insists that I get pictures from the top of the tower and familiarize myself with the climb and the viewing platform to give my writing more integrity. It will not take long, I promise. I'm working on a tight deadline."

"Don't care to hear your reasons. The answer has not changed, Ms. Ogilvie-Smythe. It is still emphatically, no."

"But Sir, this really is important. Can't you make just this one exception?"

"No."

"So, if it is not convenient now, then how about some other day this week?"

Looking at me as if I was either deaf or daft, Bill went on to explain that there were five broken steps undergoing repair and it would be at least a week before anyone could safely climb the tower.

"How and when did the steps get broken? Could a body being dragged up the stairs bumping and dragging have damaged already old and crumbling wooden steps?"

A deep sigh from this man whose late onset misogyny had grown, over the years, to nearly match his homophobic stance.

"You are entirely too imaginative, young lady. The steps are constructed of metal, not wood and thus, they rusted and broke clear through in places. In fact, as they showed signs of being dangerous at the end of the summer I was forced to close the Monument to climbers earlier than usual. Dragging a body up the stairs? Where do you get this stuff? Read too many Agatha Christies, do you?"

Realizing that no amount of pleading would get me up the tower until the repairs were completed, I gave up and turned to walk away. Behind me I heard Daphne's *sotto voce* comment and wanted to pop her in her aristocratic nose. But as I had caused enough commotion for the time being, I kept walking.

"She's been under a lot of stress lately. You know, learning how to run the inn. One of those academics who finds it difficult to learn new skills not of the *brainiac* kind."

I gritted my teeth and ignored her until Bill's voice reached out like a hook stopping me dead.

"Has it occurred to you that as I am the keeper of the key to the Monument that Edwin would have had to steal my key to get inside? Unless of course I gave it to him."

I turned. "Did he? Did you?"

"I did not lend him my key. Nor was my key ever missing.""

I retraced my steps to where the two of them stood. Damn Daphne had a wily expression going, as if she'd known all of this all along and was working in partnership with Bill.

"Is there only one key, then?"

"No, there are actually two keys. I possess one and the other one is kept safely at the police station."

"So, that doesn't seem to be a problem. Edwin knew about the other key and somehow obtained it. Therefore, he didn't need yours."

"Not quite so fast. It gets a bit complicated, young lady. To get to that key he would have had to enter the Police Chief's private office without arousing suspicion. But first, and this is very crucial, his first obstacle would have been getting by his Rottweiler secretary Alice Cannon. Without the Chief's uncanny ability to recognize every unmarked key he'd have had to spend hours, days, coming and going to test them. You see, Chet Henderson enjoys a little game involving his knowing each and every key and where it unlocks and no one else does. Bit of a sticky wicket as you Brits are wont to say."

What Bill was suggesting was that maybe he himself had made the key available. From not knowing anything to sticking his neck out in that way threw me. My investigation was beginning to look as full of holes as a good Alpine Swiss cheese.

"A bit of mystery I'd say, Miss Ogilvie-Smythe, wouldn't you agree? Difficult to envision a man being overtaken by unhappiness to the point of choosing to take his own life who goes to such pains in the process. And why? Imagine his climb up into the freezing monument with the goal of jumping off when he might have chosen a far easier way to go. No, I think not."

My tongue was tied. What was going on? At his house he'd been so very coy. He'd offered damned little in the way of solid information. His litany of reasons why people, progress and sexual orientation irked him had been of more interest to him than discussing a murder. Yet, there he was hinting that he might qualify as a suspect. Was the whole thing just a game to Bill as it seemed sometimes to be to Daphne, that traitor?

"Why are you telling me this, Mr. Windship? You said you were not a murderer and now you toss in this key question. Why?"

Bill smiled enigmatically, turned and entered the door of his shop. Before I could take a step toward him I heard the door locking. I found myself staring at a poster attached to the door advertising WWII war bonds.

"Hey, think we ought to invest?" I ignored Daphne's smart ass remark. My head was filled with the thick fog of confusion issued by the enigmatic man. I wanted to punch something, but not being a violent person, I simply stamped my foot and walked away.

Fifteen

Two nights later, as we entered Sal's Place for dinner, Daphne greeted the hostess, "Hi Antoinette, is Sal here tonight?" The reason for our visit was two-fold. I'd yet to dine there and Daphne had been raving about the great Italian food. In addition, she'd told me that Mario, Sal's manager, had taken Edwin under his wing and occasionally gave him a free lunch. In return, Edwin told him stories of the old days. Mario too, was writing a book. Isn't everyone?

"Mario's in charge tonight, Daphne. Sal's off exhibiting his paintings in New York." Antoinette the hostess picked up two menus and led us to a table. As the restaurant was situated down a few steps from the sidewalk, having formerly been a cellar, we were looking out at a half wall of cement. However, someone had cleverly painted wine bottles, eggplants, tomatoes, and other colorful images on the wall and the effect was charming.

Suddenly, from out of the kitchen swept a tall, handsome, dark-haired, olive-skinned man of a "certain age" who swept Daphne off her feet in a bear hug.

Returning her to the floor, they kissed each other Mediterranean style and then Daphne introduced us. Kissing my hand in the out-dated continental style, he exuded what I like to call a *slithering snake-like kind of sexuality*. I much preferred James' solid, trustworthy, hometown looks and manners.

Turning back to Daphne he drooled, "Ah, if it isn't the woman of my dreams. Where have you been for so long? I have been lost without your ethereal magnificence shining on my humble life. I shall have to whisk you off to my villa in the hills and never let you go."

Give me a break, I said to myself. I stood there hoping that my friend had not succumbed to Mario's sleazy idea of romance. Some men just exude mistrust.

"If the villa's in the hills of Tuscany, sure. Not tonight, however. We're here for the magnificent food, of course, but also for some information."

Leaving with a promise to bring us a bottle of the newest Calabrian wine, Mario walked toward the bar and I took the opportunity to lean toward my friend to say, "Please tell me that you do not believe that slimy man has special feelings just for you. No slight on your beauty and charm but the man is a snake."

Daph feigned hurt followed by a light laugh. "Give me some credit woman. He's a full-blooded Casanova but isn't it fun to play along and get some needed perks? Good men are thin on the ground here, you've got to admit. I might have to start subscribing to Match.com"

Mario returned with a towel-wrapped bottle in an ice bucket and proceeded to uncork it, turning his snake eyes on me. "I am most honored to have you here as the friend of this gorgeous woman who has for three years been fending off my romantic advances."

"One day I will weaken and then I will come to live right here and eat up all your profits, Mario." Daph put on her most adorable, simpering voice and the slick man ate it up like pasta fagioli. She added, "You Italian men like your women full and rounded, right? I can do that. But for now I need, we need some information on your friendship with Edwin Snow, the recently made dead."

"Ah, the old man. Yes, I liked him. He had many stories to tell about the old days. He had known Provincetown since it was a little Portuguese fishing village and up through its days as an art colony. He knew Eugene O'Neill and John Reed and, of course, the artist Edward Granger. I offered to introduce him to Norman Mailer, a frequent diner here, but he refused. Told me the man was a 'reprobate' and he wrote 'nasty and naughty books,' if you can believe it."

We all laughed and Mario poured the wine for Daphne to taste.

It occurred to me that Mario just might be a font of useful information. If Edwin had really trusted snake man, he might have dropped the name of his arch enemy, the man Edwin was sure would, one day, improve his aim and kill him.

"Mario, did he perchance tell you much about the book he was writing?"

"Not much, I'm afraid. Mostly he talked about the old days but not about his friendship with Granger, no."

"How recently before he was murdered...er, died, had you spoken to him, Mario?" I asked.

"Actually, just two days before he jumped. He was here for lunch at my invitation. The man would never have paid our prices. I liked him and felt sorry for him so I gave him lunch every so often. When Sal was out of town, of course."

"Did he give any indication that he was considering taking his own life?"

"Let me think. Of course, he was not a happy man. That goes without saying." Daphne and I nodded like twin bobble heads.

"But, wait, yes, there was one thing. Something odd. He hinted that he was being blackmailed but he did not show any fear or distress. In fact, I might venture to say that the man seemed rather amused."

"Did he provide any clue as to who it was blackmailing him, Mario?"

"No, but he distinctly said that he refused to '*pay a dead man's debt.*'

Mario smiled his snake smile and turned his full attention back to my fashionista friend who that evening was wearing a full-length, green, jungle-patterned, skin-tight, Diane Von Furstenberg wrap dress. A perfect foil for the snake.

As the two played their little cat and mouse game, I pondered old Edwin's enigmatic words. He refused to "pay a dead man's debt." It didn't take long for me to figure out exactly who the dead man was and what that debt might have encompassed. Maybe, also who might have been doing the blackmailing.

The evening ended with Daphne refusing Mario's invitation to fly off to Tuscany and me wondering how I could prove my latest hunch.

Daphne stopped by the inn on her way to the gallery the next morning. On the kitchen table were the latest architect's plans and sketches and my "case" notebook open to the list of questions I'd asked Rosita Gonsalves on her Facebook page. Daphne gazed at both with half-hearted interest. But I knew she had noted how few answers I'd managed to get out of the lady.

"Not much luck with our local portrait model, as I can see. Looks like you'll have to employ sharper tactics, Sherlock. The woman is an obstacle to a murder investigation. Time to put some real pressure on her. Let's drive down to Asheville and put the squeeze on her, pal."

I put down the blueberry muffin that I'd been torturing and which lay on the plate looking like blue-stained bird food. "Really Daphne could you please stop talking that way. It creeps me out. See, even that sounded like you. Your fractured American-English is infectious and I for one do not want to be infected."

"So, was she surprised that her erstwhile, almost husband is now dead?"

"Not much reaction. However, she absolutely refused to discuss leaving Edwin Snow at the altar. I went out on a limb and told her that Bill Windship said she left Edwin for him. She neither denied nor admitted to it; however, get this, she hinted that Bill should be so lucky."

"What about her daughter? Can we contact her?" Daphne asked, grabbing a muffin and cup of tea for herself.

"I was able to find out that her daughter's name is Edna but nothing more. She is not on Facebook and I couldn't even find an address for her anywhere. Of course, I don't know what last name she uses or where in New Hampshire she lives. A big, fat dead end."

"So, she had the kid after she left here and then what? How did she support herself and the brat?"

"As you can see, she lives in Asheville, is widowed and her husband was a farmer who raised pigs and grew corn. She sure made it a long way from the sleepy little village of P'town of her youth, didn't she? From quahogs and cod to corn and pigs." I poured more tea into my empty cup and gave up on the muffin.

100

"A long way geographically but not exactly upwardly mobile, I'd venture to say." Daphne spread a liberal amount of butter on her third blueberry muffin. I groaned. I'd just have to reign in the sour grapes. Daphne never gained an ounce although she ate like a truck driver on a long haul. One day however, one day when menopause hit us both, then we'd see who'd been smart about her diet.

"What if Rosita was in the village the night Edwin took his plunge, Daph?" Daphne looked up from her concentration on plastering the muffin like a brick layer.

"What are you suggesting?"

"Think about this possibility, Liz. Rosita was living for a time right here in town, right under our noses. She could have passed herself off as a transsexual. She could have called herself Ross. She came back to see her two former lovers before they all kicked. Let's face it, as you have wisely pointed out, old folks like to sometimes tie up loose ends. Maybe she wanted to see both Bill and Edwin, one last time. For old time's sake. Granger is gone, so she settled for two other former lovers."

"Not bad, Liz baby, not half bad. But why disguise herself as a transsexual?"

"Damned if I know. I just like the ring of the story. Let's say she wanted to remain incognito except to the two of them so, that way she just blended in.

"Well, that puts her right on the suspect list then, doesn't it?" Daphne munched away and I tried to work on my new theory. But, soon Daph was off and running with a theory of her own.

"What if she *was* here and she and Bill got going hot again and Edwin found out and the men fought over her? The three of them up in the Monument when the fight broke out. Over goes old Edwin and the two lovers are protecting one another. Bill could have brought a nice, long rope with him. Maybe he planned to tie up Edwin and leave him there to freeze. But he had another idea and tied the old guy's ankles and tossed him over. Bill and Rosita would have stood there singing, *Humpty Dumpty had a great fall.*"

"Gob-smacking brilliant, Daph."

"Do you think so, gal pal?" Daphne grinned between bites and sips.

"Don't kid yourself, Daph, it's absolutely ridiculous. But, moving on. Bill Windship called this morning."

"Confessed to the murder, finally?"

"No. Called to say we could climb the Monument this afternoon, at last. Warned us to wear rubber soled shoes and plenty of warm clothing. He also mentioned gloves because the metal stair railing will be extremely chilly. So, let's dress for an Arctic exploration and get a look at where Edwin Snow II spent his last minutes alive."

"We? I've climbed it and promised myself to never do it again. When they install an elevator, I might go back for the nice view. It's a long, boring, tiresome climb and when you are coming down you get dizzy and your legs begin to get wiggly and you feel lightheaded." Daph grabbed her head and mimed woman about to faint.

"Look, Daph. If this is going to be truly painful for you, I can do it on my own."

"I think that's what I've been saying, pal of mine."

I headed to the front hall closet hoping she'd relent. I didn't want to climb alone. I pulled out scarves and hats and gloves and began dressing. Hopefully, she'd be inspired and not betray me.

Daphne's cell rang to the tune of *New York, New York* and, as she listened to the caller, she smiled wryly at me standing there muffled up like an Eskimo.

"So sorry, Liz. No Arctic expedition for this girl, today. Got to run. Got a fish on the hook who demands an introduction to the artist before she'll put down a nickel for a painting. Actually, lots and lots of nickels. *Ta da.* Have fun." She was out the door.

Waddling along Bradford Street I was unaware of the police cruiser coming toward me until James called out. "Hey, pretty lady, if you hop in my car, I promise to turn the heat up high."

"James. Don't laugh, just don't laugh. I have a good reason for all this."

"I would hope so. You are just too bright to be doing something that looks so very weird without a real good reason. Wanna hop in and tell me about it?"

102

He made a u-turn and pulled up beside me. "Hi, Ranger Rick." Gad, I am beginning to sound just like Daphne, I thought as I sidled into the cruiser with difficulty.

"Hey, delicious woman. What's up with the Eskimo getup?"

"I'm meeting Bill Windship at the Monument to climb to the top in search of clues. He said it will be very cold and damp inside so I should dress for it. Want to join me? Daphne managed to wiggle out of it. I could use your expertise. They must have trained you in police school to search for clues." I gave him my most mocking smile and leaned in to meet his on-coming lips. My neck scarf got in the way and poor James got a mouthful of cashmere.

"Funny lady. Love to join you, but take my advice, you will be sweating like a hog by the time you are halfway up to the top. The climb will kill you in all that muffling. Prepare to peel. Hm, that sounded juicer than I intended." We laughed like silly school kids and I was reminded, once again, of why I liked him so much.

Bill was waiting outside the Monument planting flats of pansies. He rose from his knees with difficulty and came to meet us. I "peeled" everything but the gloves. It would be a long way up holding onto an icy railing, I reasoned.

"I can't imagine what you expect to find up there but, I am pleased to see that you've arranged for James here to accompany you. Wise choice."

His look clearly said that a mere female could hardly expect to handle this assignment without male supervision, if not total control over the situation. "Well, two are heads better than one." It was not for me to teach old Bill a thing or two about modern females so best to let it go with an inane comment.

Bill's condescending look surely said, *Right, as long as one of the heads is male.*

As we climbed the stairs I said to James, "Will it anger the Chief that you are spending time doing what may be a wild goose chase? Oughtn't you to be keeping busy off doing a drug bust or something important, James? Perhaps, a dead manatee to see to?"

"Only do drug busts on Tuesdays and we don't have manatees this far north so just another boring crime-free Provincetown day. Might as well tag along with Miss Marple."

"I wish I had her knack for crime solving but thanks for the comparison. When were you last inside here, James?"

"Last year. On my day off I decided to try it. Can't live in town and not have climbed to the top, after all."

We were nearly at the top and my legs *were* beginning to feel like jelly despite all the beneficial walking I did, just as Daphne had warned.

But far worse than leg weakening was the putrid smell emanating from the viewing platform. I quickly pinched my nostrils between my fingers and grimaced. "Gad, what is that? It's just ghastly."

"Sure is... Probably a dead squirrel that got trapped inside and died."

"Maybe a whole family of squirrels, I'd say. Whew, that is really bad."

James reached the top and stepped onto the viewing platform before I did. "Yup, got to be decaying critters. Let's take a quick look around and get out of here."

This was my first time up at the top of the two hundred and twenty-five foot granite Pilgrim Monument. From my reading of the town's history, I'd learned our imposing tower had the distinction of being the only all-granite structure in New England. On a less odorous day it would have been quite lovely. Hanging onto my nose, I stepped over to take in the view. Breathtaking. Both the stench and the amazing panorama before me.

"I can't get beyond the incongruity of the man's crushed cranium." Standing a few feet from me, James said this seemingly to himself, not to me. He was puzzling what I already had the answer to. It was time to share.

"James, I have a confession to make." He turned. The sun shone onto his handsome face and my knees, already weakened from the climb, turned to mush.

"Not another one. The last time, you nearly caused me a stroke waiting to hear that you were married with a brood of, to quote you, 'spoiled *Brits'* at home. You're not a royal hiding out here, are you, love?"

Whew, that was close to another truth yet to be revealed. "No, nothing like that. It's about the murder. I haven't been wholly truthful with you regarding something I checked out with an expert friend back in London. My old childhood chum works for MI6 and he's in the forensics department. I asked him how Edwin Snow might have torpedoed head-first because it seemed odd to me."

Telling him what Nigel Hoppington had told me, I watched his eyes light up with that flashing combination of blue and green and gold. "That's it." James said looking relieved. "That's what has been teasing my mind since that snowy morning. The blood all around Edwin's head and the injury that had most like caused his death; the top of his egg shaped head was crushed. That appeared to be proof positive that the man landed directly on the top of his head. I knew that was problematic but I couldn't put my finger on just why. It's been rolling around in my brain since then. Of course, the man would not have landed like that naturally, now would he have? I don't have any background training in forensics so it just didn't congeal but it did toss around a bit in the old cranium. Good detective work Liz."

"Well, I too, like you, felt that there was something curious about that landing. That's why I checked with Nigel. Did Chief Henderson ever mention it to you as being strange?"

"No, never. Sorry, I don't mean to infer in any way that the Chief is sloppy at his job. It's just that between his gout and lumbago he's in a lot of chronic pain. I try to relieve him of as many duties as possible but he's an old warhorse and just refuses to retire. His wife, Trudy, died a couple of years ago. They had plans to go south and he wanted to learn to play golf and all kinds of fun things they had on their retirement agenda. But, when she died suddenly, he just closed in and made his job his life. He's got nothing else. I'm afraid he simply doesn't have the energy for a murder investigation. If you and I could get enough proof to convince him to reopen the case and we do all the work, well, not that I'd expect you to do police work, Liz but you could assist."

"Don't worry, James. I understand. We work well together and with all those cozies I've read, I feel as if I've attended the

Cozy Police Academy for Amateur Sleuths." We got a good laugh but I was careful to hang onto my nose. The stench was just unbearable despite the spring air coming in from outside.

"Unless he was dead before...." James moved over to take a look over the side. "If his killer crushed his head up here and then tossed him to stage a suicide, then that would explain it, now wouldn't it?"

"Yes. It certainly would. But, there would be blood up here." I looked at the floor and saw no trace. Although it had been two weeks. Rain and snow had come in since then.

James chewed on the information, thoughtfully. "But, what if he was killed elsewhere and dragged up the stairs? Again, because the killer wanted it to look like a suicide."

"It certainly has troubled me no end as what pretext a person could use to convince a frail, old man to climb hundreds of steps on a cold and snowy night. To look at the view? In that weather, the view would have been totally obscured, anyway. None of it has made sense to me, James."

"If someone did drag him that someone would have to have been young and strong. Right?" Asked my handsome swain.

"You're correct. But, what young person would want to kill Edwin Snow? Seems highly unlikely he'd have a young enemy. Everything points to an old person. Someone anxious to prevent some secret or scandal from the old days from being exposed in Edwin's book. Right?" I looked at James and he nodded. Our minds were coordinated and functioning smoothly as one. It felt good. Not that I hoped for more murders in our sweet little seaside village but, this working together was most rewarding. And, kind of sexy.

"Come on. Got to get you away from this awful stink. I'll come back with a flashlight and check closely for evidence. A bit of cloth, a dropped, monogrammed lighter. You know what I mean; the kind of thing Agatha Christie wrote into her books."

Arriving at the bottom of the stairs we stood in the shadowy entry hall before stepping back out into the sunny day. I tried to imagine two elderly people coming there to recall the old days. As Daphne had said, "Old people do odd things knowing the end game is near."

I reached out and took hold of James' arm. "Before we leave and Bill overhears us I need to tell you something else I picked up just by chance the other night. Daphne took me to dinner at Sal's Place and we talked to Mario the manager. He's a friend of Daphne's Do you know him, James?"

"Oh, yes, Mario, the Romeo. Well known around town. I hope Daphne isn't foolish enough to be involved with that Casanova. He's bad news for women."

"No, Daph is smarter than that. However, he mentioned that he liked Edwin and sometimes gave him a lunch at the restaurant and the old man often talked to him openly. It seems that the old man mentioned that he was being blackmailed."

James's eyes lit up. "Blackmailed? By whom?"

"Don't know; he never gave him a name however, according to Mario, the old man acted kind of peculiarly about the whole thing. As Mario said, he seemed to be either smug or amused by the fact. But here is the really interesting thing: Edwin said that he had no intention of 'paying off a dead man's debt.' What does that mean to you, James?"

"Well, I suppose it referred to something he knew about someone who is already dead but why worry about blackmail if that was the case?"

I didn't offer what it meant to me. I still needed one more piece of vital information before deciding if my inkling carried any viable weight.

We stepped out into the sunshine to find Bill sitting on a bench drinking from a thermos cup what appeared to be black coffee. "Well, find a Maltese falcon or a suicide note?"

James stopped to talk to Bill while I wandered off to look at the spot where the body was found in the snow a fortnight before. Since then, the snow had melted and the grass had begun to green so it was difficult to believe that there had so recently been a stain of human blood against the stark white on that very spot.

It occurred to me that the melting snow cover would have worked most efficiently to wash away any clues. Nothing to see there. Then, my eye was caught by something shiny reflecting the overhead sun.

I bent down to see what was glinting in the brilliant sunlight at the edge of the path where the grass met the pavement. There, just lying as if it had been dropped minutes before, was a tiny silver ring. Definitely a female's ring although in P'town that was a risky judgment call. Perhaps even a child's ring. It was pretty tiny. Why hadn't the police found it, I wondered? What about combing the scene of the crime? Then, I answered my own question. If it hadn't been dropped recently it would have been easily hidden under the snow. If the killer had dropped it. I wrapped it in a tissue and slipped it into my pocket.

"Like a ride back to your place, Liz? I'm heading that way."

Sitting in the police car, we were both quiet and I had time to think about the tiny ring. I wondered if it just might be the metaphorical glass slipper I needed to identify a very dangerous Cinderella.

Sixteen

Temperamental and tempestuous April had slipped into a glorious May and the villagers who had spent long months hiding inside their warm homes were beginning to crawl out of their protective shells like hermit crabs. I awoke on a glorious morning knowing it was time for my first swim of the year. As a child, a virtual fish-child, I'd set myself the challenge of being the first one at school to take a swim in the spring and then the one to take my last in the late fall.

One year, I actually joined the Hastings Polar Bear Club for their annual February plunge into icy water from which they ran quickly to the Hen and Wolf Pub for hot toddies and lots of good cheer. I fully intended to carry on this tradition in Provincetown.

Pulling on my bathing suit, I found that all the good living had added a bit of unwanted padding. Mostly I blamed the experimenting with recipes for both my book and the up-coming inn season breakfasts. Daily swimming would solve that problem however. Wearing an oversized man's shirt and ratty cut-off jeans over my black bikini, I set out for the stretch of beach to the west of MacMillan Wharf. Daphne was just raising her hand to reach for the brass lobster knocker on the kitchen door as I opened it and we nearly collided.

"Hey, where are you going in such a hurry? Got a fire to get to? Your best friend is here for a cuppa."

"Hi. Sorry, I am going for a swim."

"Right. And I am growing a third ear, the better to hear you with. You know, if you get to doing this regularly, the village will tar you with the bonkers brush. We do not swim here until nigh onto the Fourth of July."

"Chickens. Come on with me, anyway. You don't have to swim. It's a great day. You can sit on the beach and watch me. I like doing this for myself. I'm not trying to impress or amaze anyone. Actually, I'm thinking of starting a polar bear club in town. They have on in Boston. You might want to be a charter member. If not, then, as you like to say, cut me some slack.

As we walked, I filled Daphne in on the climb to the top of the Monument. She suggested the awful stink was rotting blood and guts but I cautioned her to keep that to herself.

"Do you think a small woman could overpower an eighty year old man if she was angry, Daph?"

"Even if she wasn't angry, why not? Her age wouldn't be a factor because a woman's strength comes from more than her muscles. A mother can pick up a car to save her child. You must have read Ashley Montagu's *The Natural Superiority of Women*. We women leave men in the dust when we set our minds to anything, even calling for unnatural strength and endurance.

So you do think Rosita came back for her bit of revenge?"

I managed not to answer. I needed some more time before sharing that tidbit.

Two local men were casting fishing lines from the shore and one of them spoke to us. "Morning ladies, come to see how it's done, have you?"

"Hi, Sam, no just go on about your business, just here for a quick swim." Daphne smiled and the two men laughed at her joke.

"Sure you are."

With that, I stepped out of my jeans, took off my shirt and raced for the water while the two fishermen stood open-mouthed.

"Lady is crazy. What the hell is she doing in that freezing water, Daph?"

"Nutty as a fruit cake but, not to fear, she's not a danger to anyone but herself. I'm her nurse. No stopping her when she gets a wild notion in her head. Valium prescription ran out. Just go about what you were doing but please try not to hook her." Daphne laughed but the two men seemed too flabbergasted by the sight of a crazy lady in the still far-too-chilly-for-swimming water to enjoy the joke.

The other man couldn't resist. "Hey, Lady, aren't you a little young for hot flashes? The wife says when she gets one she wants to race out of the house and jump into the bay, even in winter. But she never actually follows through."

I simply smiled and continued to enjoy the cold water. "Come on in, it's great."

Later, back at the inn, Daphne carried the newly painted and faux marbleized table she'd recently finished for me into the sitting room to my applause. "It is so lovely, Daph. You are so very talented. The lady paints pictures on canvas, does murals on walls and takes a junky table found at a yard sale into the realm of a precious treasure. And she is also my best friend. Now, if you could just cook."

Daphne ignored my last remark, placed the table in the spot waiting for it and took a little bow. "Not bad if I do say so myself."

"Come on into the kitchen and try my new chocolate raspberry layer cake with mocha ganache. Renew your strength after all that heavy lifting."'

"Bring me up to speed, girl. I've been in Boston for three days. Are you and James the copper married yet? Baby on the way to make me an aunt, maybe?"

"Get a grip, girl. We are just having fun. He's a sweet guy who just happens to be very sexy and he seems to like me. He's working on the case with me."

"Do tell. The way he looks at you−wowzer! I just wish some guy would look at me like that. What's stopping you from taking it to the next level, Liz? You're getting long in the tooth, you know. Your hormones are drying up and wrinkles are on the way. Better pop out a little one soon or you'll be on the shelf lonely and whining. Women of our−your age, are like yesterday's produce. Looking a little wilted with a few rotten spots but cleaned up and propped up they can see another day. It looks to me like the universe has sent you a bargain shopper and you'd better not let him go or it's off to the rubbish tip for you."

"How romantic you are Daphne. Give me a break. My biological clock is still ticking along happily, not feeling pressured at all. Eight years of university education, a busted career in my chosen profession, and a new career as innkeeper, so, I'm just getting started. In fact, I may not want to have children anyway. Where do you get these wild ideas? That is absolutely *the* wildest theory regarding a woman's body that I have ever heard. Please let it die within this room. I fear the villagers may decide to burn you on a pyre if you don't watch your back. You are just inches from being called a witch."

"Hey, this cake is better than sex. Not that I can remember sex. It's magnificent, orgasmic, in fact. If you haven't already named it, I'd definitely go with, 'Better 'n Sex'."

"Right. That'll guarantee sales of the book. On another subject, while you fill your face. Daph, I think I might be getting close to being prepared to go to Chief Henderson with what I know." Daphne nodded as she stuffed cake into her mouth as if she knew it was her very last meal.

"I'm beginning to think a woman *was* involved. Maybe even Rosita."

"Gob, dis is gweat cag."

"Daphne, do you suppose you could stop filling your gob for just a minute and speak in the language we share."

Daphne swallowed, washed down the cake with tea and said, in her quirky way, "Did you know that George Bernard Shaw said something to the effect that the problems that arise in dealings between Great Britain and the U.S. are based on the fact that they are separated by a common language?"

"Oh I give up. You are hopeless. Here, have another piece of cake; it will only add another 3000 calories to your day and you have a high revving metabolism so what will it matter? I myself must go to wash my hair and pass an iron over my gorgeous new ball gown in preparation for attending the Blessing of the Fleet Ball tonight."

"Oh, boy, James'll probably pop the question tonight right on the dance floor. Bet he has a ring box in the pocket of his tux. It's the traditional thing to do hereabouts. Whoopee, this could be the night. I promise to get set planning the wedding shower tomorrow."

"Nut. Get out and never, never darken my door again, crazy woman."

Daphne left when she was good and ready. I left her in the kitchen expecting to find only a few dark brown crumbs left on the cake plate.

112

James rang the kitchen door bell precisely at seven. He was delicious looking in his tux and it was obvious his longish hair had been trimmed a bit. Handing me a yellow rose corsage, his smile set off sparks in my heart. Maybe we should just stay in and do something else. No, mustn't waste the gorgeous black dress and sexy high-heeled sandals. Later.

"Great dress. Thought you were going to whip up something from the living room drapes, however." James said. I stood mystified. The living room drapes?

Silence. "Oh, now I get it – Scarlet O'Hara, right? Your iconic all-American movie. I didn't see it until I came to the states."

It passed through my mind that I hoped the villagers could not tell the difference between a fifteen dollar costume jewelry pearl necklace from Marshalls and the seven-thousand dollar pearls with a six diamond clasp I'd received for my sixteenth birthday. Or my Vera Wang dress. I had been, after all, working hard at being one of them

Standing there taking each other's measure, James made an audible swoon and I imitated it but even louder and more like a wolf call. He hugged me and as we laughed at our own silly antics. Once again, I thanked Cupid for inspiring this romantic and passionate relationship that was also great fun.

"You are the most gorgeous woman in the entire world. I am the luckiest guy on the planet. Step back and let me take this all in, woman. Wow, that is the sexiest dress in eight counties and love the pearls. My Mom always wears pearls. My Pap forked over two hundred dollars one Christmas so she could have a real nice string of them with earrings to match. She's pretty proud of those pearls. Wears them like she's the Queen. Your Queen. Not that you or my Mom can afford that quality but these are lovely."

You cannot begin to imagine James Finneran. One day soon I would have to come clean, I reminded myself. The "Lady" title, the huge inheritance from my grandmother, vast properties in England and Scotland that would one day be mine. But, not just yet.

We danced all night to the local orchestra made up of two storekeepers, an inn keeper, the guy who pumped gas at the

Bradford Street Shell gas station and two fishermen. Fishing boats were in for the fête from George's Bank where the best fishing was always to be found. Men and women went out there for days at a time. The Blessing of the Fleet was an annual event everyone in the village came out for. Emily Sunshine was there manning the drinks and snacks table wearing a vintage twenties dress that sagged on her tiny frame.

"Aren't we lucky? I just love living here, James." He whirled me around the floor as if we were on our own, private cloud.

"So, does that mean you're planning to stay? Not returning to England anytime soon? And if so, I wonder if you might agree to go steady with me, Liz O-S?"

Unable to come up with a clever response I simply gave him a doe-eyed look as I leaned against his shoulder and kissed him on the cheek. Grinning like a fool, he dipped me and planted a kiss on my mouth right there in front of everyone. To my great embarrassment, everyone clapped and hooted.

In the early morning hours after the ball, I awakened suddenly to find that I was alone in the bed. The wail of fire engines and the siren of a police car seared my sleep-addled brain. Pulling the covers over my head and hoping it was just a dream, I knew better. I even seemed to know, by some kind of sixth sense, where the emergency vehicles were headed.

Seventeen

I was up and climbing into jeans and a t-shirt and down the stairs headed for my Jeep as if Beelzebub was hot on my heels. The bright orange flames shooting into the sky were easy to spot as I drove fast along the highway toward Pilgrim Lake Hill Road. The scene before my eyes was indeed surreal. Huge, mountainous, flames appeared to be coming up and out of the highest dune as if it was a roaring volcano about to burst its full anger and power upon the sleeping village.

As my reluctant Jeep climbed the steep hill, suddenly there it was, not a volcano but what had been, until that night, a fine Victorian mansion. Although all the tall, stately windows glowed orange as if a party was going on inside, it was the rotund, glass solarium on the south side that was putting on a show. I pulled to the side of the road just as glass flew like glittering rain, backlit and, had it not been for the ugly truth, a lovely, breath-taking spectacle.

The lovely, old Snow mansion.

Neighbors in pajamas and robes huddled off to the side where a white-haired woman was pouring coffee at a table set out on the side of the road. One gray-haired man hugged a huge Persian cat to his chest. A woman held two leashes at the end of which were exact duplicate tiny black dogs. That led me to wonder what had happened to the old man's pit bull, Patton.

Chief Henderson walked over with a cup of hot coffee in his hands looking disheveled and in pain. "You know, Miss, I'm just getting too old for this stuff. Come and join us. Mary Malone makes a fine cup of coffee. Hell of a night." He held out his hand and I shook it. "Police Chief Chester Henderson."

"So nice to meet you, Sir."

"Never mind that formal stuff, Miss. Oh, sorry, I guess you folks from England prefer formal, uh, havin' a queen and all. I know who you are from my right-hand man and sometimes my strong legs. In other words young Officer Finneran's who, as I understand it, had taken a shine to you. My Trudy and I met while I was still a young cop. Welcome to Provincetown. Knew your aunt and she was a right fine woman."

I was unable to keep my eyes from the fire. *"The fascination of the abomination."* How aptly Joseph Conrad had put it. Despite the horror and shock, it was difficult to tear my eyes from the spectacle. However, watching the violent death of such a magnificent piece of local architecture caused the heart to sink.

The streams of water from four fire trucks, Provincetown's two, Truro's one and one from Wellfleet, seemed to be no more than a slight annoyance to the raging flames gobbling up the house. The sounds were terrifying, snapping, crackling, smashing and a sound like a violent winter wind. But also, something else. Way in the background. What is that? I asked myself. Human voices? No, it couldn't be. Funny, it did sound like people riding a roller coaster, simultaneously thrilled and terrified. No one else seemed to have heard it though.

Comments in response to the sight before them flew like bullets. "Oh, my God!" "There it goes!" "Just downright heartbreaking," "Such a terrible loss." The old glass conservatory collapsed in on itself like a house of cards as the huddled neighbors watched. Mary Malone grasped at her chest as if her heart would burst forth if she did not hold it back. This was my first time seeing the old Snow mansion. I'd heard that it had once been a showplace but Edwin hadn't cared for it and it was badly in neat of paint and repairs. Edward Granger had evidently admired it. He painted it three times in different lighting.

The sweet voice behind me pulled me around to face Mary Malone. "Dear, please join us for some nice, hot coffee. I also have tea, a nice English breakfast variety."

"Oh, thanks. I'm Liz Ogilvie-Smythe. I own the Cranberry Inn."

"I know, dear. I'm Mary Malone. Knew your dear Aunt Libby very well. Miss her terribly. Now though, we have you to take her place. Come, join us, dear."

"So nice to meet you... of course under tragic circumstances."

"Well, probably just as well, dear. I say, let them all free at last."

Before I could respond to ask who the *"all"* might be, the Truro Fire Chief came over seeking coffee. "Hell of a night. Hate to see the fine old architecture go. This one was one of the finest, indeed. Some of the real dogs you don't mind losing but this place was an honest beauty. Would you maybe have a couple of aspirins for an old man, Mary, dear?"

Mrs. Malone left and then reappeared with a bottle of aspirins and after the chief took two, she offered them around like a box of chocolates.

"It occurs to me to ask Mrs. Malone, er, Mary, was someone able to take in Mr. Snow's orphaned dog?" I hoped the poor orphaned dog had not been caught inside the inferno.

"Oh, yes, dear. Not to worry. I took Patton to live with me after Edwin passed. He's just fine although, of course, a bit lonely for his master, but he's settling in nicely. Left him in the back room so he couldn't see this. It would just add to his unhappiness, you know."

"What happened, Mrs. Malone? When did it start?"

"I woke as always at two to let Patton out. He has a bladder problem and needs to go every four or five hours during the night. I set my alarm, let him out, and off he goes. But tonight, at the end of the front walk, he suddenly stopped, his legs stiffened and his nose went into the air. I couldn't imagine what he smelled but expected it was just a skunk. Hates skunks, he does. Then I smelled it, too. That was when I turned and saw that the windows over there were all aglow like there was a party going on and all the lights were on.

"How frightening for you, Mary."

"Yes, but not entirely unexpected. It was time. They deserved it. This way, they won't bother anyone else."

I was nonplussed. Who could she mean? Who deserved to be cooked in a hot fire? The voices I'd heard? If there was someone inside why wasn't anyone else upset? But, upset wasn't what Mary Malone was. She was pleased.

"Now, I'm not one to place blame, but your Aunt Libby should not have done that to Edwin. Not that he wouldn't have done the same to her if he'd had the chance. She just beat him to it."

I opened my mouth to ask what Mary could possibly have been talking about just as James approached looking like a well-dressed chimney sweep. He started to pull me into his arms and then thought better of it. The combination of his soot and ashes-covered tux and the impropriety of the situation hit him, and he let me go.

Mary looked at James and then back at me with a sweet knowing smile and moved away so that we could be together, as privately as possible in the situation. "Does everyone in this town know that we are dating, James?"

"I'd say that after seeing us on the dance floor last night, you can expect inquiries in the coming days regarding our wedding date and which caterer we'll be hiring"

I flinched. I felt very deeply about James, but marriage was something I'd managed to fend off for years and still had no real inclinations toward taking it on. It was something that, of course, we'd have to discuss eventually, but not at that moment. Before I could respond, James apologized for slipping out of bed without waking me.

"Sorry I had to slip out of that lovely warm bed. But you never heard my cell and you were sleeping like an enchanted princess, so I just jumped back into my tux and headed here. Taken a lot of ribbing for the formal dress for a fire. But I suppose I won't get busted for being out of uniform, considering the situation and everyone having been at the ball last night."

"I suppose it's a complete loss?"

"Yup, not a chance of saving it, poor old place." James looked crestfallen, bless his sensitive heart.

"Kind of poetic justice. The family line ended with Edwin Snow and now the family home is gone."

"Any idea how it started, James?'

"Not until the team can get inside and take a look. Going to take a while to get it cool enough. The place was stuffed like a warehouse. I was able to get inside before it became completely engulfed. Don't know how the old man lived there. He would have

had to follow narrow trails through high and wide piles of stuff of every description."

Eventually, the fire trucks prepared to leave. The Fire Chief, Ben Sears, gathered the upset neighbors together to explain that it would be best if they stayed in the village overnight. He suggested the Howard Johnson's Happy Holiday Motel. I simply could not see those saddened, dislocated people shipped off to the out-dated and mildewed, 1950's motel.

"Please, everyone, I'd love to have you as my guests at the Cranberry Inn. Just made all the beds with brand new sheets." I smiled at the group and they smiled back. They went off to gather what they would need for the night. Mary gathered up Patton and carefully put him into the car holding his head so that he would not see the burned out rubble that had been his home.

The next morning everyone gathered in the dining room for a full breakfast that was enjoyed by all. Afterwards, everyone went their separate ways. Some to shop and some to visit village friends. Mary asked me if it would be an imposition to leave Patton there for the day while she went off to visit her sister in Brewster. "I can take the bus but Patton hates buses. Doesn't mind a car but he gets very nervous on a bus."

"No problem, Mary. It will be fun having him visit for the day. The backyard is fenced in so, he will be quite safe. Enjoy yourself."

I drove Mary to the bus and returned to the inn to strip beds and try and do some writing on the cookery book. However, my mind could not shake Mary Malone's odd reference to something or someone who deserved to be burned in the conflagration. My concentration was interrupted by Patton scratching at the French doors leading out to the back deck. Opening the door, I found him standing looking very proud of himself with a long bone in his mouth. "What do you have there, dog? Who gave you that bone? That's odd. Well, I'd rather you didn't bring it in the house so..." Skidding by me, he headed directly for the front room. Down the polished floor of the hall and around the corner he went, with me hot on his heels.

As the dog took the corner into the living room like a NASCAR racer, I caught a vase full of beach grass nearly in midair as it flew from a lamp table. Scatter rugs went flying as Patton headed for the large antique Oriental rug looking as if he might be considering digging into it to bury his treasure.

"No, no Patton! Naughty boy! Stop!" Softening my tone like a good canine psychologist, I said, "Oh well, you've had a tough night, old boy. How about you give me the bone and I will give you a scone? Believe me, it's a good deal."Patton didn't agree. He kept the bone tight in his jaws. He seemed to be laughing at me for even considering that he'd so easily give it up.

"Hello, anyone here?" James called from the back door. I gave Patton one last look of disdain and went to greet the now cleaned up, handsome policeman. Looking around for my overnight guests he inquired as to how it went.

"Just great. What a nice group. We had a lovely time. Come on, fresh tea and scones in the kitchen. Oh, but first, would you please help me get Patton and a big bone back outside? He insisted on bringing it in. Couldn't bribe him with a scone."

James headed down the hall and I followed. "Okay Patton, the law is here. Prepare to be cooperative. Should I read him his Miranda rights?" James grinned at me and then went back to negotiating with the determined dog. But the Indiana Jones of canines with the bone held tightly in his endearing, grinning white and black face had no intention of cooperating. Law or no law.

James bent down over the dog and, patting and praising him for being a clever boy, tried to get the bone away from him while I ran for a better, more convincing treat than a scone. The steak I was thawing for our romantic dinner.

"Damn, I thought so. Give it here boy." James' reaction sounded odd.

I handed James the partially thawed, boneless sirloin. "Our dinner, right?" I nodded sadly.

A deal was struck once Patton took a sniff. The trade completed, I took Patton by the collar. Returning to the kitchen after I led the delighted dog out to the backyard, I found James looking quizzical in the kitchen. Looking down at the bone that he'd placed on a long sheet of paper towels, he scratched his head and shook his head slowly. Quite a strange reaction to a stray dog bone.

"What, James?"

"I'm pretty sure it's a human leg bone. Where did he get it?"

"Damned if I know. Well, I mean, he was in the fenced yard the whole time so he must have dug it up out there." I slumped into the wing chair by the kitchen fireplace and James sat in the one opposite.

"James, if it *is* human, then the rest the body is probably out there as well, right?"

"Could be. Sorry but I'll have to get someone here to spot where he got it and dig for more. I hate to have to wreck your nice grass and flowers, Liz."

"No, don't worry about some old grass and flowers. We have to get to the bottom of this. First a mysterious death, then a mysterious fire and now a human bone. Gad, James, what next? Alien abductions?"

Eighteen

James called from Boston just after three in the afternoon, four days later. I hadn't seen him at all in that time and we'd only talked a few times. He was busy working with the arson team. I was sitting in the sunroom looking at the handsome Victoriana Gothic Snow mansion gracing the page of a book on the great art of the twentieth century I'd borrowed from the library.

Entitled simply, *Ned's House* by Edward Granger, the house had been just lovely. Edwin Snow's father, also Edwin but called Ned, had evidently treasured his home as evidenced by its pristine condition when the artist painted it. There it was in its glory days. The Snow house sometime in the nineteen-forties at the end of the period of summers the Grangers had spent in Truro. I'd done my homework on the house Granger had immortalized. Looking freshly painted with curtains in the windows, neat trim, gardens overflowing with colorful flowers and a Model T Ford parked over to the left side. The wrap-around porch had wicker furniture set out just waiting for ladies in white dotted Swiss summer dresses and straw hats of the period. The Snow house, sometime in the nineteen forties. I felt deeply grateful that Granger had captured it and made it immortal. Gone but still alive and well.

Peering as closely as I could with a magnifying glass, I searched for what my sixth sense told me was there…but hiding. Deep in the shadow created by a huge overhanging maple tree branch, there it was—a young man's face. Edwin's? Half in deep shadow, the other half caught just enough light however so that I could tell it was his. But, I was looking for it. Granger had seen him and included him and yet, I wondered if the art experts had picked him out from the fool-the-eye dappled shadows. Why I thought I'd find Edwin watching, I could not say, just a hunch.

The strident ring of the kitchen phone that I intended to have replaced but hadn't gotten around to on my unending list of things-to-do, pulled me out of my reverie. James's voice brought me back to earth and I smiled as I always did at the lyrical sound of his brogue that came and went in intensity depending on to whom he was speaking. I liked it when he used it on me. It sounded like a gently flowing brook on a summer's day.

"It's a human leg bone, all right. My guess is it's been dead about sixty years or so."

"Oh, James." There, words failed me.

"I'm heading back to the Cape in few minutes. I'll pick up a nice steak to replace the one we had to sacrifice to Patton."

"Great." I answered, "But make it a *boneless*, please."

Next day, the nice men sent to do random digging in my flower beds assured me that there were no more bones to be found. James oversaw the operation and when they left, came into the kitchen for tea. "Oh James, I wonder if my Aunt Libby was involved in something unsavory."

"Now, love, one bone does not a murder make, necessarily. Sometimes the old cemeteries give up bones and dogs drag them away. There have been less than careful burials in the past. Not burying deep enough or in improper soil. Erosion takes its toll and bones appear. Sandy soil is particularly problematic."

"So, what happens now?"

"Nothing much. This is not a first, according to the Chief. Early tribal sites and old gravesites do, on occasion, throw up human bones."

Daphne knocked and then let herself in through the kitchen door. "Hey James, Liz. What's this about a human leg bone in your garden? Everyone's talking about it."

Looking from Daphne to James, I asked, "Does everyone in this village tune into some extra-sensory communication band that I don't know about, James?" Handsome James just shrugged.

"No kidding, a real human leg bone? What was your aunt up to? Well, I suppose it does cause one to surmise about what she did with difficult guests." Daphne was enjoying our gruesome find entirely too much. I gave her a look of disdain, but she simply grinned like a fool.

"So, what happens next?" Daphne asked James, ignoring me entirely. "Do the police send out an all-dogs roundup bulletin

123

until they manage to put together a complete skeleton? By the way, are we talking about a really, really old bone like from a Pilgrim or an Indian ah, pardon me, indigenous person?"

"No, it's only about sixty years old, Daph." James answered my whacky friend in his usual kindly, patient way.

Daphne turned her attention back to me to deliver her take on the bone-in-the-garden question. "Hey, if your Aunt Libby was a murderess, the Lizzy Borden of P'town, she might have killed guests she took a disliking to, or, maybe anyone who didn't appreciate her cooking. You could use this to your advantage, Liz. People love that kind of stuff. Millions flock to walk through the famous Lizzy Borden house in Fall River. Money in the bank, girl."

Mary Malone's strange reaction to the fire at the Snow mansion, her reference to something she did for Edwin that went unappreciated as well as mentioning something my Aunt Libby had done to Edwin, a kind of joke or hoax, that caused trouble between them, all sat like fiery hot peppers in my stomach.

Of course, I'd never met my aunt. I'd made her into an icon of good cooking, conscientious housekeeping and a greeter of happy visitors. What if she had been something quite different?

Daphne continued, despite my growing annoyance with her latest flight of fancy. "Great sport staying in a place where a Lizzie Borden-type British lady topped off difficult guests and neatly dismembered them before burying them in among the peonies. You could rent out shovels and let guests have a go at it. Haunted houses are all the rage these days. The way I see it, the quirkier this town gets the better. I didn't settle here to be bored."

I looked at James, "Everyone says Aunt Libby was the soul of goodness and kindness. I just don't want to think of her as a cold-blooded murderer."

Before James could respond Daph was at it again. "Have you ever noticed how the neighbors always say that in news interviews after the guy next door chopped up six members of his family? *He was such a quiet amiable fellow, loved cats and dogs and little children."*

"Oh, Daphne."

124

"Got to head back to the station and let the Chief go home for his lunch. See you ladies, anon. And, Daph, don't spread your latest theory around town, just yet, please. In fact, how about never?"

James headed back to the police station and eventually Daphne went home to see what frozen goodies she had in her freezer for her supper. James would be back at six and we'd finally grille a steak. I had just enough time to shower, wash my hair and slip into a sexy sundress before James arrived with the *boneless* steaks, a bottle of red wine and a bunch of pink freesias at six on the dot.

Sitting on the terrace waiting for the gas grille to finish the steaks, James brought me up to speed on the final report on the fire. "Ed Wilson, the Fire Chief, and the arson squad sent down from Boston finally got inside what remains of the Snow house. One room right in the center of the house remains standing and pretty much undamaged. The fire appears to have started in a back room next to the conservatory, a kind of potting shed. A gas can was found there. Definitely arson."

"Who would have done such a terrible thing, James? I cannot imagine why anyone would want to burn the lovely, historic house." I reached for the bottle of red wine and re-filled our glasses.

"Too early to tell. Interesting though, right in the center of the house was what had been the original structure on the property. A thick-walled stucco place, kind of like a southwestern adobe that the mansion was built around. Because of the thick walls and heavy wooden doors with wide iron strapping, the room nearly escaped completely the fierce fire."

"What was in there, James?"

"Looked like the old man used it as an office. Someone had obviously tossed the room completely. Drawers turned out, files strewn all around. I'd say someone was looking for something.

"The manuscript?"

"That would be my guess." James checked the steak.

125

"So, isn't that pretty solid proof that it was someone not from   here?"

"Why would you say that, love?"

"Because," I said as I reached for my wine glass "every man, woman, child and dog by now knows the status of the manuscript. Everyone in the village knows that I don't have it and may never unless I follow Edwin's command and find his murderer. Therefore, if the arsonist was looking for it at the Snow house he or she is obviously not in the village information loop."

"Right. Of course. You know, love, you really ought to go into police work. No, scratch that. It's a lot safer writing those cozy mysteries you love reading to get your teeth into crime."

"James, have you ever heard of the liberation of women? I am not a hothouse flower. Women do the same things as men, these days." Another discussion for another day.

"I do know that, love. But I'd prefer to protect my lovely woman from ending up in a shallow grave and dug up by dogs."

"Oh, James, you are far too romantic." James only smiled his leprechaun smile

"So, I'd say the arsonist, who may also be the murderer, tossed the house looking for the manuscript. Then, having no luck, his anger and frustration grew and finally, he lit the match." Said the wise policeman.

"Or, having no luck, he figured that if he burned the entire place the still-hidden manuscript would go with it. A clean sweep." I added.

"You, my gorgeous, irresistible temptress are a genius. A sleuth extraordinaire. A paragon of female detective prowess. Come here and let me kiss you." I did.

"Unless." Kiss interuptus. "What if the arson had come there believing that old Edwin had barrels of cash hidden in the house? Typical miserly trick."

"Hm." James scratched his chin and I went into the kitchen to toss the salad.

Returning to the deck I asked, "Do you think that we have one mystery or a handful, James?"

"Good question. One does wonder if they are all connected in some way. Murder, arson and stray bone."

"Don't overlook blackmail." I added, making our case even more perplexing. "I believe we need to check on Edwin's bank transactions in the past year. Large withdrawals to pay a blackmailer. Despite Mario the Lothario's description of Edwin's smug attitude maybe he actually paid up."

"Aha, think how easy our task will become if, in fact, old Edwin had paid by check?" James grinned and placed the perfectly cooked steak on the cutting board.

"Yes, and if Edwin had suddenly stopped paying, refused the blackmailer any more money, why not murder?" I said as I scooped salad onto the plates and James sliced thin the steak.

The sleuthing business was growing to encompass every waking hour. Summer was coming at me fast and soon I'd be too busy for crime solving. Despite that fact, I was a person who completed every task given me. So, there was no way I was going to drop the ball. Or, as it were, the bone.

Nineteen

The mystery of the leg bone in my back garden took a weird turn the following week until Daisy Buchanan of the Land's End Nursery and Garden Center dispelled what had begun to look like a local massacre back in the village's history.

Finding bones suddenly became a village pastime. People brought in every manner of bone in every condition to the police station and old Ted Bump even brought in an entire bucket full demanding they be tested because he was sure they were, "murdered people what got buried on my land. Ted's bones turned out to be goat bones from his pet goat herd that the man had buried himself over the previous fifty years as his goats had died and he'd forgotten he had done it. In addition, brought in by men, women and even children there were beef bones, ham bones, fish bones, chicken bones and even seal bones. Each person was treated with respect. The bones were accepted, placed in plastic zip lock bags and labeled with the finder's name and each person went away feeling that he or she had done his or her duty nobly.

Everyone was on the lookout for human bones. Finally, Chief Henderson put his foot down. "This has gotten completely out of hand. One damn human leg bone and the town goes wild. Stands to reason, burying people in sandy soil for four hundred years is going to cause some to get tossed around. Add together dogs and bones and you get trouble. No more bones will be accepted by this office. Do I make myself clear?" The Chief told James and James told me.

While the bones episode was racing around town, Daph and I met at Beasley's for lunch on a sunny Saturday to review the clues. Daphne had become my often unwilling but occasionally helpful, sounding board. I knew she was growing bored with the case. Cases. After all, we'd hardly had one conversation in recent weeks that did not have to do with the mysteries. I didn't blame her. This was my case and although she'd been pretty patient, still it wasn't her whole *raison d'etre* as it seemed to be mine. I was the one doing the sleuthing and it wasn't everyone's favorite pastime. Obviously, not Daph's.

Sitting in a booth at Beasley's under old movie posters, I imagined us as Sherlock and Watson. I sat under Katherine Hepburn and Humphrey Bogart on the *African Queen*. Daph's, totally appropriate poster was *Rebel Without a Cause*. The table was covered in blue and white checkered oil cloth and the salt and pepper shakers were in the shape of Harley Davidson motorcycles. Definitely, a time warp scene.

Beasley's had quickly put together a new spring menu to accommodate the earlier than usual visitors. Nothing like the possibility of a murder to flood the town with early tourists. That day's luncheon special was fresh asparagus, spring leg of lamb, roasted baby red potatoes and early greenhouse-raised strawberries atop an old-fashioned, biscuit-type shortcake.

As we waited, Daphne mused, "When we have an entire skeleton we can display it in the Provincetown Museum next door to the Pilgrim Monument. Label it Pocahontas or John Smith, depending on the sex. Do we know the sex of the bone, Liz? Did James say?"

"I think any part of a body has indicators as to the sex of the person. But I do believe the pelvis and the skull are preferred for identification. But even if we were to find all the bones, a complete skeleton, I don't think it's legal to keep it and display it."

Daphne responded, "Drat. Hey, maybe Emily Sunshine could be helpful on a cold case. Maybe good old Eloise can identify the bone's owner."

"Not crucial to the investigation, Daph. Right now, we need to convince the Chief to reopen the Edwin Snow case and prove it was murder, not suicide. But, the Chief is still sitting on a gate."

"By the way, that's *sitting on the fence,* Liz. But I get your drift. You know, you really ought to try harder to learn American slang." Daphne picked up the salt motorcycle and inspected it closely. "Nice detailing for a cheap knickknack."

I ate the delicious food but my mind was elsewhere. "What if Edwin hired someone to kill him to make it look like suicide? People do that to make sure the life insurance gets paid. But to whom would he have left his life insurance in that case? Rosita? His dubious daughter, Edna?"

"Hey, look up there, a pig flying."

"You could try and be helpful, you know. Rather than treating this like a game." Daph's casual attitude was getting on my nerves.

"Okay, how about this Madame Sleuth? Maybe, just for kicks, old man Ned Snow and his creepy son Edwin joined forces killing people. You know, loners who happened by and an assortment of hikers, bikers and hookers. Hey, good title for a mystery. *Hikers, Bikers and Hookers.* Don't you just love it? At last, they'd found something to share– murder."

"Hey, not bad," I considered Daphne's proposition, despite its absurdity. "Suppose some relative found an old postcard saying he or she stayed at the Snow house and then…nothing. Years later, based on that postcard, the relative came looking for answers." Daphne grinned but I remained serious.

"It isn't your worst idea, Daph. Not nice and neat and ready for the jury but it isn't entirely nutty, either. Congrats!"

With that she took both the Harley shakers in hand and drove them wildly in the air for effect, nearly hitting my nose. I shoved them away but she continued her childish antics.

"Well, our darling Edwin *was* a pre-med student; he'd have known how to dismember bodies," Daphne added before I tossed a rolled up paper napkin at her.

I groaned. "Do you consider anything out of bounds for your sense of humor, Daph?"

"Lighten up, Liz. You'd think you were a good pal of old Edwin. He was miserly, nasty, sneaky and a complainer of the first order. What's your problem, anyway?"

"Doesn't it make you feel even a bit sad, Daph?"

"This all is making you sad, Liz?"

"Even you, cold-hearted woman, must admit that the story of Edwin is fraught with bad decisions and missed opportunities that rendered his life a sad tragedy. You've got to feel sorry for someone who wasted his education and came home to vegetate in the small village where his family was scorned. Then, he lost the only girl he'd ever loved. It's a Shakespearean or Greek tragedy, Daph."

"Oh, get a grip on reality, woman. *Humpty Dumpty had a great fall.*" Daph picked up a piece of garlic bread and dropped it onto my plate from her outstretched arm. Not an egg but I got the picture, anyway. Never should have told my friend what Emily Sunshine shared with me about Edwin's unhappy childhood. Poor "Eggy".

I tried to maintain my cool, professional stance but finally lost it and we hooted together until Mr. Beasley gave us the stink eye.

"Poor, poor Egghead Edwin turned into an omelet," said Daphne laughing like a fool."

"Egged to death," I added, equally crazily. It felt good to be so silly.

Laughing until our sides hurt, but attempting to keep it under control so as not to be the only people ever ejected from Beasley's, we finished our lunches. Daphne had to get back to the gallery to meet a potential customer. I sat finishing my tea. In the quiet space left by the removal of Daphne the Jester, what I overheard next changed everything. I wasn't aware of two women coming in and sitting in the booth behind me, so deep in my thoughts I was.

Twenty

"It never occurred to me that they might be from my pile of bones. I'm so embarrassed. I've just been so busy with spring planting. I simply forgot about the bones. My boyfriend Peter was going to put them through his heavy-duty mulching machine. It would have turned them into useful bone meal. If he hadn't had to go off-Cape to a conference, the bones would have been safely buried and no one would have been any the wiser."

I leaped off the bench as if it was an ejection seat. Turning to look into the booth behind me, I saw Daisy Buchanan of Land's End Nursery, our local green thumb and expert on everything that grows. Across from her sat my friend, Tish Souza.

"Hi, Liz. What's new?"

When I again found my voice, I mumbled, "Daisy, what did I overhear about a pile of bones? Sorry, I wasn't being a nosy parker but bones are kind of a hot topic in the village right now."

Daisy motioned me to come and join them. I did. I waited. Finally, the latest mystery took on a whole new aspect.

"I'm just so embarrassed, Liz. It's all my fault! I've been so busy. I simply forgot the pile of bones out behind the greenhouse."

A sentence I'd never imagined I'd hear from the lips of such a fine woman, the woman who was going to be my surrogate green thumb and turn my back garden into a productive herb and vegetable wonderland was also a bone collector.

"A friend of Peter's owns a huge butcher shop in Springfield and he offered me a truck load of bones. Bone meal is excellent for gardens, you know. Peter has a high-powered mulching machine that would have turned them into fine mulch. But Peter had to attend a landscapers' conference in Ohio. So, the enormous pile, unknown to me, was being scavenged by local dogs."

Daisy smiled guiltily. I nodded. Tish laughed. Dee Dee delivered their desserts and we shared the news with her. The

132

bones mystery had been solved. Well, not completely. The bone Patton had found in my garden could not have come from the greenhouse pile. My backyard was completely fenced in so, Patton could not have left and come back with a bone.

In the realm of sometimes truth is stranger than fiction one more human bone showed up. The universe can be perverse. Sometimes the seemingly impossible becomes possible. Sometimes, just when we think things could not get any crazier…they do.

Standing on my back doorstep obviously waiting for me to come home was Tish and Manny Souza's daughter Shelley. "Liz, at last, I've been waiting about twenty minutes. Oh, sorry, that sounded terrible. I mean, no reason you shouldn't be gone when I come to your house. Oh, I am blabbering here."

Aware that usually happy-go-lucky Shelley was obviously uncharacteristically upset and shaking I quickly opened the door and guided the teenager to a chair at the kitchen table. Plugging in the kettle I looked back at Shelley who was tearing a paper napkin into tiny bits and creating a pile that would make a fine bonfire for a mouse. Neither of us said anything until the hot, sweet tea was served.

"Drink it up, Shelley, it'll relax you."

"Sorry about being so impolite outside, Ma would give me you know what if she knew."

"Don't worry; your secret is safe with me." I smiled, hoping to put her more at ease.

"It's this thing. This ugly thing that scared the living hell out of me when I was picking spinach and chard in my Dad's garden. It was just sticking up, like pointing at me. Ugh."

She pulled a piece of paper towel out of her canvas L.L. Bean bag and pushed it quickly across the table to me as if it burned her fingers. My first reaction was to let it sit there unopened, forever. However, knowing Shelley wanted me to see what she'd found, I proceeded to look inside. "Oh."

"Right. Damn thing nearly knocked me on my ass. What the heck is it, Liz?"

Before I could answer, Shelley said, "It's a damned finger, isn't it. So what was a finger doing in the vegetable garden? Did my Dad plant it there? *I don't think so.*" Despite our mutual disgust and surprise at sitting with a whitened finger bone between us, we both began to laugh uproariously. A shock will do that.

"But why did you bring this to me, Shelley? You should take it to the police station."

"That's what Mom and Dad said but I'm not comfortable there. When I was young and dumb, two summers ago, I was picked up for carrying a six pack of beers to a beach party and since then, I'd rather not deal with the cops. Mom suggested that I bring it to you because you are working on the Edwin Snow case. She assumed you are also working on the bones case. Mom said that you are the smartest person around."

"Well, please thank your mother for her confidence in me. Yes, definitely a phalange."

"Yuck, you mean it's a man's *thingey* and not a finger?"

"No. No, I mean a finger." I quickly swallowed a laugh.

"Oh, ya. That's a lot better. I really thought you meant that other thing." Shelley blushed. "So, now that a mysterious dead person has given us the finger, what do we do?'

Our laughter served to lighten the heaviness of a reality I was not prepared to deal with. Not wanting to upset Shelley any further, I simply offered to deliver the skeletal finger to the police station.

"Thanks, Liz. You are a pal. Well, gotta go. Mom's expecting me to take over the store while she goes to her needlepoint class. But you can be sure I am never going to look at a ham bone, chicken wing or a standing rib roast the same ever again. Do you think this is important, Liz?"

"Yes, I think it is very important and you will get credit for finding it. Hope that takes the onus off your feelings about the police. All kids get into trouble of some kind. I'm sure when I tell the Chief what a good thing you did by reporting this, he will forget your crime spree of two years ago."

"Thanks. I'm outa here. Bye."

The bone case was taking on a whole new aspect. I headed into the Police Station to find James busy talking to a couple whose outfits, complete with cameras strung around their necks, gave them away immediately as tourists. From what I could make out from an unobtrusive distance of about ten feet, was that the woman's purse had been grabbed on the street and they'd come to file a complaint.

The red-faced husband said, "Ya, a floozy with bright pink hair and wearing a long sequin covered cape over what looked like green tights and a matching bra. Unbelievable! What kind of a getup is that for a purse snatcher?"

Not sure what the man expected a purse snatcher to wear, I continued to eavesdrop. James looked my way surreptitiously. Turning back to the man he put back his proper cop mask.

"The wife and I came here because it seemed like it ought to be a safer place than the Jersey shore with all those mafia guys vacationing there. But since we got here we've seen more damned crazily dressed people. You got some kind of early Halloween thing goin' on here, officer?"

The man went on to say that his wife's purse had been snatched by the person in the pink wig. James managed a glance in my direction and I held up the plastic bag containing the skeletal finger remains.

Assuring the couple that he would take their description out onto the street and track the thief, he suggested they go and have a nice cappuccino at the Green Genie coffee shop. He took their cell phone number and promised to contact them within the hour. The couple departed although their facial expressions displayed a lack of confidence in a man of the law who would live in a town full of weirdly dressed residents.

James quickly moved to my side and took me by the elbow. He steered me into the meeting room where the attorney had announced Edwin's bequest to me. Déjà vu.

"Where? Who? When?" James looked through the clear plastic and, as I had, knew immediately that the bone did not belong to a goat or a seal.

"Shelley found it in her Dad's vegetable patch."

"Time to back off, Liz, please."

"Pardon me, James, I do not recall you taking over as my keeper." I was coming on a little too harshly considering I knew James had a perfect right to be worried about me.

135

He looked so sweet and concerned that momentarily I considered taking his advice and backing out of the case. I'd certainly have enough on my plate with the inn during the busy months ahead. Agatha Raisin's strident voice shouted inside my head. *A good sleuth never backs down. Finish the job and show that arrogant male what you are made of, woman. Never let down the side.*

Unfortunately, Agatha provided no avenue for rebuttal or I would have shouted back, *James is hardly arrogant and I have nothing to prove to him. He is just concerned for my safety.* But I knew that my favorite sleuth was right and no matter what the risk, I was not about to butt out. I was not a quitter.

"Please, Liz, this could be dangerous. We have a possible three crime situation here, two current and one cold case and if you continue digging, you could be the fourth...situation."

I'd told him about Daisy Buchanan's bone pile but we both knew this finger bone had not come from there.

Leaving my concerned boyfriend with the phalange, I left the station. Meaning to head back to the inn, I had a sudden idea. Instead of turning down Honeysuckle Lane, I kept on going down Commercial Street in the direction of the Fairies in the Garden Shop. A loud commotion behind me grew louder and louder until I just had to turn to see what was going on.

About six feet tall and wearing a bright, shiny pink wig, a silk cape covered in sequins flying out behind him like a super hero in a comic book and exposing lime green tights and matching bustier, the superhero aka Bernie Williams, nearly knocked me down as he flew by. He was carrying a bone and swinging it like a baton.

As he passed, he shouted over his shoulder, "I didn't do it, the bone did! I'm telling the truth."

Summer cop Eddie Mason, hired back early to help with the crowds the Boston newspapers had brought to town, also shot by me in hot pursuit. He jumped over a dog sitting in the middle of the sidewalk and when the pink-haired runner tripped on the uneven surface, Eddie caught him by the flying cape. Sequins went flying like confetti. The bone took off like a missile, landing at the feet of the aforementioned dog who gave it a thorough sniff before rejecting it. Still adamantly protesting his innocence as the cop clamped on the handcuffs, Bernie's wig fell onto the road. The dog also checked it out with even less interest.

Back at the station the prisoner told his tale. James and I laughed when he told me the whole story of Bernie, aka Busty Betty, at the Crown and Anchor where he performed nightly. His specialty was a Barbra Streisand imitation that was absolutely phenomenal.

"According to Bernie, he found the bone wedged into his dog's house. When Bernie retrieved it, he recalled his college anatomy and was sure it was human."

"Wow, wonder where the dog got it."

"Hang on. It gets better. He said, "I had it under my arm and I was headed to the station when it grabbed a lady's purse. Next thing I knew this guy was yelling and chasing me. I thought he was a guy I owe some money to so I managed to lose him when I turned down Mayflower Lane and ducked into the tumbled down fish packing plant. The damn guy was shouting, 'Thief, thief.' Wasn't about to try and deal with him. Then, I looked down and saw what I'd done. The bone had done. It had grabbed a lady's purse, damn it.' As best as I can remember his testimony."

I laughed in amazement rather than humor. "You have a great memory, James."

As it turned out, the bone had belonged to a robust steer and had evidently come from Daisy's bone pile. Bernie was released, the purse returned and the couple left in a huff promising never to return to Provincetown. James laughed when he told me the man was overheard saying to his wife that they'd never come back to "this town full of dizzy whackos in Halloween costumes."

Bernie was been hauled off to the police station minus his pink wig and I'd continued on to the Fairies in the Garden Shop. I knew I could count on being brought up to date on the bone-wielding Bernie by James, later in the evening. Like have a police band radio, I knew everything that went on in James' professional life. The little bell on the door made a Tinker Bell jingle as I entered Emily's shop. Once again, my sinuses screamed their objection to the atmosphere of competing attar of roses, cinnamon, citrus and assorted other scents.

137

Emily stepped through the beaded curtain from the back room wearing a Donna Reed era housedress with high top pink sneakers and a gray felt beret.

"Hello, Ms. Ogilvie-Smythe. Isn't it a lovely spring day? Hot chocolate?"

"Yes, it certainly is nice out there. (Nicer by far than in this un-breathable atmosphere!). No thanks. Just finished an iced coffee. How are you Emily?"

"Just jolly. Thanks for asking. How are you, Liz?"

"Great. Emily, I've come to ask a favor. It would help the police a great deal," I fibbed, "if you could look into your crystal ball, er, Eloise and see if she has any clues to the bone found in my back garden?" Lying and playing into the hands of crazies was becoming quite natural. I wasn't sure I wanted this newly acquired talent.

My Scottish Granny always said, *"T'is easier to catch flies with honey than vinegar."* So, honey dripped from my lips until I was sure I might suddenly take off and fly around the shop like one of the ubiquitous fairies on a sugar high.

Emily looked doubtful. It passed through my mind that this request might be outside her purview. Could bones communicate once they were separated from their skeleton, I wondered? It also occurred to me that I'd been thinking far too many unscientific thoughts lately for a student of hard science.

"Perhaps in doing so, you could help the victim to be at rest." Emily's response could be seen in her eyes. She liked the idea. Maybe this could work, after all.

"My powers are generally used to bring people together or ask important family questions of the dear departed. But I suppose I could try. Eloise could, that is."

"Try is the best we can ask for Emily. Thank you."

We sat. The crystal ball gave me the creeps. It seemed to be alive and waiting. Waiting to cause trouble.

Emily moved the orb closer to her and began speaking intimately to the glass ball. It occurred to me that there was not much difference between Eloise communicating with Emily and my hearing the sound of Agatha Raisin's voice in my head. Oh, I thought, I will need much more than a few weeks on an analyst's couch. Maybe a month in Monte Carlo.

My poor head was so congested; I worried that I might begin to hallucinate from pressure brought to bear on my brain. Had that angel doll sitting on the shelf straight ahead of me just winked? No, not possible. I must be drunk on flower scents. A whole new kind of high.

Emily's voice seemed to come from a long distance away. "Sorry, I don't think this is the kind of thing that Eloise can do." Emily's voice sounded shaky and perhaps, I thought, scared.

I remained as silent as the grave (pun definitely intended).

"Hm. Very interesting." Emily looked up at me. "Sorry, Liz. Princess Proudfoot says that the bone belongs to someone in her tribe." With that, Emily pushed Eloise away from her, covered *her* with a lace cloth and closed her eyes. Subject closed."

"Wait, Emily. Are you saying the bone in my garden was from an Ind...Native American?

"Not surprising. Disgraceful how the old tribal burial sites were tossed to construct modern buildings. The Princess says that the bone must be returned to the ancient burial ground off of Shank Painter's Road or something..." She stopped before finishing the sentence.

"Or what Emily? What?"

"Or, there will be more troubles. More retribution."

What could I say to that? It was obvious that Emily had no intention of helping.

"That's all. Eloise has shut down. Good day Liz."

Twenty-one

Unable to put off any longer the many inn-related responsibilities waiting for me, I headed back there. My goal was to have the inn ship-shape when Katy Balsam arrived from college just before Memorial Day to take over her duties as manager. In the meantime, I had to interview local girls interested in housekeeping positions, order supplies and deal with the kitchen re-do. My time with Emily had produced nothing of value except to verify my opinion that Eloise ran the show.

Sitting at the kitchen table with the Dean and Deluca catalog in front of me, nearly drooling with anticipation, I organized an order for new pots and pans and time-saving kitchen gadgets. I could not resist ordering a Panini maker and a waffle iron that made the delectable cakes in the shape of sailboats. But, despite my anticipation, my mind was not fully on the project at hand.

Emily's behavior in conjunction with Eloise's had disturbed me more than I wanted to admit. The woman obviously knew lots and lots of secrets but she was standing obdurately in the way of solving the town's mysteries. Damn her. And her orb.

The ringing of the front doorbell surprised me. Since I had my friends trained to come to the kitchen door, I concluded that whoever was there ringing the bell was someone I did not want to see. Oh, how correct I was.

Standing there in the warm sunshine on the front stoop was a droopy young man in an even droopier, too large for his slight frame, old-fashioned chauffer's suit and cap. After two years in town, I'd grown accustomed to costumed people everywhere but this was somehow quite different. Behind him, parked at the curb, I could see a Boston taxi cab and a face I wished was still across the wide Atlantic Ocean. My heart sank fifty fathoms.

"Hello, Miss, I'm delivering Lady Gwendolyn Ogilvie-Smythe. Her card, Miss."

Oh no! Not now! My first thought was to slam the door and move a large piece of furniture in front of it as a barricade. When Lady Gwendolyn paid a visit, the world was always turned on its head.

Then, completely out of character, my mother opened the cab door and stepped out. As far as I knew my mother had never opened a car door for herself. Will wonders never cease!

The last thing I needed at that moment, or, at any time, was my bothersome snob of a mother. Alighting from the cab, Lady Gwendolyn, wearing furs from head to foot on the sixty-eight degree day, called to the chauffer to return immediately to unload her luggage. When I spotted the suitcases that filled the trunk plus the two cases that had traveled on the front seat with the driver, I knew without a doubt that life as I presently knew it was over.

"Mother, what a surprise."

"Oh, Elizabeth darling, what on earth is that thing you are wearing on your head? Have you become a hippie late in life? God its tropical here. I certainly hope you have central air. I shall expire."

My hand went to the scarf covering my hair that I wore when dusting. I pulled it off and stuffed it into my jeans pocket.

"Mother, you might remove a few animals from your body and find that it's not that hot. Come in."

Lady Gwendolyn, my officious, snob mother, took three steps into the front hall and stopped dead. Gazing around with her proud eagle eyes, she harrumphed loudly. "So this is where that foolish woman ended up. That is what comes of marrying out of one's class. Did you know that two dukes and a count wanted to marry   Libby?"

No point in defending my ostracized aunt at that juncture. Let it go, Liz. You have never won any argument or ever made a convincing point with this woman, so don't try now.

"I'll make some iced tea, Mother. Hang those furs on that coat tree over by the stairs. Make yourself at home in the living room and for God's sake give that phony chauffer a big tip; he's melting in that suit. Where *did* you get him that terrible chauffer's getup?"

141

"At a costumer's shop in Boston. I could not allow him to drive me in one of those disgusting muscle shirts and droopy pants, could I?"

"No, I'm sure his driving skills were greatly improved by the monkey suit."

Returning with a tray of tea things and cookies I found my mother engrossed in a photo album put together by Aunt Libby.

"Look here, darling. This is me at the Fairfield School for Girls. Did you know that your Aunt Libby and I were chums there and she introduced me to her handsome brother, your dear PaPa? She invited me to a hunt weekend at the Smythe's country house in Sussex and there was your dear Papa in his military uniform. Oh, he was so chic. What wonderful memories reopened for me by these old photos. If only she hadn't betrayed us all."

"How nice, Mother. Now tell me, what on earth are you doing here?"

"That tone of voice hardly makes me feel welcome, Elizabeth. I've left Percy. I don't want to talk about it. My psychologist advises that I not burden you with our troubles. We both love you and will continue to but I simply cannot live with him any longer."

"You've left Papa? But why? And why come here? You could have gone to the country house or the Riviera or rented a flat in London. Cry on the shoulders of your friends. Why, for heaven's sake come all the way here?"

"Well, I thought my darling daughter would be happy to see her Ma Ma but this is hardly the reception I hoped for. Don't worry, I'll be gone in a fortnight."

"*Two weeks*! Well, you can't because, because…every room is booked."

Having let that lie slip I had no idea of how I could pull it off. Every room was tumbled, beds were stripped and bathrooms smelled of bleach. But, if forced to, I'd invite everyone I knew to a stay with meals included just to stand behind my word.

"Mother, be serious. I have a business to run. I do not have the time to entertain you."

"Oh, Darling, I don't need entertaining. I will entertain myself. I intend to walk around and get to know the village, gossip

142

with the humble villagers and hand out coins to the dirty, unfortunate children."

"Oh, that attitude will make you welcome, indeed. Mother this is not England. People here are not snobs and the children are not dirty and unfortunate." In the back of my mind I could see my haughty, bejeweled mother giving fashion advice to a gaudily dressed female only to discover that *her* name was Tom or Mike or Henry.

"And anyway, I can sleep in your room. Certainly you will not deny half a bed to your dear Ma Ma. I'll be gone in no time at all. After my heartbreak heals."

"Well, on that subject. Where do you plan to go from here? In fact, do you have even a semblance of a plan for your future?"

"Of course I do. I'm going out to the west coast to spend time with an old beau who's been after me to visit for years. He's in the movie business or the music business or something very exciting out there. I just plan to be a gypsy for a few years after so many years of living in your Pa Pa's huge, crushing shadow. Being an indentured slave wears one down, darling."

"Two things, Mother. Gypsies travel light. I'm not sure you can survive with a backpack as your only luggage. And second, when have you ever been a slave? You have never lifted a finger to do anything for yourself except perhaps in the privacy of the bathroom."

I went to answer the ringing phone and Lady Gwendolyn returned to her photo memories.

"Sorry, Daphne, can't make it to book club tonight." I put my hand over the mouthpiece just in case my mother's keen hearing was still working.

"What are you talking about? That's ridiculous. What on earth would keep you away? Another murder, right in your kitchen?"

"You'll never believe it but my mother is here. She left my father and she plans to stay around for a fortnight. God, I think I'll just drown myself."

"Hey, bring her along. Love to meet the old gal. So would the girls. Do bring her along."

"No, Daph. Really, don't even suggest it. She'll bring a plague upon your good house. She'll just ruin the evening. She takes over wherever she is and tries to run everything."

"Oh, get off your high horse, Liz. She's your mother all the way from jolly old England. She's missed her darling daughter. She'd love to meet your friends."

"Right. Imagine Geraldine telling her about her sex change operation. Of course, Geraldine *would* reinforce my mother's present attitude that all men are brutes. But, honestly I just don't think it's a good idea."

"That's it. I'm coming right over to invite her myself."

"Daphne, honestly, believe me, please. She is a snob and a harridan and she's pushy and arrogant."

"Cool. She should be very entertaining. By the way, we've got three new members. Say, you could just send her along and you stay home if you don't want to come yourself."

"Damn Daphne, you ought to be her daughter. You are a lot like her. See you at seven."

An hour later, James's appeared at the kitchen door causing Lady Gwendolyn to immediately transfer her fascination with modern kitchen gadgets such as the microwave oven and the amazing wire whisk to him. She had wandered around the foreign territory of the kitchen exclaiming over such things as the potato peeler, the Cuisinart food processor, the French press and the pasta machine. However, of particular interest was the microwave that she at first took for new-fangled, kitchen television. As I explained the function of this space age appliance, my mother's reaction might have been in response to an account of the practical uses of alchemy.

Making introductions, I could see my mother sizing up the handsome police officer and doing some secret drooling. Too sophisticated and British tight-lipped by far to let her favorable impression of him show, I knew she was having lascivious thoughts about him. Even if he was a member of the "inferior" Irish "rabble."

Finally, Mother announced that she was off to take a brief nap, "To restore myself before heading out into the village to view the natives." I was sure she expected them to be wearing feather headdresses and wielding tomahawks.

"James, I'm so sorry, she is such a snob. Just showed up unexpectedly this morning. I don't know what I am going to do with her."

"Sweetie, she's your Mam. How bad can she be?"

"Don't ask. Why are you here, anyway? Sorry, that sounded terrible, James." I kissed him deeply and then motioned for him to sit at the kitchen table.

"Brace yourself, Liz. Found a torso in Mary Malone's garden."

"No! Are we real or are we characters in a cozy, James?"

"Mary happened on it while digging to put in a new plant. Missing one leg and one arm but otherwise, a complete torso, head and all."

"So, what do we do next?"

"You, my love, do nothing but get the inn up and running and write your cookery book. And, of course, entertain your loving Mam. I, the law, will pursue this mystery."

"What about Mrs. Malone? What do we really know about her? What was her reaction to such a find in her garden? What about her husband? Did he disappear one night and she told everyone he had left her for a belly dancer or some such?"

"Don't know the woman real well but the Chief says she's the sweetest lady on the face of this good earth. Makes cookies and brownies for every town function, runs the scholarship bake sales and knits little caps for all the new babies in town. Last year, she took the CPR course so she could save a life if it became necessary. Chief vouches for her not to have murdered anyone."

"So, that leaves the Snows. What about the old man, mean as a wet hen and he certainly had enemies aplenty. You don't rob people of their homes and land without making murderous enemies. Maybe one of them tried to murder old man Ned but got murdered himself, instead."

"It was a woman. Doc took a look and checked the pelvis," James said.

"Oh, James, this case is getting weird."

"Welcome to crime fighting, love."

James went off to help the Chief's secretary, Annie Cannon, search through the dusty files from sixty years ago looking for reports of missing females. I went into a black funk. In just a few short hours I'd be introducing my black widow spider mother to my best friend and a handful of other women I liked and hoped to continue to be liked by. However, probably by the end of the evening my social life would be a shambles.

Ten minutes later, James called my cell. "Hi. Forgot to tell you. In the stucco room in the middle of the Snow mansion the arson team found an old steamer trunk full of women's clothing. Real 'flashy stuff' as Bob Gerard said.

Twenty-two

The rest of the day I spent doing laundry, cleaning bathrooms and endeavoring to explain to my mother why I did not have servants to do such menial work.

"You have gone mad child. Why would you not have help to do such odious jobs?"

"Mother, this is America. I like doing my own work. This is a labor of love and pride. I love this place and I enjoy taking care of it. I have a serious business to run. I have no time for entertaining you. Perhaps you should contact friends and drum up some invitations to visit them. You'll only be bored to death here. There is nothing in this village to interest you. You know you hate being in the country and sea air gives you headaches. You need to leave."

"Oh, balderdash. First, I want to get to know your little, provincial village. In fact, I am having my fortune told tomorrow. I read an ad in your little newspaper and I called to make an appointment. You just keep ruining your fingernails and your posture and I will just head out into the village to find my own entertainment, every day."

Mother went off in a huff leaving behind her a trail of very expensive scent. I could hear her high heels clicking down the front hall and then up the stairs. Only then, when she was not there to witness, did panic set in. I simply could not let Lady Gwendolyn and Emily/Eloise meet. It would be tantamount to splitting the atom. Boom.

Later, when I told my mother that I'd be attending my monthly book club and that she was welcome to come along, explaining that she'd be utterly bored and probably prefer to stay at home and watch some telly she became all excited about coming along. Damn.

"How lovely. I am anxious to meet your new little American playmates, darling." I flashed to the sandbox in the park near our London flat where my governess took me to play with other little rich girls. Did my mother expect girls in pinafores with their hair in plaits?

Unfortunately, seven p.m. did arrive and I had to face the fact that my mother's visit had been real and not the result of my having fallen into a bathtub and been concussed. Never had the possibility of a temporary slip into unconsciousness seemed so promising, however.

When my mother finally floated down the stairs at seven fifteen, much to my chagrin she did so as if she was on a Paris runway. "Mother, don't you have anything less...obviously expensive to wear. Everyone will be in jeans and t-shirts. You will be so out of synch. Better to try and fit in than flaunt your wealth."

"Darling, you know MaMa always sets the pace. They will love seeing this designer frock."

"Whatever. Let's go."

Arriving at Daphne's house, I worked at holding down everything I'd eaten that day. My mother could, with the wave of her diamond-heavy hands, ruin my new life. To the villagers I was just one of them, a regular, hard-working, friendly villager. I had attended town meeting and I took my own trash to the dump, gave to the Fund for the Families of Lost Fishermen and baked goodies for the scholarship bake sales. A bona fide villager. Or as my mother, left to her own haughty devices would call me now (please, I beseeched the Gods of incognito rich, titled girls, don't let her use the term tonight to my new fiends), "a rag tag commoner."

The front door opened and there stood Daphne wearing anything but casual herself. I wondered if they'd had a wardrobe confab over the phone in secrecy. White stovepipe silk slub jeans that might have been painted on, topped by a silk gypsy blouse encrusted with red, blue, yellow and black embroidery that must have cost at least eight hundred dollars at Ralph Lauren, screamed wealthy.

The dripping diamond earrings might look to the others like great paste costume jewelry from T. J. Maxx, but I could recognize a Tiffany earring anywhere. Even on the ears of my traitorous friend.

Damn you, Daphne, (I said to myself), you planned this outfit to impress my mother. Obviously not to be outdone by Lady Gwendolyn, Daphne had purposely dressed the part of the wealthy woman she was. So much for her witness protection program pretense. We had once kidded, after I discovered her secret life, that, if found out, she could plead having stumbled onto sex tapes of the prime minister. In a quirky place like Provincetown that would diminish the onus of having pretended to be just a wage-earning villager.

"Welcome, ladies. Lady Gwendolyn, it's so lovely to meet you." Taking both of my mother's hands in hers, Daphne drew the woman into the living room totally ignoring me.

Mother entered the room to face the bevy of females and facsimiles thereof as if she was stepping onto the stage of the Haymarket Theatre in London. Then, the leading lady turned back to me and oh so graciously reached out her hand to pull me into the circle as if just remembering that I was there. A bit player.

What on earth was Daphne up to? We had agreed not to let on that we were both refugees from wealthy (titled) families. But there she was putting on airs like a grand duchess. Where was her hip talk? This was just too much. It had already been a darned difficult day only to conclude with my best friend blowing our cover and treating my mother as if they belonged to the same polo club.

The solution came to me like a meteor on a collision course with my brain. I'd simply convince these good, real, honest people that my mother was a prize-winning fraud. Otherwise, my cover would be blown and I was not ready, at least that soon, to be exposed for a wealthy woman. I liked just being one of the villagers. As if on cue, my mother decided to begin her dropping of facts like crumbs but these were gold-encrusted crumbs.

"Dear, you look so familiar. I could swear I knew you in my youth. Well, I would venture a guess that you are the spitting image of your mother, am I correct? Didn't I meet her at a ball at Baliol Castle sometime during my coming out year? Not that I dare mention what year that was." A little girlish laugh for the rapt audience.

"Yes, now I remember. Of course, Alexandra Crowninshield. Darling girl, you could be her with only the addition of a beehive hairdo."

I had to hand it to my almost ex-best friend for her next move. Daphne very cleverly dodged the social bullet by simply beginning the introductions and letting the matter drop. Once Mother was ensconced on the couch next to Geraldine (who used to be a man) I ceased to be concerned. Whatever happened from that point on was completely out of my hands. Talk about sunspots and planet alignments!

Geraldine, wearing a tight black, scooped neck, cleavage-exposing sweater with slim black designer jeans and a wide red snakeskin belt with matching high boots, grinned broadly and patted the empty seat beside her on the couch. I must note here that although casual was the norm for most occasions in the unpretentious village there were certain exceptions and exemptions. Geraldine was still fully enjoying her newly won female life and her knockout New York designer wardrobe.

My mother was immediately enraptured as she and Geraldine shared their opinions on the "beastliness of men," the season's new fashions, their favorite designers and their shared contempt for American wines. Fortunately for us all, Geraldine did not share the details of her sex change operation.

Taking Daphne aside, I asked, "Do the girls know about your elite British roots?"

"No, of course not; do they know about yours?"

"They do now, don't they? Mine *and* yours. Nice work, pal." I glared at Daphne in contempt.

"Oh dang, I guess they do. Hey, we'll just tell them later that your mother's a big fake and we set it up for me to put her on. No problem. Just a bit of sport. They'll have no problem accepting that Lady Gwendolyn's a British housewife who enjoys putting on airs. After all, you are such a regular girl, Liz."

"Bite me." I snarled at Daphne before laughing. After all, great minds work alike and since we were both on the same page, all should be well.

"After all, it's not like anyone *ever* takes me seriously. You, on the other hand, are a worry wart and too dead ordinary to come from the upper class." I gave her a withering look, sat across the room from my mother and leafed through the cozy book samples on the table, hoping my mother would disappear in a puff of smoke.

Amazingly, the evening went fairly well. I left feeling confident that my mother had been more entertaining than toxic and I would not have to leave town in the dark of night. But Mother's visit wasn't over yet.

The following day, as I was hanging freshly washed kitchen curtains when my mother burst in with her big news, the following day. I had thought she was sleeping in but she'd slipped out and actually walked *on her own legs*, the four blocks to Emily's Fairies in the Garden shop without my even knowing it. Sitting in the kitchen watching me work until she insisted I sit, *after* brewing her a cup of mint tea, I sensed something big coming. Like the change in the air before a storm or, the horrifying, high-pitched buzz as a bomb is dropping.

"Where did you go without my knowing it, Mother? I would have made you breakfast. Did you go to Beasley's?"

Then it was out and could never be taken back. "You will never believe what I wandered into, Dear. A little shop full of wonderful scents and silly angel things. But no matter, I met the most fascinating woman named Emily Sunshine. She tells fortunes and she told me, via her crystal ball, that my future lies in California."

My stomach fell like a failed cake. The damn had broken. The levies had failed. I had no idea of how to stop the runaway train now that it was out of the station. I couldn't muster enough metaphors for the awful thing that was to come.

"Mother, you didn't. The woman is a fake, a charlatan; you mustn't believe anything she told you." But her expression said otherwise.

What could I do but brace for the worst and then hope I could find a patch large enough to close the whole in my ruined life when the maelstrom passed. "Oh, whatever she said about your future, about California, that you will become friends with Brangelina, it is all fake. Contrived. Balderdash, Mother."

Mother just smiled a serpent's smile as I rambled on nearly incoherently. "Mother, Emily could just as likely have told to take up charity work and live in sack cloth or join a monastery. Or, simply that you ought to change your lipstick color?"

"Now don't be so flippant, Elizabeth. MaMa is not as shallow as that." Right!

I bit my lip and tried to think of something more shallow than my mother but only came up with the image of my father's foot bath. My mind wandered to the real estate market and how much I might realize from selling out and moving to Istanbul to sell scarves.

"I know you will be disappointed, darling, but MaMa must be on her way tomorrow."

A brilliant light shone upon my antique pine, well-worn but steadfast kitchen table. Had she really announced her immanent departure? Had the God of Innkeepers, whose name I did not know but who must have been watching over me, come to my rescue? What my mother said next, in another context might have brought forth laughter. Instead, in this framework, it brought joy to my heart.

"Yes, Hollywood is calling. My fortune is waiting for me there. Won't Percy be surprised when he sees my name up on the huge screen in his man cave?"

"Mother, what on earth are you talking about? Hollywood? And, where did you pick up that expression, *man cave*? Really, Mother, Papa would never call his study that."

"Geraldine taught me that and I think it is just delightful. Men are such Neanderthals; the cave image is quite apropos. I am heading west as soon as I can arrange for transportation."

"I'll drive you to Hyannis or Boston or Providence, whichever airport you choose to fly out of Mother, dear."

Twenty-three

With my difficult mother off on her way to Tinsel Town, feeling like a new woman, I returned to the inn after driving her to the Hyannis airport. Nothing like the insertion of a much greater problem into one's current mélange of problems to put things into proper perspective. What was a little bit of murder, arson and a torso in the pansies compared to a few days with Lady Gwendolyn?

Stepping from my sunny yellow Jeep, I realized that Daisy Buchanan and the wonders of Land's End Nursery had been to visit. Our joint plans for my gardens; flowers, vegetables and edible herbs, would be such a wonderful addition to the charms of the inn when completed. That day, Daisy had planted black-eyed susans and shasta daisies in huge clumps all along the driveway. Just as I'd envisioned them since the day I first came to the Cranberry Inn.

James drove in behind me. "Well love, the torso in Mary Malone's garden tipped the scales. Takes a lot to excite the Chief these days. I'm sure he's in more pain than he lets on but he perked up when we found the mysterious torso. Wants answers to everything. He's sure that all the mysteries somehow tie in together. As he said, 'Figures that old buzzard would not leave this mortal coil without leaving behind a real mess.' Never heard the Chief so poetic."

"So, a full investigation is underway?" I asked, feeling pleased.

"Yup, nobody missing in town at that time but we'll reach wider for missing persons who might have been visiting here around sixty years ago." James pulled me into a big hug. "Got to hand it to you, Liz. You have the mind of a sleuth. In the body of a goddess."

I smiled, pleased that there just might eventually be justice for the miserable old man and punishment for his killer. I kept mum however on my next plan.

"Oh, I forgot to ask. Did you ever check with the bank to see if Edwin made any large withdrawals or wrote any large checks?"

"I checked and he didn't. In fact, the man lived on almost nothing. Took out forty dollars a month in cash and all in small change. Drove the teller nuts. Brought in an old ratty canvas sack to pick up his coins. Dead end if he was being blackmailed. I'd say he managed to avoid paying."

"So, he must have fended off the blackmailer somehow. Makes sense that the blackmailer would have been pretty frustrated and murder might have been the result. The thing that sounds strange, however, is the description of Edwin looking smug and almost amused by the blackmail attempt. At least, according to Mario at Sal's Place. A rather odd reaction wouldn't you say? I mean who is amused by blackmail?"

"Only the odd, I'd say."

Wednesday morning found us at Mary Malone's cozy house sitting in comfy chairs with antimacassars. I had weakened and decided to share my plan with James. After all, the Edwin Snow death was now officially a possible murder case. In addition, with arson, blackmail and a cold case torso in Mary Malone's garden, it seemed we ought to achieve more working as a team.

Patton had just been bathed and coiffed at veterinarian Taylor Eastman's pet grooming parlor where mostly dogs but the occasional cat came out looking "best in show." Patton was grinning from ear to ear looking spit and polished and seemed to be seeking compliments. "Oh, Patton, you are so handsome. What a fine looking fellow you are." This got me lots of wet doggie kisses. Mary laughed and it was obvious that she was enjoying her new companion.

We had come to discuss a female partial skeleton found in her garden but Mary appeared undisturbed. Greeting us at her front door wearing a butter yellow sweater set with a pearl necklace, a matching skirt and old lady, sturdy, white tie shoes she might have stepped out of a children's book. A beloved grandmother greeting visitors for tea.

"Come in children, come in. Isn't it a fine day? My flowers are coming up daily. I love this season, don't you?"

"So nice of you to have us, Mary, and yes it is a grand day indeed." The lilt of James' voice spoke of four leaf clovers and warm from the oven Irish soda bread. The man was certainly a charmer but a never a phony, instead, a man as solid and sincere as the rolling, green hills of Eire. Definitely a keeper.

"I wonder dear," she said to James, "if you'd put this fellow out into the backyard. He's needing a bit of fresh air, been in all morning keeping me company. Now that you are here, it's time for him to go and frolic about a bit. Such a good companion he's become to me."

James led Patton to the back door and out he went, but instead of frolicking, the dog walked to the very center of the fenced-in yard, lay down with his chin on his paws and gazed in the direction of his former home. Of course, there was nothing to see but a raked-over blackened scar on the land. I wondered if tears were running down the handsome white and black face spoiling his body coiffure.

"Coffee or tea, dears?"

"Whatever you are having Mrs. Malone. Thanks."

The conversation took off on its own independent course as Mrs. Malone told us stories about the old days in town and about some of the old town characters. She told us about the fish weirs just offshore that trapped tinker mackerel and how she and Edwin, when they were youngsters, would go out to buy a bucket of them from the old fisherman who tended them. "His name was Harry Mutt so all the children made fun of him calling him Dog Man and Mixed Breed. Children are often not very kind."

"Was Edwin a good friend to you, Mrs. Malone?"

"It's just Mary, dear. And yes, we were the best of friends all through childhood but later, when he came back from Yale, he'd grown mean. Just like old Ned, his father."

"Do you recall anything odd going on over next door, Mrs. Malone, way back?"

"Odd, you say? Well dear, you've come to the right place. There were a lot of odd things going on over there all the time. I know everything about that balmy family. You see Edwin and I are, well we *were,* until he died, the same age. I was born in this house on a stormy November day and two months later Edwin was born next door. Didn't run off to the hospital back in those days to have babies. Well, the closest hospital was in Plymouth anyway so why set out to drive a hundred miles and just have the little one on the way. Better for a woman to stay snug in her own home and her own bed with the local midwife there to attend to her in her important moment. Ours was Maggie Crocker. She delivered ninety-six babies in her long career. Imagine that? Everyone called her Mother Goose, just like in the nursery rhymes, because she kept geese."

"What wonderful memories you have, Mary." I was fascinated and wanted to hear more. I nearly lost track of why we'd come but the afternoon was young and all I had waiting for me was an eight bedroom inn waiting to be prepared for the long busy summer season. *C'est la vie.*

"My mother survived but Edwin's did not. The poor little motherless tyke was nursed by my mother. She told me how she'd have one on one side and the other on the other side and that is why we grew up more like siblings than just neighbors. My mother never understood why sweet Annabelle Jenkins ever married that nasty thieving Ned Snow in the first place. But once he had a son, my mother at least expected him to take some interest in the tiny, innocent baby. But he couldn't have cared less. So poor Edwin spent most of his childhood in our house. My mother took him in like a stray cat. Fed him, made sure he put on his boots and mittens, made his school lunches and patched up his skinned knees. Edwin loved my mother like she was his own. Old Ned Snow just went about his business *stealing* land for back taxes and putting people on the street with never a fare thee well. Never even knew where his son slept of a night. Imagine?"

"So, you and Edwin probably had no secrets then?" Time to detour the fascinating trip down memory lane at this juncture before we got too far off of a winning tack. Mary's lead-in seemed a good opportunity for me to take the tiller. James' eyes said *tread carefully*.

"You know how it is, Liz. When you get to the teen years, boys get weird." That brought laughter. Mary put her hand on James' hand. "But, probably not you, dear boy. I suspect you've always been sweet and reliable. James actually blushed.

"What I mean is," she turned toward me, "boys are so silly and immature and such–what is it my nieces say, oh yes, 'dorks'. Well, that was when Edwin and I began to drift apart. However, the drift became a chasm when he returned from Yale and just stayed. He had no ambition. He was wasting all that fine education. I blame that strange group he joined at Yale, Skull and Bones."

"Did you talk after that? When he came home and just hung around?" I hoped she would tell us why he made such an odd life choice.

"No, well, by then I had met my husband-to-be. Although I had loved Edwin for all of my growing up and actually believed he loved me and that naturally, we'd marry one day, I finally realized it was not going to happen. My Charles was a good man. I decided not to wait so I married Charles."

"Did his father mind his being home again?" James asked.

"From what I could tell Edwin and old Ned just sort of bumped along on their separate roads through life as they always had. Lived in the same house but they might have been living in different towns." Mary looked toward the place where the house once stood.

"Did his father support him?" I asked.

"Didn't need to, Edwin had a sizable trust fund. However, until he turned twenty-one, he received only a small, monthly stipend. Later, when he came of age, he had control of his own money. Up until then however, the old man paid for school and books and such, although, most reluctantly. I do remember letters to me from Edwin when he was still at college complaining about how he had to beg his father for money when his monthly stipend didn't stretch far enough.

Her eyes misted over and we looked away to give her time to gather her emotions.

"His letters to me were few and far between by then but I do know that there were times at Yale when he went hungry. I started sending him care packages. Son of the richest man in town and I was using my allowance to send him cans of baked beans and Spam and boxed cookies."

"Can you tell us about Edwin and Rosita Gonsalves?

"Always liked Rosita. That is, until she left poor Edwin standing at the altar feeling like a fool. I was there that day and my heart just broke. I suppose that time stands pretty much alone as a day when the entire town felt pity for poor Edwin Snow. Over the years I've thought about how strange it was that the two women who caused havoc and loss in Edwin's life were Portuguese."

"Edwin's mother was Portuguese, Mary?"

"No, no, dear. It was his father's kept girl. That tramp, Estrella. She came to live with old Ned while Edwin was away at college. No shame at all. It was she who convinced the old man to cut his own flesh and blood out of his will and leave his millions to her. Traipsing around like she did half naked in front of proper neighbors. Well, she got her just desserts, now didn't she?"

Silence. James and I shared a look of confusion. Had Estrella's just desserts been murder, I wondered? I could feel James having a similar thought. So, Edwin had come home and killed the interloper who was after his father's wealth. Made sense. Then, afterwards he gave up on any plans he'd had for a career and just slipped into a miasma of guilt and ennui. He lost all interest in life and since everyone expected him to be like his father anyway, then why not fulfill their expectations? A psychologist's dream patient. I pulled my mind back from my sleuth's daydream. However, it seemed we might have the answer to the cold case: Edwin as murderer of his father's wild, gold-digging mistress.

I opened my mouth to speak but James put his finger up to his lips and we sat silent. I knew he feared interrupting the flow of the story. Once again, Mary picked up where she'd left off.

"Ned, of course, had no concern for the scandal he was involved in. He lived with her openly and she flaunted her flashy clothes and jewelry all over town."

James had said the arson squad found a trunk full of women's *flashy* clothes in Edwin's office that survived the fire. So, they belonged to old Ned's mistress. But, why would Edwin have kept them? Well, no accounting for the deranged mind of a killer.

"When Edwin found out that the old man had written him out of the will in favor of his girlfriend Estrella, he came to me. Knew I'd never judge him and would always be there to soothe his wounds, just like my mother. But, I wanted to be more than a surrogate mother to Edwin." Mary sighed deeply. "I remember him sitting in my kitchen just seething. Why, I thought his head would go up in flames, he was that mad."

"What did he do? Did he move out of his father's house?"

"No, he just dug himself in like a mole refusing to leave his room. But I knew he snuck out after dark and went into town to drink with his pals. The few pals he had left, by then. Then one day, like a miracle, Estrella was gone. There at breakfast and gone by midnight. Everyone just figured she and the old man had quarreled and she left to punish him." Mary grew quiet, contemplative.

"If she was a local girl Mary, hadn't someone missed her? Wasn't Estrella reported missing?" James's mind grabbed onto this story like a tick on a deer.

"She was a half-breed. That's what the Portuguese-Indians were called back then. No longer politically correct, according to Bill Windship. But, you know what I mean. Estrella was sort of adopted by a local family, Norm and Millie Tavares over to The Point took her in. Never legally adopted her but just as well. Estrella was a wild thing. Nothing but trouble from the day they gave her a home. She was pure blooded Wampanoag on her mother's side and her father was from Portugal. Both of them drowned on a trip back from Boston on a coastal schooner but the baby was found floating on top of a trunk in the bay. Everyone else drowned. After she turned sixteen she took her mother's Indian name, Proudfoot. Princess Proudfoot she called herself. The old man only encouraged her by watching her dance around like a wild Indian in the backyard."

Proudfoot. Princess Proudfoot! The name ricocheted around in my brain as if it was a squash court. Then it came to me. Emily or, Eloise, had contacted a Princess Proudfoot. Nosy Emily would probably have picked up that Estrella was related. She made it her life's mission to know everything about everyone, even going back into the history of the village. Was her story about the old sacred tribal burial ground just a ruse to put me off--or a solid clue? Did Emily know that Edwin killed his father's mistress? And if she did know, then it made sense that she might have been blackmailing him with this knowledge. But why? What could Emily have hoped to gain and now that he was dead why not tell what she knew? I couldn't wait to share this with James.

Mary perked up and continued with her story. "Before the tramp left, I'd see through the windows at night when they had the place lit up like a bonfire. They'd be dancing and snuggling, it was disgusting. Old Ned was ancient by that time but he was sashaying around like he was a boy. Well, he'd never cared what anyone thought of him anyway. Then Estrella was gone. Edwin came home to stay and the rest is history, as they say." Mary's face clouded over and she sighed deeply. Patton scratched at the back door and Mary rose to let him in. Patton came to sit at Mary's feet looking up at her with concerned eyes.

Pouring more tea for us all, Mary continued her story although it was obvious that something vital was missing. She'd slipped a piece of the puzzle into her pocket. I could see the hole but was at a loss to fill it. "Ungrateful boy. Not a word or thanks. Made me wonder why I'd even bothered doing it for him."

"Mrs. Malone, did you ever speak to Estrella when she was living with Edwin's father?" I asked, hoping Mary's answer might lead back to the question of what she did for Edwin for which she'd received no thanks.

"Occasionally over the garden fence but she was not our kind. My husband used to make furniture for people, special things with fine details and his workshop in our cellar is still there. It was just a hobby but he was good at it. He had all the right tools and he was so proud of them. I oil his tools and keep everything really nice in his memory. Once she ordered a table from him but he refused to make it because she was living in flagrant sin and he told her that in no uncertain terms. That was the end of any neighborly communication. My husband died soon after."

"Then she disappeared from one day to the next, Mary?"

160

A simple, "Yes" and Mary appeared ready to shut down just like the controlling Eloise. But I was not about to let that happen. Not when we'd come so close. I looked to James and he gave me the silent high sign.

"So, once Estrella was out of the way the inheritance reverted back to Edwin, correct, Mary?"

"Well, yes, dear, that was why...well now how about some nice chocolate chip cookies?" We were so close. There was no way I was going to let Mary avoid what I was afraid she had to tell and was trying to skirt around as if it shouldn't matter. I was sure that for all the years since Estrella disappeared Mary had neatly compartmentalized her deed and labeled it, *Naughty but Necessary*.

"You would have done anything for Edwin wouldn't you, Mary?" I hoped the affection and understanding in my voice would earn the woman's confidence.

Mary leaned down to scratch Patton behind the ears. Returning to our eyes intent upon her she paled and seemed to slip into a semi trance. Her words got a bit slurred as if she'd been into the elderberry wine. She spoke, but not to us. Looking into space she spoke to Edwin. Wherever the old coot had gone in the after-life.

"I had to impress you with just how much I loved you. I was sure you would be grateful and realize what a great sacrifice I'd made for you and love me back. I was widowed by then and I could have made you happy. Not like that Rosita who gave her favors to others and left you to be the ridicule of the whole town."

Before James could speak I was jumping into the ring. "So you took matters into your own hands didn't you Mary?"

James looked at me with wide eyes. He reached out and took Mary's hands in his.

Mary turned to James and smiled at him but said not a word. I worried that the thread had been broken and we'd find out no more. There was a long silence and then Mary began speaking again. She was calm and seemingly transfixed on what she saw in her mind's eye, a place far away in time and space where the present company could not follow her.

"Edwin came home that last summer before everything changed for good. That was when he found out what his father had

161

done. That awful Estrella taunted him, telling him what she was going to do after his father died and she was a rich woman. She was going to Paris and Rome and she was going to buy furs and jewels and on and on she went."

"Did he confront his father about the will, Mary?"

"No, dear. No one ever confronted old Ned. No one. No, Edwin just simmered and drank and ran around with a rough crowd. That drunken artist and his wife and their city friends took him under their wings and taught him lots of bad ways."

"So, that was when he began seeing Rosita Gonsalves, Mary?"

Mary didn't answer but once again slipped into a kind of free association drift and I was sure the scene she was seeing was not the present but something that happened over sixty years ago.

"When Edwin went to New York that winter weekend like a fool traipsing after those artsy people, I happened to be out in the yard on the Saturday. It was a mild day but there was Estrella muffled up in furs the old man had bought her. I suddenly had such a fine idea it startled me. It would be so simple. So neat and clean. I called to her and invited her over to tea. Old Ned was down with the gout and the doctor had him all drugged up for the pain. He slept right through and woke around midnight to find her gone.

"I invited her to come in by the cellar door and slipping behind her silently, I locked the door. There she was in her leopard coat looking like a trapped animal. I had set the perfect trap for the jungle cat. All it took was hitting her over the head with an axe and then there were all those lovely saws and rippers just waiting to send the slattern to H. E. L. L."

We both sat shocked but silent. Equally surprising as her grisly story was Mary's tone that she might have used to report on a successful bake sale. Mary smiled a sweet grandmotherly smile at James and patted his hands. Was she expecting congratulations for her heartfelt deed?

"So, you took Estrella's body and cut it up and buried some of it in your garden and hid some bones around town in other people's gardens, Mary?" The handsome Irish cop's voice was unsteady, shocked that the cookie-baking woman could have done something so dastardly.

"Oh, no, dear, at least not right away. No, I dragged her out into my backyard and dug a hole and pushed her in. I was still young and strong and she was only a bag of bones anyway." Mary laughed at her own macabre joke but James and I sat quietly, barely breathing.

"Some time later, after I read a very good mystery, I think it was either Agatha Christie or Somerset Maugham…no, I think it might have been Mary Roberts Rinehart. No, now I remember, it was Poe. I got the idea of cutting her up and doing what a maniacal killer might do. Figured if the police ever came looking and found her, I'd say the old man went wild and did it. I'd say I was too frightened for my own life listening to the horror over there that I couldn't even pick up the phone to call the law. I knew I'd be believed because I, unlike Old Ned, was loved and respected in town. In addition, I'd say that I feared for my own life so I kept mum. It began to seem like a lot of fun. Like a movie."

"So, you cut Estrella in pieces and did what with the pieces, Mary?" James looked gray.

"Well, I tried to get into the mind of a terrible murderer. First I cut off one leg and then one hand. I planned to cut her all up like a Sunday roast and then spread the pieces around the town. Wasn't that a good plan? Sounds like a really scary movie, doesn't it, dears?"

We nodded. Mary's mind was going fast. She did not see anything wrong in what she had done to Estrella. After all, she'd been motivated by the deepest of love.

"Well, I soon grew tired of that, you see. After I took her leg and buried it in Libby's garden and her hand in the Gonsalves' garden, that was it. Changed my plan."

"Mary, why Libby's and the Gonsalves'? Was there some important meaning behind those choices?'

"Yes, dear. Libby always loved a good mystery. Thought one day to tell her and we'd get a good laugh out of it. The hand though, in the Gonsalves garden, was a kind of tribute. To Rosita. You see, although I'd been very angry with her for leaving poor Edwin at the altar, I later came around. One day, Rosita's mother told me that she knew where her daughter was and that she'd had Edwin's baby. Well, you can imagine my shock. Told me that

Rosita had written to Edwin telling him about the baby and asking for financial assistance. He'd flatly refused her. The Gonsalves didn't have much at the time. With all those children and just a little store to support them, they couldn't help their daughter. So, as I had plenty of money, I began sending her checks each month for the little girl, Edna. Edwin's child." Tears ran down Mary's face and I handed her a tissue. She smiled and patted my hand.

Poor Mary had *slipped a cog* right before our eyes. For some reason, it occurred to me, I was sounding very much like Daphne. Oh, well shock does funny things to a person.

A deep breath and she was back to her story. James reached under the table for my hand. Together we waited for what was to come.

"Can you imagine? Edwin actually laughed when I told him I'd killed Estrella for him so he could be happy again? Ungrateful man. Then he went and proposed to Rosita Gonsalves. Treated me like some kind of hired help. Like he'd hired me to kill the interloper so he could ride off on his high horse with the prettiest girl in town."

"Did he ever mention it again, Mary?"

"No. Not until recently, that is. We hadn't spoken a word in years and then one night not long before he died, he came to the door and asked if he could come in. Well, I was all alone and a little company is nice now and then; even an ungrateful rat like Edwin Snow III."

"What did he want?"

"He got to recalling lots of things about the old days but I knew he was up to something. All that fondness for the old days was just a way to try to get to me. Soften me up. He asked me to do something for him, a special favor. He was having some trouble and he wanted me to help him, as he said, "Because you've done something like it before." When he told me what he wanted, I flatly refused to help him. He was really angry and called me a hypocrite. He had the audacity to say that once someone has done one murder the others came easily. Imagine that."

"He asked you to murder someone, Mary?" James looked shocked but I had an idea of who that someone had been that

Edwin wanted disposed of. A thorn in his side. Someone demanding some of his precious money. The blackmailer.

"I refused to listen to why he wanted that sweet woman killed. Such a kind and sincere person, so concerned with the welfare of the town's citizens that she hardly deserved what he had in mind."

Emily Sunshine. Blazing before my eyes in neon letters the name slipped into the gaping hole in the puzzle. Hypotheses: Emily found out about Edwin's father's mistress, the change in the will and the sudden disappearance of Estrella. Of course, most likely it had been Mary Malone who'd told her in deepest confidence. How opportune. Edwin Snow was the richest man in town and Emily had the goods on him. Why not blackmail? Emily certainly wasn't getting rich telling fortunes.

No time to think this through any further as Mary began her slow motion slide toward the floor. James reached out and prevented her from hitting the wood floor. Placing her on the nearby loveseat he looked completely crestfallen. It occurred to me that with his sweet sensitivity to people's troubles it was a good thing he worked in a small village rather than a city. I covered Mary with an afghan and reached out to James who came into my arms for a reassuring hug.

Coming out of the faint, Mary Malone's first words were, "More tea, dears?"

Twenty-four

Police Chief Chet Henderson sat behind his desk and Mary Malone sat across from him. It was the day after our amazing meeting at Mary's house and she seemed not to have been adversely affected by all that she'd told us.

Mary sat there as if she had been invited to an afternoon strawberry social. The Chief offered her tea and she accepted. Annie Cannon the Chief's ever so efficient secretary served our hot drinks and a plate of her homemade chocolate pecan cranberry cookies. We all settled in as if ready for a pleasant talk. However, if Mary was ready and willing to repeat her story for the Chief, there was unlikely to be a pleasant out-coming.

Annie with her notebook on her lap waiting to take down the discussion, the Chief sitting behind his desk with the painting of his dear, departed wife Trudy hanging on the wall behind him, Mary in the hot seat, James standing by the desk and I sitting across the room might have been a tableau of a Norman Rockwell painting entitled, *The Town Sherriff Entertains.*

No one was prepared for the Chief's abrupt official opening to the meeting.

"Mary dear, did you kill Edwin?"

"Gracious no. Chester, dear, how could you entertain such a thought? All right, I must admit that I did entertain that idea but soon passed on it. After all, I loved the man. Even after he grew to be as nasty as old Ned. No, instead, he did it himself when he jumped. The man was of no use to himself or anyone else now was he?"

"But you did kill Estrella Costa, correct? And Edwin wanted you to kill Emily Sunshine, is that also correct, Mary, dear?" James and I had gone over every detail of our meeting the previous day with Mary for the Chief. He was right on top of it and in his best form regardless of the constant pain he lived with.

"Oh, dear me, Chester, why don't we just forget all this nastiness, shall we? It's all over now. No good can come of digging up such old doings. We shouldn't beat ourselves up about things that happened so long ago."

"Oh, how I wish it were that easy Mary, dear."

It seemed to me that Mary's mental state was so fragile that at any moment she might just shut down. Hide from reality in a place where all of the answers we needed would be forever unavailable to us.

As the Chief reached for the bottle of aspirins and a glass of water it occurred to me that one more vital question had to be asked before Mary slipped away from us as it seemed she might be doing.

"May I ask Mary a question, Sir?"

The Chief smiled at me and nodded. I stood and moved my chair up next to Mary's and she turned to face me. It was now or never.

"Mary, the night of the fire at the Snow place you said something that I've been wondering about. You said something to the effect that the fire would have driven something, *some things*, away. The fact seemed to please you very much. What were those things to which you were referring, Mary?"

"Dear, Elizabeth, the ghosts, of course."

"The ghosts? Do you mean that the Snow house had ghosts?"

"Oh my, yes. Although they used to reside at the Cranberry Inn, your Aunt Libby's place. But that's a story you should ask dear Emily to tell. It's her story, too. She was there that night when they were sent away."

When the Chief had heard enough, he had James drive Mary home before he called Doc to have him schedule an appointment with a good psychiatrist in Boston. Mary was hardly a flight risk and the sixty years ago murder of Estrella would require some deep thought for Chet Henderson. Much to his chagrin, the Chief's beloved hometown was becoming a hotbed of intrigue. In other words, a damned nuisance for a man who ought to have retired already and was now re-considering just that move.

Later, James and I sat in a window seat at Napi's sipping Mojitos trying to gel the surprising day into something we could manage. The very cold case of the wandering bones could be closed. But we still had other mysteries to unlock. I didn't say so at that time but I was pretty sure I knew who set the Snow house ablaze. I just needed a little more information that meant another visit to the miasma of the Fairies in the Garden shop. I sneezed in negative anticipation and James handed me a crisply ironed white handkerchief.

I took a deep drink of the cocktail that tasted like summer in a glass. I needed some answers from Emily to close the arson case. What a complete surprise I had in store. Striving to keep my face unreadable to my favorite Irish cop, I said, "Just one more thing I want to check out, James."

"You have that mysterious look on your face, woman. Just promise me it's not a dangerous mission you're pursuing. This thing is still volatile until we put it to bed. Not everything is known yet for sure. No danger, okay?"

"Don't worry, no danger." I crossed my fingers under the table.

"Hello! Emily! Anyone here?" I called out but the shop felt empty. Well, empty only considering that there were no customers and Emily was not in evidence. But empty of stuff it was not. Even more stuff than usual it looked like. The smog, however was the same as always. It had reached critical mass and, I believed, couldn't get any worse. Not that that helped my stricken sinuses.

"Why, hello dear, come to have your fortune told today?" Emily came through the front door that she always left unlocked when she slipped out to get some lunch. She was looking very pretty in a turquoise cotton dress. More bright color than I'd had ever seen her wearing.

"Well no, actually I have two reasons for being here. I realized recently that I failed to pay for your services on the two occasions when you…and Eloise were so helpful to my inquiries."

"No dear, not necessary. After all, you are helping the police with their investigation so as a good citizen it's my duty to assist for free."

"That's very kind of you but I really feel that I should pay you."

Emily smiled and motioned me to sit at the lace covered table. She placed her hands on the table, palms down, waiting. I felt obliged to say something.

"All right well, perhaps I could treat you to lunch one day soon." Emily nodded.

"Well, today I am here for some personal information. Well, not exactly personal but about my house and the Snow house." Emily's eyes changed; I could have sworn they went from light blue to deep violet with silver sparks.

"I simply can't imagine what your house and the Snow house might have in common, however I will help if I can." Emily's hand began to shake as she pulled Eloise toward her I noted. Had I hit a nerve?

"Actually, I don't believe we will need Eloise's help on this one, Emily. I just need some information on a subject that I thought might be in your purview. Ghosts."

"*Ghosts.* Oh my dear, that term is not used in my work. They are non-corporeal spirits. 'Ghost' is a term made popular by Hollywood."

Or Shakespeare. Deciding not to get into a discussion of Hamlet, I moved on hoping to catch the woman off guard.

"You once said that my inn had ghosts. I wonder what you based that comment on. Did my aunt complain of things that go bump in the night, maybe?"

"Your aunt was a lovely woman, Liz. A smart business woman and a generous member of the community. She was very kind to me when I first arrived in town years ago. She helped me to approach my...Oh well, that's hardly important anymore. She let me stay at the inn for a couple of weeks until I found this storefront with a small apartment upstairs for me to live in. I couldn't have managed without her."

"That's very nice to hear Emily but what about the ghosts?"

"Well, she had some gho....non-corporeal spirits left over from long ago when the first family built the house. It was a successful sea captain who went off whaling for years at a time and while he was gone his wife fooled around with a young sailor who

169

rented a room in the house. The young man had been badly injured aboard her husband's ship and she took him in and nursed him back to health. They fell in love and when the captain returned and found out he killed them both. The captain's wife and her lover remained to haunt Libby's inn. But have no fear Liz, they are gone now. Definitely gone."

"Gone? Exorcised?"

"Moved on."

"How do you convince ghosts to move on, Emily?"

"As it happened, this woman from Philadelphia came to stay at Libby's inn one summer years back and, like the man who came to dinner, she just stayed and stayed. She did séances and fortune telling. It was that clever woman, Maude Muckle, who taught me all I know about the crystal ball and tarot cards. When I opened this place it was basically a gift shop. But once Maude trained me I found that I had a real calling and from then on I had a better way to make my living. Libby asked Maude to do a séance so she could talk to her ghosts because at that time she did not yet know their identities. The first séance went nowhere but the second was a great success. If you could call a truly frightening night of howls and blood and mayhem a success."

"So, the murdered lovers appeared? Is that what happened?"

"They more than appeared; they put on a show. We sat there around that table and watched them being slaughtered by the furious sea captain. He used an axe. He split them asunder and there was blood and guts everywhere, even hunks of flesh landing on the lace tablecloth and into our teacups. I will never forget that night. But that is not all that happened; it got even wilder when Edwin showed up."

"Edwin. What was he doing there? Had he been invited to the séance?"

"Oh no, he hated such things, disapproved of any kind of mystical stuff. He and Libby were still on and off in their friendship at that time and he just happened to drop by. He saw us all there looking like frightened rabbits, and although afterwards he claimed he never saw anything but a bunch of silly woman sitting around a table in candlelight drinking tea, I knew he saw them too.

170

Libby was always such a daring and independent woman. I know I said she was friendly with Edwin, but he also got on her nerves. She loved a good joke and he was an easy mark. She got a clever idea while he was standing there calling us names and telling us we were all crazy. She whispered to Maude that she should try and convince the ghosts to move on to Edwin's house. Imagine that?"

"Can that be done? Can you convince ghosts to move from the place they are attached to just by telling them they ought to?"

"I am no expert but Maude evidently was because she made up some wild story about how Libby's house dishonored their memory or some such and that they would be happier in the Snow house. She even gave them directions. What a hoot. Well, Edwin that miserable excuse for a man just harrumphed and slammed the door behind him when he heard Maude's words."

"What happened to the ghosts?"

"As I recall, Libby never had another peep out of them from that day forward."

Hardly an answer to the question but I decided to move on before she shut me out. She most certainly knew a whole lot more than she'd ever let on without prodding. So, I decided to prod.

"Do you know if Edwin believed they came to live er, dwell in his house after that night even though he feigned disbelief in such things?

"I believe that after that night he became a believer. But when he came to me just before he died, it was something else troubling him more than ghosts."

"What are you talking about, Emily?"

"Doc had told him that he only had only a short time to live. Had a tumor or some such. He was upset, of course, but also, he couldn't sleep because of *them.* They were tossing things around and making a terrible mess of his orderly life."

Remembering the description James had provided about the condition of Edwin's house, I doubted that one more mess would upset him.

"Yes, Edwin lived in what appeared to be a tightly packed warehouse but to him it had order and the piled boxes and rolled up rugs made him feel that he was safe in a kind of fortress. He liked living that way and he was persnickety about how things were kept. The so-called *ghosts* made a mess of things regularly and they were driving him crazy. He said they were tossing out closets and drawers."

That explained the tossed office at Edwin's house. But what were the ghosts looking for? Asking myself that question I began to doubt my own sanity. Was it the sea air, the shock of losing one career and beginning another, totally unrelated to anything I'd ever imagined for myself? Surely, if I, a scientist, was asking about ghosts I needed immediate professional help. Well, I had no choice but to follow along on the present line of inquiry.

"What did you do for him, Emily? Did you help him get rid of his ghosts?"

"Oh, no, I hated that man and wouldn't have done a thing to please him but he offered me the opportunity to vex him." Emily smiled. "The few times he came here I could see he really believed I could help him. Well, I suppose he was just so desperate he was ready to try anything."

"It occurs to me, Emily, other than an exorcism, how would one get rid of pesky ghosts?"

"That's not really my territory but in my profession you do hear about other similar – sciences. I've heard that the most successful method is to burn them out. Burn the place they have come to inhabit and that sends them off to their final resting place."

Now we were getting somewhere. I was sure that Emily had passed that information along to Mary Malone however, would she admit it to the authorities? Not that it would help poor Mary at that point. Still, it would help to solve the mystery of the arson of the Snow house.

"Did you ever tell Mary Malone that?"

"Yes, I might have" Emily answered coyly. Why do you ask?"

I looked at my watch and rose, thanked Emily for her time and rushed away on the excuse that I had a dentist appointment. What I really needed was an eye, ear, nose and throat specialist.

I left the Fairies in the Garden shop gulping fresh air like a woman drowning. Now, if only I believed that Edwin had been so driven to distraction by the so-called "ghosts" that he had chosen to jump to his death, all the mysteries would be solved. But I knew better.

Like the pieces of colored glass in a kaleidoscope, a design began to form in my over-taxed mind. I walked to MacMillan Wharf and sat in the warm sun on a bench surrounded by squawking seagulls. If Mary had somehow trusted Emily with the secret of having killed Estrella, but Emily suspected that the sweet, old woman was covering for her beloved Edwin, then, why not blackmail him? Surely, anyone would sooner suspect Edwin of murder than kindly, grandmotherly Mary Malone. Maybe Emily hounded the man to his death. Suicide as an escape? No.

Twenty-five

I sat in the Chief's office while he reminisced. I'd brought him his favorite cranberry pecan scones and he told me about his dead wife, Trudy. Then, he moved along to the period a few years later in his time as a widower when he was ready to meet another woman.

"You know, when that pretty, little lady first came to town, I was a recent widower. Trudy had been dead for almost two years and I was feeling mighty lonely. Trudy always told me, in no uncertain terms, that I was to find me a new wife to take care of me should she pre-decease me. Well, let me tell you, it didn't seem right but then pretty little Emily Sunshine showed up. Truly a ray of welcome sunshine. Summoning up all my courage, I asked her out to dinner."

"Good for you Chief. How did it go?"

"It didn't. Turned me down flat. Oh, she was sweet and kind but she said she just didn't date. She gave no reason but with my self-confidence being pretty fragile, at the time, I never asked again. Never asked anyone."

"Oh, Chief, any woman would be lucky to get you. Time to try again." I thought but didn't add, *But definitely not Emily because I expect she will soon be in either the state penitentiary or the state hospital for the criminally insane.*

James appeared with Emily at his side. She'd been away at a gift show in Atlanta and had just alighted from the Greyhound Bus as James passed on his way back to the station. James had seen the sign on the Fairies in the Garden shop when he went, on the Chief's orders, to bring her in for questioning. It said that she'd be back on Tuesday but although it was Tuesday, James had no idea of when to expect her. He was headed back to report when there she was. Inviting her to come with him because the Chief wanted to speak with her, she'd left her suitcase in the pharmacy with Miquette, the pharmacist, and went along.

"Good day, Emily, just a few questions." The Chief stood, gentlemanly. I hoped his sights were not set, once again, on dating the little woman whose sidekick was a crystal ball. It did, however, occur to me that Emily might be incapacitated without her trusty companion, Eloise. I'd never had a conversation with her minus the glassy, controlling orb.

The Chief, naturally, led off the questioning. "Emily we need to talk about your relationship to Edwin Snow III. Just take your time and tell it like it was. Everything you can remember about what Edwin talked about when he came to you for help when he was troubled and anxious." The Chief pulled the ever-present bottle of aspirins and accompanying glass of tap water toward him.

After a brief pause, during which Emily flicked a piece of lint off of her violet linen jacket, checked her curls that never moved because of copious amounts of hair spray and smoothed her white skirt, she spoke. What came out did so like a corked volcano suddenly free to burst its top, to the utter surprise of us all. I wondered if Emily had been preparing herself for this moment and could hold back the roaring lava no longer.

"Miserable of old miser. Laughed at me when I told him who I was. Wouldn't part with a nickel for his own flesh and blood. Got what he deserved. I gave him my birth certificate and a letter from my mother but still he refused to accept my story. I hated the man. *Hated him.* Got even by toying with his little egg head."

This took the poor unprepared Chief by total surprise. As if hoping to escape the lava flow, he rolled his chair back a few feet until it was stopped by the bookcase behind him, toppling two books onto the floor.

James interjected when it looked as if the Chief was having difficulty finding words to lob back at Emily. "So, Emily, you were blackmailing Edwin because your mother, Rosita Gonsalves told you he was your father but he refused to recognize that fact. Correct?"

"He was also going to make my mother look like a common whore in that stupid book he was writing. I meant to see

175

to it that he didn't do that *and* I just wanted what was rightfully mine."

Chief Henderson, at last in control of his voice, motioned to James to let him take over. "Did you attempt to blackmail Edwin Snow, Emily?"

"At first, yes. But that was going nowhere so I had to change my tactic." Mary stated, matter of factly.

"I'm told that you sometimes vexed Edwin purposely just to upset the old man. Was that part of your new tactic, Emily?" I asked hoping the Chief would not object to my sticking my nose in. He nodded at me and I knew that I was okay.

"I wasn't sure where it was going Chet, Dear, at that time. I just knew that I was getting even for what he did to my mother. Anyone would have done the same. Rich as Croesus he was and yet he never sent us a dime. We'd have starved before Mom married that sweaty, stinking hog farmer if Mary hadn't sent us those checks every month." Emily was nearly foaming at the mouth.

"When was the last time Edwin came to your shop Emily?"

"Let's see, that would have been the night before he jumped from the Pilgrim Monument, Dear."

"What was the reason for his visit on that night, Emily?"

"He wanted something, some information that only Eloise could provide."

"You will need to tell me what that was. In detail, Emily. Do you understand? Every word that you can recall."

"Certainly, Chet. I am a good citizen and if I can help then I certainly will." This abrupt change from flaming lava to perfect citizen didn't fool me. The woman who, as Daphne had put it, *knows where all the bodies are buried in this town,* held the best hand in this card game. I was becoming a font of metaphors.

"Please remember, Emily, that you must tell us the truth so that we can help you if you are innocent."

"Innocent? Innocent of what, Chet?" Emily actually looked confused. But, as I had seen her in the course of her so-called "profession", I knew that she was an Academy Award class actress.

"Emily, I may as well tell you that someone saw Edwin Snow at your back door on the night of the snowstorm. You say he was there the night before his death but it seems he also showed up shortly before his fall from the Pilgrim Monument. Is that true?"

Emily coughed and then continued in a shaky voice. "Eloise was having an off night when he came that first time. We couldn't get what he needed so he returned the following night. He was troubled by his memory's loss of some important names and dates for his silly book and wanted Eloise to contact Edward Granger." Emily took a deep breath. "That's when I got the idea."

"The idea?" The Chief reached for the aspirins but realized that he'd just taken two and put back the bottle. "You know, Emily, somehow I cannot imagine anything being important enough for the old, frail man to wander into town during a terrible snowfall."

"Well, he did. Do you want to hear this or not, Chet?"

Emily was becoming the inquisitor. Could she get away with taking over the investigation, I wondered?

"Proceed." Chief Henderson put his aching feet up on the stool under his desk and leaned back as if preparing for a tall tale. Two hundred and twenty-five feet tall, I wondered.

"I quickly decided that I could get even with him for all the misery he'd caused me and my dear mother over the years. As I've struggled to hold my business together through good times and bad, increasing rents and higher and higher heating and electric bills he just sat around counting his money and doing no good with it." Her voice rose to a crescendo as she twisted the handkerchief in her hands as if she was wringing her denying father's puny neck.

"So, I looked into Eloise and..."

Chief Henderson groaned audibly. "Sorry Emily, go on. But, please, just do stick to the facts."

I was tempted to remind him that Emily's so-called "facts" came from a galaxy far, far away. But instead, I held my tongue.

"The plan to finally get even came to me in such a rush I felt dizzy. Looking into Eloise's face I told Edwin that Edward Granger had a message for him, a very important message. The old man's face lit up like a Fourth of July firecracker and I knew I had him. Funny thing is, at that point I wasn't exactly sure of how I was going to do it but I was sure that the good fairies would watch over and guide me to a solution. Not for getting the money I deserved, no, that was a lost cause by then but at least, I could get my *soupçon* of revenge."

"Emily, does this idea include getting the old man to climb all the way up the Pilgrim Monument?"

"I'll get to that, Chet." Emily gave the man a look of annoyance as if she might be cheated out of her full performance. Checking her plastic curls, once again, she continued.

"Actually, I didn't need Eloise that night. I let her rest and I took over although, of course, Edwin thought she was contacting that drunken artist Edward Granger."

"What on earth could you have told Edwin that would have convinced an old man to climb way up there, Miss Emily?" The chief moved forward to the edge of his chair, cigar burning down in his ashtray right under the **No Smoking in Public Buildings** sign.

Emily's smile had the quality of a snake eyeing a tasty mouse directly in its path. "It was just so simple. I told him that everything he needed was safe in a journal the artist had hidden up in the monument in a secure place and it was just waiting for him."

We all gasped. Emily sat like the Cheshire cat. Was she purring?

The Chief used the old inquisitor's trick of saying nothing thus unnerving the suspect which, according to the police interrogators' manual, usually brought forth jewels. Eventually the little woman could bear it no longer and spoke.

"You know how old people are. That night, despite the snow, Edwin Snow just had to have a few bits of information that only a dead man, Edward Granger, knew. Edwin was dying, the doctor had told him. So, he had to rush to finish the book."

The Chief groaned, either in physical or mental pain. "So, you convinced the old man to climb with you to find these secret journals that you knew were not there. That sounds a bit silly, Emily."

"Not so silly Chet, when you consider that I hated the old man and anything that annoyed him pleased me. I knew where the key was in your office because I'd worked here cleaning when I first came to town. Remember that, Chet?"

Chief Chet nodded.

"I slipped in the back door that is never locked because of the public restrooms. Only I knew that the door to the main hallway was also unlocked. It was easy. I knew all the secrets from my time here. I slipped in and took the key to the Monument and slipped out undetected."

The Chief looked over his shoulder at the pegboard where at least a hundred keys hung on key chains, bits of string and what appeared to be plastic tie wraps. He shook his head in disbelief. Or, admiration?

Chet suddenly jibed the boat around onto a new tack thus, tossing us all into a muddle, if not the sea.

"Tell me, Emily, that crystal ball of yours, it's just a lot of show business, right?"

"Chet, that lump on your hip is benign. Don't worry about it anymore. Don't waste your time and money on having it biopsied, it's just a pocket of stray fat. Happens with age, particularly in men with gout."

Chief did a double take and coughed to cover his astonishment. Actually, the week before, the chief had driven all the way to Hyannis to have the suspicious lump biopsied and the report had come in just that morning. The doctor had told him on the phone just minutes before James arrived with Emily, *Don't worry Chet the lump is just a pocket of stray fat, happens later in life.*

I decided that I'd better jump in before the situation steered too far off track and Emily was giving us all health advice. "So you and Edwin climbed up to the top of the monument and you hit him with what, a baseball bat or maybe a metal rod, and then you tossed him over. Is that correct, Emily?"

"Ah, you have a fine imagination, Liz. You ought to write mysteries, you have a knack. Must be from reading all those silly cozies you and your friends read instead of serious literature. Softens the brain to read such dribble but those cozy writers do make a nice bit of change selling that foolishness. No, Liz, that's not quite what happened. You see, I am not a murderer, although you would all like to think so."

If surprise had a sound, it rang loudly and clearly around the office at that moment. Like a bell rung too close to the ear, Emily's statement of denial shook us all equally. But something that popped into my head at that moment troubled me, far more.

What if clever Emily had decided to name Eloise as the killer of Edwin Snow III? A very fine ploy for an insanity defense if ever there was one. I was sure at that moment that that was exactly what the woman had in mind. You had to be pretty foxy to get people to pay for what she offered them in the guise of "science." If anything, Emily was a wily fox.

The Chief spoke. "All right Emily, just take us through what happened the night old Edwin climbed the monument believing that there was a journal waiting up there for him. Just take us along with you and him, step by step. If you didn't murder him then you'd better have a pretty good explanation of how he ended up dead on the snow with his skull cracked. I can tell you, based on a credible source, that the man's head was smashed in before he landed. So, if you didn't crack him on the head and he didn't smash in his own head then how did the poor man's skull end up like a broken egg, *before* he hit the ground."

Interesting, I thought, how the egg reference kept cropping up in discussing Edwin Snow. *Humpty Dumpty had a great fall.*

Emily sat up straighter. "I do admit to considering killing him. After all, he denied being my father, denied me my rightful inheritance, insulted me repeatedly and scorned my dear mother, however..."

"Let's just cancel the dramatics, Emily, and cut to the chase."

Emily nodded at the Chief. "Before I closed up the shop and left for the Pilgrim Monument, I put an axe in my backpack, just in case. I keep it for chopping ice off the sidewalk so my customers don't slip. I didn't actually believe that I'd have the courage to use it but it was like a security blanket. The snow was coming down hard as the appointed hour approached. Part of me hoped that Edwin would chicken out on such a terrible night but part of me believed that he wouldn't dare. He needed what Eloise had promised him if he was going to complete that silly book before he died. The clock was ticking."

"So, you helped him climb all those stairs not sure what you were going to do when you got to the top, right?"

"Not quite. I refused to tell him which stone the journal was hidden behind. Eloise had told me, I told Edwin, so he'd need me there to identify it. I offered to go up first, find the hiding place and remove the journal. Then, he'd come up."

"Wait, why did he fall for that, Emily? I mean, you could have found it and brought it to him. Why climb himself at his age and in his condition?"

"Lack of trust. Old Edwin was agreeable to letting me go first to find it but he didn't' trust me to bring it to him. Of course, I played it just right to instill that idea in his head. He was afraid I'd steal it and publish it myself. Edwin trusted no one."

The Chief groaned. James shifted his feet and I just sat there incredulous to think how this seemingly harmless woman could twist people around her finger and wondering if we'd ever know the real truth. Chief motioned for Emily to continue.

"By the time I arrived at the Monument, I had a half hour to climb and get ready for the old miser. I even briefly began to feel sorry for him. But that wasted feeling quickly passed. The man had caused me years of misery so he deserved what he got, snow or not."

"Get back to the axe, Emily."

Emily smiled her most ingratiating smile at Chet. "Waiting for the old man I reached around and felt the axe in my pack and wondered if I, like Lizzie Borden, could give her father forty whacks."

"Emily!" His shocked tone did not seem to reach her.

"It was very dark. No lights around the top since the town budget slashed them. Used to be so nice looking up at the beacon glowing over the town every night. However, strangely enough, there was a full moon that night and even though the snow was still falling a modicum of light shone in to provide a weak spotlight. Hidden in the shadows, it passed through my mind that it would be fun to pretend that I was Edward Granger. I could speak to Edwin

181

in a deep voice and really scare the beans out of him. He was so easy to frighten." Emily smiled but the Chief frowned.

That's when it occurred to me that it must have been Emily who'd dropped the cement block and lobbed the rock at poor old Edwin. Murder attempts or simply harassment? Then, as if Eloise was there reading my private thoughts, Emily spoke and really spooked me.

"If I may digress for a moment, Chet, I must confess to dropping the cement block from the roof of the Canterbury Tales Leather Shop and throwing the rock across Commercial Street at the old misery but I only meant to scare him. I wasn't trying to kill him, just unnerve the silly old man. I used to play softball in school and I was pretty good. I did scrape his nose with the rock although that was just pure luck. Never make it to the Red Sox, I guess."

She looked directly at the chief knowing he was an avid Red Sox fan and this might have been just a lighthearted moment among friends but for the true nature of the scene that Emily was directing like a professional.

"What did you do to Edwin, Emily, up in that cold tower?" I could tell that the Chief's reserve of energy was growing thin. It was almost two in the afternoon and none of us had had our lunch.

"I heard the old bat huffing and puffing and groaning. Then, after a good long time, he was there, at the top of the stairs. He didn't see me in the deep shadows. Quite frankly, Chet, I had expected that the old man would die on his way up and save me the trouble. I knew immediately that I couldn't use the axe on his ugly egg head. I thought about simply jumping out of the shadows and yelling BOO!"

"So, you didn't hit him with your axe?"

"No, Chet, I did not. In the darkness, when I first arrived, I went to adjust the axe because the handle was sticking into my back. I rested the backpack on the ledge and removed it and that was when I heard something fall. I reached over the ledge but it had dropped further than my arm could reach. Then I remembered the large Limburger cheese I'd purchased at Souza's that morning. Well, no time to search for it then so I adjusted the axe and slipped further into the shadows. One look at the axe and I knew that I

182

couldn't split that man's head like kindling. Even filled with hate as I was."

I looked at James and wordlessly, by holding my nose, reminded him of the disgusting smell we'd encountered up in the tower. He grinned and nodded knowingly. Limburger cheese, of course.

"Edwin stopped on the next to top step. He was gasping for breath and clutching at his heart. He let out a terrible gasp and a kind of gurgle." Emily stopped talking. No one spoke.

Emily slipped back into her old, sweet, pink and white persona. "After all the misery he'd caused my mother and me, I suddenly found myself feeling sorry for the miserable old miser. Imagine that!"

Frozen in our seats, we remained like marble statues.

"I moved out of the shadows and he recoiled in fear. I suppose he thought it *was* Granger's ghost. He shot out both hands in an attempt to push me away from him and in so doing lost his balance. Down he went banging into the wall, bouncing on the steps, hitting the banister, like a plastic toy, tumbling and rolling. Suddenly, I was racing after the miserable old man's falling body." Emily's voice increased in volume and grew shaky. "After all, even though I hated him he was my father and I had to do something. Not that I expected him to be alive after the first few hits against the stone wall or the metal steps. I think I heard bones breaking but never a word from him. No screams so he must have been quickly dead. But still…"

The Cief stared at Emily, his look seeming to alternate between compassion for Edwin and confusion as to how he would handle so peculiar a case. We all drew in a huge collective breath and waited. How could any of us have expected a third possibility? Not suicide and not murder. Edwin Snow had died by accident.

"There is nothing more deceptive than an obvious fact" Sir Arthur Conan Doyle, *The Adventures of Sherlock Holmes.*

"When he hit those jagged, broken steps that I'd carefully maneuvered around and evidently he had as well, on his way up, he sort of catapulted forward and flew headlong onto the cement floor at the bottom of the steps. I froze in place at the top of the final stretch of stairs. I watched him land squarely on the top of his

Humpty Dumpty head. His skull cracked loudly. Inside the icy, narrow tower I heard that crack reverberate off the granite walls." Emily slumped in the chair.

With her last words, the sun disappeared, as if on cue. Dark clouds rolled across the sky blotting out the light, and, off in the distance, a rumble of thunder punctuated Emily's astonishing story.

The Chief was the first to speak. "What did you do then, Emily?"

"When I finally reached him he had no pulse. So, I dragged him outside and through the snow and left him there like a broken doll. I watched as the snow increased, covering his body in a white shroud. Then I cleaned up the blood at the foot of the stairs with buckets of snow. I'd found both a bucket and a broom there and between the two I left the entryway as clean as a whistle. Wouldn't want Bill to be troubled by such a mess."

"Chief, may I ask Emily just one more thing?" I asked and the chief nodded.

"Emily, I assume that your mother sent you here to see if you could win over your father and I am sorry that he made it so difficult for you. I just wonder if you might satisfy my curiosity," I turned around to take in the other faces there, "and I am sure, that of many others in town who have heard the story. Why did your mother, Rosita Gonsalves, leave Edwin Snow at the altar?"

"Mother didn't leave that miserable old coot at the altar. He rejected *her*. When she told him the night of their rehearsal dinner at the best restaurant in town, at that time, The Captain Winslow Tavern, that she was pregnant with his child, he nearly tore her head off. He didn't want children because he was afraid of passing his genes along. Well, at the time he didn't know about genes but he was sure that his father and he had some kind of bad blood that made them mean and he didn't want any child to suffer as he had. My mother had brought out the good in him but he feared that the bad blood would be passed on to a child thus, there must be no offspring. Of course, it was too late for Mother, I was already started. What was she to do? She ran. She went to Bill's house and he took her in because he'd loved her since they were children. He tried to convince her to go away with him but she was so confused and hurt she just needed to get far away from the town. She decided to make a clean break, have her baby in a distant city and do her best to care for the child Edwin had rejected."

I needed verification of my theory of why Edwin showed up for a wedding and faced a church full of guests who he knew would see no bride that day. "Emily, did he ever tell you why he showed up for his own wedding knowing that Rosita would not be there to marry him?"

"Don't look so puzzled, dear. There's a simple explanation. The man was desperate. No one liked him and he didn't have the talent for making them like him. My mother had but she was gone. He had driven her away. So, and here I am guessing because I never asked him, he decided to show up and appear to be left at the altar. He figured that the town's pity was, at least, a, shall we say, caring emotion. No matter how much they disliked him, only completely heartless people would fail to feel sorry for the deserted man."

Just as I'd seen it in my mind's eye. Poor, poor lonely, unloved Edwin.

Chief pulled himself together, took a deep drink of coffee and then stood and came around his desk until he was looking down on the tiny woman dwarfed by the large chair. His business-like demeanor spoke volumes.

"Thank you, Emily. I want to believe your story but first I need to see that axe of yours. Just in case it has evidence of blood on it. I'm afraid we will have to hold you overnight until we check that out. Where is that axe now, Emily?"

"Gone to sea."

"What? You threw it into the sea, why? Do you realize that that just compounds our case against you? We have to prove that you did not split Edwin Snow's head with it."

"Well, I guess you will just have to trust my word based on all the years you've known me then won't you, Chet? I can assure you that I did not use the axe but I just wanted to toss it away anyway."

185

"Where did you toss it Emily? The wharf? The beach behind your shop? You just pinpoint the location and we'll go and look for it."

"I tossed it onto the fishing trawler that came in that night. After I left the monument, I headed down to the wharf and watched them pull in and tie up. That's when the idea came to me for getting rid of the damned thing, just in case. Although I never used it, I watch those T.V. shows where someone gets convicted for something they didn't do just because they own a weapon. So, after it seemed that everyone had gone to bed on the trawler, and a few of the men had gone up the wharf headed home, local men, I tossed it onto the deck. I watched it fall onto a rolled up sail or bag or such so it made no noise at all. No one on the boat would know where it had come from. I felt much better after I tossed it."

"Damn, Emily, I have to make a case to try and save your neck and you are not making it easy for me, now are you?"

"Guess not, Chet. Sorry. Will they let me take Eloise to prison with me, Chief?"

Twenty-six

Emily spent the night in a cell made comfortable with a plump down pillow, sheets and quilts supplied by me from the inn. James and I looked in on her later to find her sleeping like an untroubled baby. The Chief had sent James to put a padlock on the Fairies in the Garden shop and a sign saying, **Closed for Repairs.** James and I went back to the inn and I made a quick pasta carbonnara for our supper. Sitting over tea and pumpkin ginger ice cream I'd made in my new electric ice cream maker, we reviewed the astounding day.

"Do you believe her, James?"

"I'm just not sure but if the axe is ever located, it will be checked for blood. All the fishing trawler captains have been notified to look for it. Meantime, the floor just inside the door to the monument will be checked with a special light that picks up blood even after it's scrubbed away with even the strongest cleaner. If Emily's story is proved credible after these checks then the next step will be up to her lawyer."

"Has her mother been notified, James? Poor Rosita, it will be so tragic for her to hear what her daughter did as a reaction to her long desperate need to know her true father."

"Chief will be calling her tomorrow. You did a great job, Liz, despite my concerns for your safety." The remainder of the evening was comforting for us both, needless to say. Then, we too slept like untroubled, if not babies, then at least, successful investigators.

It was only later that next day that I remembered the one more thing I had figured out that I needed to tell James. I reached him at the police station. "Hi. What's up, lovely Liz?'

"James, remember Mary talking about the ghosts in Ned's house?"

"Sure, burned the buggers to cinders didn't that nasty fire?"

"Well, as you and arson squad are still questioning who started it, if not how it started, I think I have the answer."

"The ghosts themselves. Playing with matches, love?"

"No. I seriously believe it was Mary. She believes in ghosts and knew that Aunt Libby sent them from the inn to the Snow house."

"Well, listen to you. A ghost believer yourself now. And the will o' the wisp and the mysterious pookah horses of Ireland, as well, I assume. Not to mention, Big Foot."

"Get a grip, James. Mary was so pleased when the Snow house burned. Well, not pleased to see the grand old place go but pleased that the fire was a funeral pyre for the so-called ghosts. And, no, I do not now believe in ghosts. I am simply reporting what was said to me. I know also that Emily told her that burning was the next best way to rid a place of ghosts, exorcism being the number one way, but burning being just as effective, Mary set fire to the Snow house. I'm very sure of it. Probably too late for a confession, however."

"I'm afraid so. She's as closed as a clam at low tide. The doctors can't get a word out of her. Her mind has slipped entirely. Probably a good thing, I'd day, less suffering that way. But, I'll tell the Chief what you've reported, good citizen."

Daphne and I met for breakfast at Beasley's two days later. James had been busy wrapping up the case and I did not expect to see him for a few days. Time to bring my b.f.f. up to speed. Daphne had been in Boston hanging her work in a friend's gallery and returned to find the mysteries all but put to bed.

All the doors and windows were open to the gentle, warm, sea breeze. Customers were wearing shorts and flip flops and the pretty, colorful flowers spilling out of the window boxes affirmed that the village had made it successfully to yet another summer.

James took me totally by surprise when he opened the door to Beasleys, spotted us, and came in. Dee Dee was delivering a fresh pot of Earl Grey tea. She grabbed another cup on her way by the coffee station.

"Hi, gorgeous women. Any place for a stray male on his coffee break?"

I patted the bench beside me and he sat.

"I come bearing news."

"Oh, goody, now that the crime wave has abated, I'm feeling bored with this quiet town. I liked it when it was still a small town but had big city crime to take the dull edge off." Daphne looked around to see what other customers were eating.

"Daphne, you are absolutely certifiable. Let's just enjoy the peace and absence of mysterious conundrums that have plagued us for weeks and weeks. Give it a rest, will you?"

Daphne stuck her tongue out at me and dove into her pancakes topped with bananas, strawberries and a monumental mound of whipped cream. In fact, the Beasley's clever marketing-major daughter, Mia, had named this breakfast offering the *Monumental Breakfast*. Bill Windshship had applauded the honoring of his beloved Monument but refused to try and eat one.

"Do you eat like that every day, Daphne?" James asked.

"You have no idea James; the woman is a trash compacter in designer clothes."

I reached for his hand under the table and squeezed it. We had tickets for that night for Bob Ballard's talk on searching for shipwrecks, particularly the *Whidah* that the pirate Black Bellamy had captained and sunk. My inn manager, Katy Balsam, was due to arrive the next day and I was preparing to cook magnificent breakfasts for the coming three months. The mysteries solved and the cases closed, a nice, warm sense of completion had settled over me.

"Okay, what is this news, big boy?" Daphne asked between huge bites.

"A special delivery letter arrived late yesterday afternoon for Emily. It was addressed to Edna Gonsalves Snow from a law firm in Asheville, North Carolina. Naturally, no one at the post office recognized the name but since the address was Emily's closed and locked shop it was decided to bring it to the chief. Of course, the Chief knew it was for Emily Sunshine aka Edna Snow. It turned out to be a pretty important announcement although unfortunately it may have arrived far too late."

We put down our forks and focused on the handsome James. I was braced for not having much time for him in the coming months. However, once the summer rush was over, we'd had a lot to talk about.

"The letter announced the death of Rosita, Emily/Edna's mother. She passed away in Asheville, North Carolina just a few days ago. Left her daughter one million dollars." James waited for our reactions. He was not disappointed.

"Wowzer, that confirms that there is indeed damned good money in pigs and corn. I had no idea." Daphne stopped eating and just stared at James.

"Oh my goodness, James, *where did* Rosita get the million? Is there really that kind of money in corn and pigs?"

"No, it seems that miserly Edwin evidently suffered a stroke of conscience a couple of months ago despite the hard time he was evidently giving Emily. He hired a detective to find Rosita and to give her a check for a million; for Emily aka Edna after he and Rosita both were gone, according to Edwin's instructions. For some reason Rosita never told Emily er, Edna."

"To think that all of this could have been avoided. If Emily had known that her father had relented, then she would have backed off. Even if he refused to strike up a cuddly, father-daughter relationship with her, at least she would have had some sense of closure. But why didn't Edwin tell her what he'd done? He put himself in harms way on purpose, it seems. I guess that's just further proof that he was a very peculiar man, indeed."

"That's an understatement, pal," said Daphne as she finished off more food than I ate in an entire day.

"Hey, wait a minute I hadn't even considered this..." Daphne tossed her fork onto the greatly diminished waffle tower.

"Daphne, what?"

"Does this mean no murderer no manuscript?" Daphne's look of disappointment caused us to laugh.

"Aha, there lies the rub. No, actually the attorney contacted me early this morning. It seems our dear James here notified him of what had transpired. Then, dear James suggested to him that solving the mystery was just as good as finding a murderer. Thus, the codicil demands ought to be honored. I will have the manuscript by tomorrow. It's being sent by overnight mail and then we can all read it and see what we missed back in the forties when the town really rocked. Imagine being here with Eugene O'Neill, John Reed, Louise Bryant and Max Eastman and then later with the Grangers and their crazy New York friends."

"I venture to say, Daphne," said James, "that you missed a great period in the history of the village when you would have fit the town's atmosphere like the proverbial glove."

"I know. Damn, wouldn't time travel be gobs of fun?'

The next morning, I was making my breakfast when the special delivery package arrived. Sitting in the sunny sitting room I tore into it and began reading.

An hour later, I called both James and Daphne promising cappuccinos and cranberry lemon muffins and a big surprise.

They arrived and we sat at the old pine kitchen table that had been my aunt's. The tattered, very shop worn and yellowed pages of Edwin Snow III's manuscript lay on the table in front of me. My pals all but drooled waiting to hear about the secrets and scandals the old man had been storing up for decades.

"Okay, are you ready?" They nodded their bobble heads. "All right, here goes. I read it through twice just to be sure I didn't miss anything important. He had only written a hundred and two pages so it wasn't that daunting."

"Okay. So, how many great scandals did he expose? How juicy were the secrets of those dudes back in the forties when a milk toast novel like *Forever Amber* got banned as porn, eh? I mean after all, compared to what people get away with today, how bad could their behavior have been?"

My Mona Lisa smile lingered too long and my audience jeered.

"Come on. Don't do this to us, Liz. Spill the beans," Daphne begged.

"Hey love, before I grow too old to laugh without cracking a rib, please." James.

"Daphne, James, I am here to tell you, the first people to hear it, that after two readings, I declare the work of Edwin Snow III to be..." I let a pregnant pause fall, giving my audience a chance to fill in the blank for themselves.

"A masterpiece? The great American biography? What, Liz, come on you are killing us here. Sock it to us, girl."

"Gibberish! Total, unqualified rubbish. The ramblings of a very disturbed mind. Not one iota of scandal or secrets, just on and on, ad infinitum grumblings about all the insults and unfair treatment, rebuffs and snubbing he'd received over his lifetime in Truro and Provincetown."

Groan. "Damn, Liz, what an anticlimax. Aren't you disappointed?"

"Not really, I guess it is what I sort of suspected, all along."

"Well, ruins my day, let me tell you. Such a long wait for this, nothing juicy at all. Damn that old man, he could have given us something to talk about." Turning to face James Daphne asked him, "So when will the DNA test come back to prove conclusively that Edwin was Emily's Papa?"

James looked confused. "There won't be a DNA test. Doesn't seem necessary since everything checks out. Why would you think it necessary with all that we have to support her story that we need a DNA test, Daphne? Edwin admitted his paternity when he sent that million to Rosita for *their* daughter. "

I blurted out before Daphne could respond.

"Blimey, Daphne, you are so right. Why didn't I think of that?

James looked from Daphne to me, totally mystified.

I reached out and put my hand on his. "James, when Rosita named her baby daughter Edna she might have named her for either Edwin Snow *or* Edward Granger. Without positive, scientific proof we will never really know."

James looked perplexed.

"I suppose it doesn't really matter. What difference would it make, at this point? If Emily's lawyer manages to get her off with something less than a manslaughter charge, she will be a very rich woman. I doubt that it will matter to Emily. Oops, sorry, Edna."

The bobble heads shrugged.

Epilogue

Dear, sweet, grandmotherly Mary Malone spent six weeks in a private, very up-scale, well-respected mental hospital north of Boston where she underwent observation. It was determined by the experts that she had suffered a complete breakdown that had erased every memory of everything that had happened regarding the murder of Estrella.

In fact, Mary, on a daily basis, believed that she was an assortment of different characters. A new personality emerged nearly every day. At various times, Emily had told her doctors and the other patients that she was Betty Grable, Harpo Marx, Abraham Lincoln and Raggedy Anne, among others.

From there she was transferred to a hospital in up-state New York where she passed away gently, in her sleep, a month later. Her home was sold to a nice young couple from California who'd always spent their summers in Truro. They opened a homemade ice cream shop, Ye Olde Penny Candy and Ice Cream Shoppe in the vacated Fairies in the Garden shop space. A pretty old-fashioned name for such new age flavors as cinnamon-bacon, celery-ginger-raisin and lavender-macadamia.

Patton came to live with me as did Emily's cat Jasmine. They were often seen sitting side by side or lying close to one another, their friendship obvious to anyone. If cats and dogs share a secret language, as I hoped they did, they appeared to be entertaining themselves on some good old stuff.

Daphne, however, was sure that there was more than friendship at work. "Don't you see, he, Patton, was Emily's father's dog and she, Jasmine, was Emily's cat. Thus, since Patton was, in effect, Emily's *half-brother* and Jasmine, in that same vein, Emily's *child*, Patton's would be Jasmine's *half-uncle*. There is a real family bond there, particularly since they both ended up rootless."

"Right." Best not to encourage Daph when she went off on a tangent like that, I'd learned.

Emily's case dragged on and on. She went through four lawyers until she found just the right one. In the end, it was determined that when she'd reached out to Edwin in his distress after the long climb her intentions were to be helpful to the old man. In addition, her latest lawyer stressed the fact that when Emily raced down the stairs after Edwin's tumbling body she truly meant to try and save him, if she could.

Where the judge came down hard was on the matter of Emily deceiving old Edwin with the promise of a journal awaiting him up in the top of the Pilgrim Monument. Naturally, this strenuous climb resulted in his death. Or had it? That became a slightly shady area that helped the little woman escape a far more dire fate.

On the stand, both the coroner and the medical examiner concurred. Edwin was pretty much a dead man anyway when he climbed all those icy steps. He could have refused but he hadn't. Nearly ninety and in frail health with a serious heart condition and a tumor pressing on a vital part of his brain, he might not have lived another day, one way or the other. Not that this totally washed away Edna's aka Emily's guilt regarding tricking the old man. (I don't think I will ever get used to calling her Edna.)

The coroner stated that "The man suffered a massive heart attack in unison with the *explosion,* in laymen's terms, of the tumor pressing on his brain. Either occurrence alone would have been fatal."

Neither of us had attended any of the trial before the final day. Life had been hectic in busy Provincetown and we'd both been far too busy. In fact, neither of us had even read the newspapers accounts of the trial during that time. Coming out of our caves in early November, we decided to drive up-Cape to Barnstable to hear the summation of the murder trial of Emily Sunshine aka Edna Gonsalves Snow.

As I said, Emily went through lawyers like Grant through Richmond and on that day we were there to witness something that it took us months to fully digest. In fact, we were still talking about it a year later and were no closer to understanding if it had been pure coincidence or something else. There are those who believe that there are no such things as coincidences. I, however, disagree. I had learned, since coming to Provincetown, that even the most earnest scientist must be open to quirks, now and then, in the fabric of space and time.

The latest lawyer had come on the scene just days before but she'd inserted herself into the picture like she'd been born for the role. Sitting in the courthouse waiting for the judge to make his appearance I picked up a Boston newspaper that someone had left beside me on the bench. The front page article on the trial that was due to finish up that day, all but the sentencing, pulled it all together neatly for me.

"The tall, attractive female attorney", the reporter explained, "has turned this trial around as if wielding a magic wand in the eleventh hour". As he said, "The defendant Edna Snow has rejected a handful of lawyers in the course of this case but she appears to have made the correct choice this time. What appeared, until just days ago, to be a hanging jury, this legal eagle has softened into twelve kinder and gentler adjudicators."

We all stood as the judge appeared and the final arguments and sentencing proceeded. Of course, everyone believed that a case so complex would take days for the jury to bring to a final verdict. Everyone had been dead wrong. Instead, the jury marched out of the courtroom to be sequestered and a mere eighteen minutes later they returned with their verdict.

Emily was given a three year parole and five hundred hours of community service. She eventually went to work at the Land's End Walk-In Medical Clinic. There, she impressed even the best doctors with her ability to diagnose ailments either by holding a patient's hand or looking into their eyes. Of course, she was just a volunteer receptionist there but even before a patient saw the doctors Emily/Edna wrote down her prognosis on a pad she kept at her desk. Later, she'd compare her diagnosis to the official record and only occasionally missed. Some people have a sixth sense. Emily/Edna was such a person. Eloise might have been hidden under the desk but she seemed to be gone, forever.

After the trial, Edna built a new house on the site of the Snow mansion using her inheritance. I offered to give her cat back but she decided that Jasmine was best living with her close "relative."

She slipped right back into her old status of a pleasant, albeit quirky, little lady. After all, Provincetown's *liet motif* is nothing if not quirky thus, Emily's absorption back into the village was just one more proof of the cohesiveness of that idiosyncratic, eclectic village.

Oh, yes, I must include the fact that Chet Henderson retired as Police Chief and James Finneran was appointed chief. Two weeks after his retirement, Chet and Edna had their first date. He continued to call her Emily. They were married three months later and were off to their honeymoon in Puerto Rico. While there, Emily purchased a new crystal ball from a local "healer." By the time they got back to Provincetown, Chet was pretty much pain-free. The new crystal ball sat in a place of prominence across from their bed in Emily's new house.

On the drive back down-Cape from Barnstable, Daphne and I chewed over what we had learned that day in court. Finally, we concluded that it was best to simply forget what was obviously just one of the strange tricks the universe sometimes plays on us mere humans. Otherwise, we'd probably drive ourselves balmy.

The day had turned dark and dreary. It had been clear when Daphne and I arrived hours before but it had rained, evidently rained hard, unknown to us who'd been holed up in a room whose windows were covered and keeping secrets about the weather outside. Except for those heading to their cars in the huge parking lot beside the handsome old gray stone Barnstable County Courthouse, a combination of staff and those who'd attended the trial, the village seemed to have cleared out completely. Dinnertime.

Daphne looked at me as we headed along route 6A or, as we preferred to call it by its old name, the King's Highway, in silence. Then, Daph turned to me and asked me if I'd thought, as she had, that Emily/Edna's new attorney seemed rather odd.

"Odd, Daph. In what way?" I smiled and she laughed. Oh yes, there was definitely something odd about the gutsy, might I say pushy, new female attorney.

196

Starting with her name. Edna Gonsalves Snow's amazing defender was Attorney Eloise Ballantine. As Daphne said, "Go figure!"

Cynthia grew up in the seaside town of Brewster on Cape Cod. She returned as an adult to live in the Captain Burgess House just down the street from the Captain John Freeman house that her family ran as a guesthouse after moving there from Boston. She has also lived on Nantucket Island, the setting for her India Street culinary cozy mystery series.

Her Narrative Maritime Americana Primitive paintings have been a mainstay of the island's art scene for decades. Now, with the publication of a number of mysteries to her credit she has also captivated readers who love vivid descriptions (painterly in their character), complex plots and a mix of quirky and lovable characters plus some of the best twisted and tangled routes to mystery solving any reader could ask for.

She and her husband downsized to a forty-five foot boat in 2004. They now spend summers on a mooring in Pleasant Bay and winters in Puerto Rico.

Made in the USA
Lexington, KY
11 May 2012